THE YEAR'S BEST

MYSTERY & SUSPENSE STORIES

1989

Other Books by Edward D. Hoch

The Shattered Raven
The Judges of Hades
The Transvection Machine
The Spy and the Thief
City of Brass
Dear Dead Days (editor)
The Fellowship of the Hand
The Frankenstein Factory
Best Detective Stories of the Year 1976 (editor)
Best Detective Stories of the Year 1977 (editor)
Best Detective Stories of the Year 1978 (editor)
The Thefts of Nick Velvet
The Monkey's Clue & The Stolen Sapphire (juvenile)
Best Detective Stories of the Year 1979 (editor)
Best Detective Stories of the Year 1980 (editor)
Best Detective Stories of the Year 1981 (editor)
All But Impossible! (editor)
The Year's Best Mystery and Suspense Stories 1982 (editor)
The Year's Best Mystery and Suspense Stories 1983 (editor)
The Year's Best Mystery and Suspense Stories 1984 (editor)
The Quests of Simon Ark
Leopold's Way
The Year's Best Mystery & Suspense Stories 1985 (editor)
The Year's Best Mystery & Suspense Stories 1986 (editor)
The Year's Best Mystery & Suspense Stories 1987 (editor)
Great British Detectives (co-editor)
Women Write Murder (co-editor)
The Year's Best Mystery & Suspense Stories 1988 (editor)

THE YEAR'S BEST

MYSTERY & SUSPENSE STORIES

1989

Edited by Edward D. Hoch

WALKER AND COMPANY
NEW YORK

Again, for Marge and Ed Blodgett

First published in the United States of America in 1989 by Walker Publishing Company, Inc.

Published simultaneously in Canada by Thomas Allen & Son Canada, Limited, Markham, Ontario.

Library of Congress Cataloging-in-Publication Data

The Year's best mystery & suspense stories. —1982-   —
New York : Walker, 1982-
v. ; 22 cm.
Annual.
Editor: 1982   E.D. Hoch.
Continues: Best detective stories of the year.

1. Detective and mystery stories, American—
Periodicals.   2. Detective and
mystery stories, English—Periodicals.   I. Hoch, Edward D., 1930-
II. Title: Year's best mystery and suspense stories.
PZ1.B446588   83-646567   813'.0872'08—dc19
Library of Congress [8406] AACR 2   MARC-S

ISBN: 0-8027-1097-2

Printed in the United States of America

2 4 6 8 10 9 7 5 3 1

CONTENTS

Contents

Acknowledgments

"Crime and Punishment" by Michael Collins. Copyright © 1988 by Michael Collins. First published in *A Matter of Crime #3*, Bruccoli and Layman, eds. Harcourt, Brace, Jovanovich, 1988.

"Flicks" by Bill Crenshaw. Copyright © 1988 by Davis Publications, Inc. First published in *Alfred Hitchcock's Mystery Magazine*.

"The Crooked Way" by Loren D. Estleman. Copyright © 1988 by Loren D. Estleman. First published in *A Matter of Crime #3*, copyright © 1988 by Harcourt, Brace, Jovanovich, Inc.

"The Reason Why" by Edward Gorman. Copyright © 1988 by Edward Gorman.

"The Spy and the Guy Fawkes Bombing" by Edward D. Hoch. Copyright © 1988 by Edward D. Hoch. First published in *Ellery Queen's Mystery Magazine*.

"The Dakar Run" by Clark Howard. Copyright © 1988 by Clark Howard. First published in *Ellery Queen's Mystery Magazine*.

"Different Drummers" by Linda O. Johnston. Copyright © 1988 by Davis Publications, Inc. First published in *Ellery Queen's Mystery Magazine*.

"The Wasp" by Peter Lovesey. Copyright © 1988 by Peter Lovesey, Ltd. First published in *Ellery Queen's Mystery Magazine*.

"Fatherly Love" by Carl Martin. Copyright © 1988 by Davis Publications, Inc. First published in *Ellery Queen's Mystery Magazine*.

"Bridey's Caller" by Judith O'Neill. Copyright © 1988 by Davis Publications, Inc. First published in *Alfred Hitchcock's Mystery Magazine*.

INTRODUCTION

The past year continued to be a strong one for mystery anthologies, with my count of thirty-four volumes only slightly lower than last year's record total of thirty-eight. Single-author collections of mystery short stories, standing at twenty-nine, actually exceeded last year's total.

I wish the news from the magazine front was as encouraging. The bright spot was the circulation gains shown by both *Ellery Queen's Mystery Magazine* and *Alfred Hitchcock's Mystery Magazine*. The gloom descended with the news that the fine anthology series *A Matter of Crime*, which began life as *The New Black Mask Quarterly*, had ceased publication. If we consider *New Black Mask* and *A Matter of Crime*—publishing from two to four issues a year—to have been a periodical, then *EQMM* and *AHMM* remain the only two professional mystery magazines in the field. The last time there were only two mystery magazines available to readers was in the early months of 1920, just before the original *Black Mask* made its debut and the floodgates opened.

Happily, there are some glimmers of hope on the horizon. In England a new magazine called *Crime & Mystery Monthly* is promised for the spring of 1989. It will be the first British mystery magazine since the demise of the *London Mystery Selection* some seven years ago. In this country a number of small semiprofessional publications have begun to appear, available almost entirely by subscription. The already established *Hardboiled* was joined in 1988 by *Detective Story Magazine*, which published three issues, and *Two-Fisted Detective Stories*, which produced a second issue. The typewriter composition and crude production no doubt prevent wider distribution of these magazines at the present time, but all three show promise for the future. Taking mystery fanzines as an example, a look at

The Armchair Detective shows how a publication can progress from an amateur effort to a professional magazine in both appearance and content.

Private eye stories were especially strong during 1988, the centennial of Raymond Chandler's birth. Five of the twelve stories included here feature established private eye series characters, though the stories themselves are far from the traditional private eye capers.

As always, my thanks to those who helped in the preparation of this volume, especially Joe L. Hensley, Eleanor Sullivan, Mike Nevins, and my wife Patricia.

Edward D. Hoch

MICHAEL COLLINS
CRIME AND PUNISHMENT

Michael Collins is the best known of the pseudonyms used by popular mystery writer Dennis Lynds. Collins is the creator of one-armed private eye Dan Fortune, who has appeared in some fourteen novels and numerous short stories. This author tackles the moral implications of modern living. He is our conscience, and we are the richer because of it.

Back around the time of *the* Revolution, I told James Crawford, there was so much counterfeiting they made the punishment hanging, drawing and quartering, boiling alive, gouging the eyes out, or any slow, horrible death they could think of, and printed the punishment in detail on the money. The counterfeiters just went on printing the phony money, punishments and all.

"It didn't stop them. They had to have money to live."

"It stopped the ones who were executed," Crawford said.

But this story doesn't start with James Crawford, it starts with Tracy Detective Agency, an international outfit with offices coast to coast and in fifty cities overseas. Mr. Donald Meredith heads the New York office. He's a big, classy man with thick gray hair going white at the temples, and a smooth pink face that gets shaved daily in his office. His muscles are hidden under a thousand dollars of gray banker's flannel, and he hasn't broken a strike, caught a bank robber, or faced a killer in twenty years.

"Sit down, Fortune."

"Hiring extra guards yourself now, Meredith?"

He's *Mister* Meredith these days, but he'd turned me down once when I'd tried to join Tracy because he didn't employ one-armed men as detectives. Besides, he called me.

"You want an easy job or not?"

"What kind of job?"

."A killing, small and simple." He tented his hands, stared me down. "We don't usually take private cases anymore, pretty

1

much all corporate and government work. But Dr. Walter Payne Crawford was a client, his son is an executive in a corporation where we're on retainer."

He laid it out short and neat. Dr. Walter Payne Crawford had been shot three times in the back of the head two weeks ago in his Oyster Bay house. Nothing had been stolen. The house was in a guarded development, no strangers had been seen anywhere in the neighborhood. Crawford had been alone in the house, no one heard the shots. The Crawfords were important people, but the police and Tracy had come up with nothing except the footprint of a workboot and a small cut on his neck. No witnesses, no suspects in or out of the family, and no motive.

"How come he was alone in the house?"

"It was the day his wife visits her mother, his son plays poker, the help takes the day off."

I must have stared. "That's a lot of coincidence. It had to have been planned."

"We don't think so. It was his own gun."

"His own gun?"

"Gun's missing, but the desk drawer where he kept it was open, he had a firing range and the police found slugs that matched. No prints. I can't waste men on a wild-goose chase after some passing psycho high on angel dust. I told the son it was a police job, but he says we owe him. It's a touchy situation, I have to give him a man."

"How much?"

"Three hundred a day and expenses. Work a couple of weeks, then back us up and drop it."

"That's not half what you're getting."

"Five hundred then. We've got to recoup the overhead."

"Seven-fifty. I don't care about your overhead."

It wasn't their full fee, but I had to leave him enough to explain to the board it was worth it.

The house in Oyster Bay was big, white, and sprawling. James Crawford looked at my missing arm, my duffel coat and beret, and wasn't impressed. That was probably why Meredith had picked me.

"My father was murdered in cold blood. I want the animal who did it caught."

"Why did your father have a gun?"

"We all have the right to defend our home."

"A lot of good it did him."

"He had to have been taken by surprise, or the killer would be the one who was dead."

I dug into the family and Crawford's medical practice and associates. Checked taxis, buses, the train for any suspicious strangers. Talked to the neighbors, the cops, his friends.

"No enemies we can find," Lieutenant Watts of the Oyster Bay Police said. "No outside business activities except investments. We can't trace the workboot to anyone he knew. No one knows how he got that cut on his neck."

"How'd the killer get the gun?"

He shrugged. "Crawford kept it in his desk."

His wife and son were the only immediate family, both lived in the house, both had ironclad alibies. Mrs. Crawford was still in tears, too distraught to even count her money yet.

"We were married thirty-two years, Mr. Fortune. Walter never looked at another woman."

Neighbors and associates agreed.

"If they didn't love each other, they sure loved the same things—money and comfort."

And added, "Honest, hardworking, dull, that was Walter."

His fellow doctors at the hospital had a mixed picture, depending on who they were themselves. The more dedicated physicians saw one man, the rich golfers saw another.

"He still had the first buck he made, and every other one he could get," an emergency room doctor told me.

"The best plastic surgeon on the East Coast, and a hell of a guy."

"Accepted no Medicare or welfare patients, never put in an hour of community or free-clinic time."

"Generous to a fault, a good sport."

"Liked by his rich friends, didn't have any poor friends."

After a week of this, I came up as empty as the police or Tracy. It was time to agree with Meredith and bow out.

"He killed my father," James Crawford said. "I want him

caught and executed. I want to stop others from killing men as
fine as my father!"

That was when I told him about the Revolutionary era
counterfeiters and deterrance, and he said, "It deters the one
who is executed."

"We're not going to deter this one," I said. "And I don't
believe it was any passing psychotic. It had to be planned, but
there're no leads, no motive, and no witnesses. It's not going to
be solved except by chance or time, and that's a police job."

"I'll double what I pay Tracy. I want you to keep going."

"Two thousand a day?"

"I want to see justice done."

Occam's Razor says the simplest explanation of anything is the
right one. Fortune's Law says that when everything is ruled out,
what's left has to be the answer.

About all that was left was hobbies. I talked again to everyone
at the yacht club and the country club, at the medical associa-
tions and in the neighborhood. Everywhere and anywhere. At
two thousand a day, I was in no hurry, but slow or fast the
answer was the same. The doctor had had no hobbies except
making and investing money.

So I sat down in the study where Dr. Walter Payne Crawford
had died and went through each drawer until I knew every one
of his investments. Call it the sensation of a possibility. A notion.
Crawford had been heavily invested in New York City real
estate. Three of the buildings had addresses on the Lower East
Side. I took the train back into the city.

The first two buildings were in the shadows where the El had
darkened the streets when I was a boy. The El had gone, but
the darkness remained. There were no front doors, only black
holes like the mouths of tunnels. The lightless corridors were
as dim and silent as ancient cliff dwellings. In the vestibules
broken mailboxes hung open. Pools of urine covered half the
grimy tile floors. Inside, the floors were gouged and splintered
to bare wood. The walls were disfigured with leaks and filth and
violent graffiti. The apartment doors had no paint, and the hall
toilets had no doors. The stairs were broken and the bannisters
gone. The stench was overpowering.

Standard slumlord operation. Buy up buildings in such bad condition it's better for the former owner to sell at a loss than fix them up, then run them down even further.. Never spend a cent on them, overcharge the tenants who are poor, intimidated, can't speak English, or all three. Lawyers are cheaper than repairs, so bribe the building inspectors, fight condemnation, pile up the profits.

The third was just up the block. Or it had been. I stood in front of what was left. Fire had destroyed the entire building from the ground floor up, gutted the top two floors leaving only jagged outside walls against the sky. A year ago, maybe two. The damaged buildings on either side had been cleaned up and more or less repaired.

When everything is ruled out, what's left has to be the answer.

A tenement fire doesn't rate much news coverage unless someone is killed, not a lot even then.

It took me most of the day in the Forty-Second Street library before I found it. The building had burned a year and a half ago, a cold winter day when the firemen had trouble with their hoses. The *Times* called it a slumlord building, gave the name of the owner: Dr. Walter Payne Crawford of Oyster Bay. The cause of the fire was the gas line of an illegal heater chewed through by rats while the tenants slept. The building's central heating system had been broken for five years. One woman died.

The *Post* coverage was about the same, but with a lot more gaudy prose. The woman had been pregnant, and a heroine.

Newsday had a wire-service photo and a caption. The photo showed two black children crying on a dirty, snow-covered street beside a fallen black woman. The caption read: *The small boys cry beside Pearlie Jordan who collapsed outside her Lower East Side apartment Monday after leading her mother, brothers, and two nephews' to safety from the burning building. The 26-year-old pregnant woman died later in a New York hospital.*

*   *   *

Detective Alex Callow nodded in the precinct squad room.

"I remember. They gave the woman a posthumous medal for saving the people she did, brought charges against the landlord. He got off with fines, orders to clean up his buildings."

"She was married?"

Callow shook his head. "Lived with her mother, two kid brothers, a couple of nephews. There was a boyfriend. Raised hell in the hospital."

"You have his name?"

"Hell no. It wasn't a police case."

"What hospital did she die in?"

"Bellevue, where else."

At Bellevue, the death of one black woman in a tenement fire a year and a half ago wasn't something easily remembered. But this one was a heroine, had been in all the papers.

"Sure," the nursing supervisor said. "She arrived in a coma, never came out of it. Smoke inhalation, burns, shock. Those run-down tenements torch like roman candles."

"Do you remember her boyfriend?"

"I wasn't on that night."

She sent me to the Medical Records librarian. The record on Pearlie Jordan showed her mother as next of kin, no mention of a boyfriend, but had the names of the nurses on duty that night. Two had left the hospital, but two were still there and even on duty. They both remembered the boyfriend.

"He took it real hard," one said.

"Sat with her the whole time," the second said, "but she never regained consciousness."

"Even after she died we couldn't get him away."

"He tried to go with the body to the morgue."

" 'It's my son, too,' he said. 'I got to stay with my son.' "

"Four months pregnant. A real shame."

I said, "Do you remember his name? Where he lived?"

They didn't. No one in the whole hospital knew his name. I went back to Medical Records. The body had been released to the mother, but the only address they had was the tenement that had burned. And the mortuary that buried her.

At the mortuary the records said Pearlie Jordan had been sent back to her native town in North Carolina for burial. The mortuary had been paid in cash, no record of who paid it.

"But we sent the papers after burial to her mother."

"To a burned out tenement?"

"No, she had a new address by then. I think we have it here somewhere."

It was another tenement not six blocks from the one that had burned. In better condition, almost livable, the dark living room clean in the light of the single lamp.

"Pearlie had some insurance," the mother said. "We got us a better place."

She was a white-haired old woman fifteen years younger than she looked, thin as a rail and stooped as if she'd spent her life in the fields of her native North Carolina. She hadn't, the stoop only the weight of her struggle to survive.

"I'm looking for Pearlie's boyfriend. The father of the child."

"What you want with Noah?"

"That's his name? Noah? Noah what?"

"You don't know his name?" The suspicion instant. Who was I to be looking for a man whose name I didn't know. "Cop?"

"Private detective. Dan Fortune."

"So?"

"The landlord who owned the building that burned was killed three weeks ago out in Oyster Bay."

"You want I should cry?"

"Executed," I said. "Like a murderer."

"That supposed to mean something to me?"

"I think so," I said.

A few times in your life there is a moment when you know you've made a mistake. A bad mistake. I knew it now.

The faint sound was behind me in the dark apartment. It had never occurred to me he might be living with the mother.

"See if he got any guns, Momma. Any tape recorders."

The knife blade behind me caught the light of the single lamp, the point drew blood from my neck.

I said, "Is the knife how you got Doctor Crawford to sit in that chair so you could shoot him?"

The old woman was shaky and scared, but she knew how to search. She shook her head to the man behind me.

"Nothing, Noah. You maybe oughta not—"

"Anyone in the hall? On the street?"

"I'm alone," I said.

The old woman went away.

"Noah what?" I said.

The woman returned. "I don't see no one, Noah."

The knife dug deeper into my neck. "How'd you get here?"

"No one out there can figure a motive. I found he owned the tenements, came up with you."

He was silent for some time.

"What do they have?"

"A footprint."

"That's okay."

"Look, Noah—"

"What else?"

"Nothing," I said, "but they will have. They'll find the gun. They'll—"

"They won't find the gun."

The old woman said, "Noah works in a foundry."

I said, "Someone will remember seeing you. Out there you had to stand out too much. Someone's going to remember you when they ask."

The knife went away. He walked past and stood facing me in the light of the single lamp.

"No they won't."

He was Caucasian. Or close enough. A white man of medium height, ordinary face, nondescript. In a plain blue suit and hat like a thousand commuters. An everyman. He sat down, the knife still in his hand. "He murdered Pearlie, and they fined him. He murdered her and my son, got slapped on the wrist, bought more buildings."

"You learned when the house was empty? Knew he had a gun?"

"They just guard at the gates. His kind always have guns. Someone had to make him pay, stop him killing more people."

"You can't stop killing with killing."

"The state executes murderers. If they can, I can."

"They'll find you, Noah."

"He had to pay for Pearlie and my son. I've never been in any trouble. I'll never do anything again. You can't prove I did anything. You made some guesses. You found me, but you've got no proof. There's no way they can prove anything, and if they try I'll get off. Tell the police, go ahead. If they want to arrest me I'll get my time in court, tell the whole story. Maybe that'd be better. Show all the other animals like him what's gonna happen to them when they murder people. Maybe it'll stop all the slumlords."

"It won't," I said. "Go in yourself, Noah. Tell them."

"You tell them. They won't even arrest me. Go on, get out of here."

I didn't argue with him. I got out of there.

In the silent Oyster Bay house James Crawford listened impassive. When I'd finished he spoke without moving.

"Is that murderer under arrest?"

"I don't know."

"You don't know? He murdered my father in cold blood, and you don't know if he's been arrested?"

"Your father made a fortune buying substandard buildings, renting them to the poor five to a room, letting them run down into garbage dumps. Just take the rent and run. Sewers an animal shouldn't live in. One place burned to the ground. A pregnant woman died."

"My father made an investment. An accident happened."

"To Noah he executed a murderer."

"He's insane!"

"He believes in capital punishment."

"You can't just kill anyone you want to!"

"No," I said, "you can't. Not in a civilized world. So I went to the police. I told them what I've told you. But he'll deny it. There aren't any witnesses. He isn't the kind of man anyone would particularly remember. He's not worried about the footprint. The gun is probably melted down in a batch of iron. I don't think the DA'll even bring an indictment."

"He killed my father! He has to be punished!"

"Get a gun and do it yourself. Then one of his friends can

execute you. Keep it up until someone is caught and the state can finish the job."

He sat there, the hate in his eyes. "You don't expect to be paid, do you?"

"I did my job. I'll send you my bill. The rest is up to you and the state. Call it justice."

I took a cab back to the station, the train into the city. In the morning, Callow at the East Side precinct said they'd arrested Noah and charged him, but the DA wasn't optimistic. I called the best lawyer I knew who owed me a favor.

The Tracy Agency put every available man on finding evidence against Noah. After a couple of months they had to give up. My volunteer lawyer put on the pressure, and the DA dropped the charges for lack of evidence.

Down on the Lower East Side, Pearlie Jordan's insurance money ran out. Her mother, brothers, two nephews, and Noah were evicted for nonpayment, disappeared from the city.

James Crawford took over his father's business. The publicity brought the city down on him—his lawyers are in court every day fighting complaints, citations, condemnation proceedings. It doesn't worry Crawford. Win, lose, or draw, the tenements will make a nice profit before he loses them or they fall down.

BILL CRENSHAW

FLICKS

*Bill Crenshaw is one of several new authors of the 1980s,
who writes mainly short stories and shows a great deal
of promise. In Crenshaw's case the promise is more than
fulfilled with a police procedural unlike any you've read.
The story is set in a movie theater playing horror films.
The Mystery Writers of America has honored it with the
Edgar Allan Poe Award as the Best Short Story of 1988.*

He knew it wasn't a question of if his beeper would go off.

This time Devin Corley was home, his apartment, had just
opened a beer, turned on the TV, stretched out on the couch.
He phoned in. Dispatcher said Majestic Theater, across town.
He started the VCR, took a last pull at the beer, gave the cat
fresh water, got a quick shower. Then he left. Speed was not of
the essence.

He knew what he'd find. A body; Ray Tasco, his partner taking
statements, popping his gum, looking amused and surprised at
once; Maggie Epps with her wedge face and her black forensic
kit, diagramming the scene, scooping nameless little forensic
glops into baggies; Joe Franks in a safari shirt, slung with
cameras, smiling like always, always smiling, always angry. He'd
give Corley grief about being away from his desk again, or being
late. Corley had been away from his desk a lot. He was always
late.

At the Majestic there were two uniforms in the men's john.
The room was done in men's room tile, blue and white, smelled
of urine, wet tobacco, stale drains, pine. Trash can on side,
brown paper towels spilling out, balled up, dark with water,
some with red smears. Floor around sinks wet, scattered
splashes and small pools. Hints of blood in wet footprints
running back and forth across the tile. In near stall somebody
retching. The uniform watching the somebody was pointedly
not looking at him.

11

"What we got?" Corley asked the uniforms.

"Got a slashing, lieutenant," said the older uniform, twenty-six maybe, Lopez maybe. Corley glanced down at the nametag. Lopez. The younger uniform looked green at the gills. Corley didn't know him, knew he wouldn't be green long, not this kind of green. Lots of greens in Homicide, green like Greengills, green like a two-day corpse, green like Corley, like old copper.

"In here?" Corley asked.

Lopez snapped his head back. "In the first theater."

Corley moved to the stall. Lopez moved beside him. Greengills went to the sink and splashed water on his face.

"Who we got?" said Corley.

"Pickpocket, he says. Says he just lifted the guy's wallet. Says he didn't know he was dead."

The pickpocket turned around, face pasty, hair matted. "I didn't know, man," he said, whiney, rocking. "Jesus, I didn't know. That was blood, oh God, that was blood, man, and I didn't even feel it. My hands . . ." He grabbed for the john again. Corley turned away.

"Any of that blood his?" he asked.

"Don't think so."

The wallet was on the stainless steel shelf over the sinks. It was smeared with bloody fingerprints. Corley took out a silver pen and flipped the wallet open. "Find it in the trash can?"

"Yessir," said the younger uniform, wiping the water from his face, looking at Corley in the mirror.

"Money still in it? Credit cards?"

"Yessir."

The driver's license showed a fifty-five-year-old business type, droopy eyes, saggy chin, looking above the camera, trying to decide if he should smile for this official picture. Bussey, Tyrone, Otis. Toccoa Falls, Georgia.

The pickpocket told Corley that he'd like seen this chubby dude asleep at the end of his row, which he'd seen him before with a big wad of cash in his wallet at the candy counter and seen him put the wallet inside his coat and not in his pants. Near the end of the flick when he got to the guy he kind of tripped and caught himself on the guy's seat and said sorry, excuse me, while lifting his wallet real neat, and he dropped the wallet into his popcorn box and headed right for the john to ditch the wallet and just stroll out with the plastic and the cash, but in the john his hands were bloody and the guy's wallet and his shoes, and then he heard screaming in the lobby and he ditched the wallet and tried to wash the blood off but there was too much, the more he looked, the more he saw, and somebody came in and went out, so he tried to hide. He didn't know what was happening, but he knew it was real bad.

There was a spritzing noise and thin, piney mist settled into the stall and spotted Corley's glasses. Corley tore off a little square of toilet paper and smeared the spots around on the lenses. He had the pickpocket arrested on robbery and on suspicion of murder, but he knew he wasn't the killer.

"Victim here alone?" asked Corley.

"As far as we know," said Lopez.

"Convention, maybe. Is Tasco here? Do you know Sergeant Tasco?"

Joe Franks leaned into the restroom, cameras swinging at his neck. "Hey, Corley, you in on this or not? The meat wagon's waiting. Come show me what you want."

Corley smiled. "You know what I want."

"Yeah, show me anyway so if you don't get it all, you don't blame me. Where've you been?"

"You shoot in here?"

"Yeah, I shot in here." He sounded impatient.

"You get the footprints?"

"Yeah, I got the footprints."

"Get the towels and the sink?"

"Yeah, the towels, the sink, and the stall, and the punk, and I even got a close-up of his puke, okay?"

"See, Joe," said Corley, smiling again, "you know exactly what I want."

"I hate working with you, Corley," said Franks as Corley pushed past him.

In the theater Maggie Epps was sitting on the aisle across from the body, sketchpad on her knees. "Glad you could make it, Devin," she said.

Corley fished for a snappy comeback, couldn't hook anything he hadn't said a hundred times before, said hello.

Franks showed Corley the angles he had shot. Corley asked for a couple more. The flashes illuminatd the body like lightning, burned distorted images into Corley's retina.

Tasco came in, talking to somebody, squinting over his notebook. "Ray, you got the manager there?" Corley called.

"I'm the owner," the man said.

"Think you could give us some more light?"

"This is as bright as it gets, officer. This is a movie theater."

Corley turned back around. Franks snorted.

Mr. T. O. Bussey sat on the aisle in the high-backed chair, sagging left, head forward, eyes opened. Blood covered everything from his tie on down, had run under the seats toward the screen. People had tracked it back toward the lobby, footprints growing fainter up the aisle.

"You shoot that?" asked Corley.

Franks nodded. "Probably thought they were walking through cola."

Corley bent over Mr. Bussey. He put a hand on the forehead and raised the head an inch or two so that he could see the wound. "You see this?"

"Yeah. Want a shot?"

"Can I lift his head, Maggie?"

"Just watch where you plant your big feet," she said.

Corley stood behind Mr. Bussey, put his hands above the ears, and raised the head face forward, chin up. He turned his eyes away from the flashes.

"What did he get?" said Corley.

"Everything," said Maggie. "Jugular, carotid, trachea, carotid, jugular. Something real sharp. This guy never made a sound, never felt a thing. Maybe a hand on his hair jerking his head back. Nothing after that."

"From behind?" Corley lowered the head back to where he had found it.

"Left to right, curving up. You got your man in the john?"

"Don't think so. Too much blood on his shoes. He walked out in front, not behind."

"So what have you got?"

"Headache."

Maggie smiled. "It's going to get worse."

Corley smiled back. "It always does."

Corley made Greengills help bag the body. He could say that he was helping the kid get used to it, that it didn't get any better, that as bodies went this one wasn't bad, but he wasn't sure he had done it as a favor. He was afraid he'd done it to be mean.

They spent half an hour looking for the weapon. Corley didn't expect to find anything. They didn't.

He had a videotape unit brought over and sent Lopez and Greengills into the other theaters to block the parking lot exits and send the audiences through the lobby.

The owner pulled him aside and protested. Corley told him that the killer might be in another theater. The owner said something about losing the last *Deathdancer* audience and not needing any publicity hurting ticket sales and being as much a victim as that poor man. "I own nine screens in this town," he said, dragging his hand over his jaw. "I'm not responsible for this. Let's keep the profile low, okay?" There was nothing Corley could say, so he said nothing, and the owner bristled and said he had friends in this town. "I'll speak to your superior about this, Officer . . . ?"

"Corley," he said, walking away. "That's l—e—y."

The other movies ended and the audiences pushed into the lobby. Corley had them videotaped as they bunched and swayed toward the street. Two more uniforms arrived and he started them searching the other theaters for the weapon.

He left Tasco in charge and went to the station and hung around the darkroom while Franks did his printing and bitched about wasting his talent on corpses and about Corley's always wanting more shots and more prints than anybody else. Corley didn't bother to tell Franks again that it was his own fault, that Franks was the one who always waxed eloquent over his third beer and said that the camera always lied, that the image distorted as much as it revealed, that photographs were fictions. He had convinced Corley, so Corley always wanted more and more pictures, each to balance others, to offer new angles, so that reality became a sort of compromise, an average. Corley didn't say any of that again. He made the right noises at the right times, like he did when Franks said how he was going to quit as soon as he finished putting his portfolio together, as soon as he got a show somewhere.

Maybe Franks really was working on a project. Maybe he should be a real photographer. Corley didn't know. He knew Franks about as well as he could, down to a certain level, no further. He imagined that Franks knew him in about the same way. It wasn't the kind of thing they talked about.

Corley lifted a dripping print out of the fixer. "Why'd you become a cop anyway?" he said.

Franks took the print from him and put it back. It was hard to read Franks's eyes in the red light. "You're asking that like you thought there were real answers," Franks said.

Corley took the prints to his desk and did what paperwork he could. He worked until the sky got gray. By the time he stopped for doughnuts on the way home, the first edition of the *News* was in the stands. It didn't have the murder.

He thought sometimes there were real answers instead of just the same patterns and ways to deal with patterns and levels beyond which you couldn't go. He thought sometimes that there was a way to get to the next level. He thought sometimes he'd quit, do insurance fraud, something. He thought maybe he hated his job, but he didn't know that either. He had thought there was something essential about working Homicide, essential in the sense of dealing with the essences of things, a job that butted as close to the raw edge of reality as he was likely to get, and how would he do insurance after that? But whatever kind of essence he was seeing, it was mute, images beyond articulation. None of it made any sense, and he was bone-marrow tired.

The landing at his apartment was dim, and as he slid his key into the second lock, he could see the peephole darken in the apartment next door. Half past five in the morning and Gianelli was already up and prowling. Corley stood an extra second in the rectangle of light from his apartment so that Gianelli could see who he was, whoever the hell Gianelli was besides a name on a mailbox downstairs, an eye at the peephole, the sounds of pacing footsteps, of a TV. Corley's cat sniffed at the flecks of dried blood on his shoes.

Corley tossed the paper and Franks's pictures on the desk,

opened a can of smelly catfood, had a couple of doughnuts and some milk. Then he rewound the tape in the VCR and stretched out on the couch to watch the program that the call to the theater had interrupted. It was a cop show. At the station they laughed at cop shows. Things made sense in cop shows. He fell asleep before the first commercial.

Corley woke up with the cat in his face again. He got a hand under its middle and flicked it away, watched it twist in the air, land on all fours, sit and stretch, lick its paws. It wasn't even his cat. The apartment had come with the cat and a wall of corky tile covered with pictures of the previous occupant. The super hadn't bothered to take them down. "Throw 'em away if you want," he'd said. "What do I care?" She was pale and blonde. An actress who never made it, maybe. A model. A photographer. Corley wondered what kind of person would leave a cat and a wall covered wth her own image. He still had the pictures in a box somewhere. He used the cork as a dart board, to pin up grocery lists and phone numbers. After eight months he was getting used to the cat, except when it tried to lie in his face, which it always did when he fell asleep on the couch. One of these times he was going to toss it out of the window, down to the street. Four floors down, it didn't matter if it landed on its feet or not.

He looked at his watch. Only nine thirty, but he knew he wouldn't get back to sleep. He might as well go in.

He stopped for doughnuts and coffee and the second edition. Big headline. HORROR FLICK HORROR. *Blood flowed on the screen and in the aisles last night at the Majestic Theater* . . . Great copy, he thought, great murder for the papers. Stupid murder in a stupid place. Not robbery. Not a hit, not on some salesman from upstate Georgia. Tasco would say somebody boozed, whacked, dusted. Corley didn't think so. This one was weird. There was something going on here, something interesting, a new level, maybe, something new. He sat for a long time thinking.

It was going on eleven by the time he dropped the paper on his desk.

"My kids love those things," said Tasco.

"What things?"

Tasco pointed to the headline. "Horror flicks."

Corley looked at the paper. The story was coverd in green felt tip pen with questions about the case, with ideas, with an almost unrecognizable sketch of the scene. Corley didn't remember doodling.

There was a tapping of knuckle on glass. Captain Hupmann motioned them into his office.

"Finally," said Tasco.

"How long you been waiting?" said Corley.

"Too long."

"Sorry." He knew the captain had been waiting on him, had made Tasco wait on him, too.

"Just go easy, okay?" Tasco said.

The captain shut the door and turned to Corley. "So where are we on this one?"

Tasco looked at Corley. Corley shrugged.

The captain started to snap something but Tasco flipped open his notebook. "Family notified," he said. "Victim in town for sales convention, goes to same convention every year, never takes wife. Concession girl remembers him because he talked funny, had an accent she meant, and he made her put extra butter on his popcorn twice and called her ma'am. Nobody else remembers him. Staying at the Plaza, single room, no roommate. They don't take roll at the meetings, so we don't know if he's been to any or if he's been seeing the sights." Tasco looked up, popping his gum, then looked at Corley.

"I think we've got a nut," said Corley. "Random. Maybe a one-shot, maybe a serial."

The captain raised his eyebrows in mock surprise. "Are we taking an interest in our work again?"

Corley shifted his weight.

"A nut," said the captain. "Ray?"

Tasco shrugged. "Seems reasonable, but we're not married to it. Might be a user flipped out by the flick."

The captain turned back to Corley. "Why did he pick Bussey?"

Corley could picture Bussey at the convention, anonymous in the city and the crowd, free to cuss and stay out late if he wanted, hit the bars and the ladies, drink too much and smoke big cigars. But Mr. Bussey hadn't gone that far. He'd just gone to a movie he wouldn't be caught dead in at home.

"He sat in the wrong place," said Corley. "He was on the aisle. Quick exit."

"What quick exit? This is a theater, for chrissake. This is public. You don't do a random in public." The captain drew his lips together. "Where do you want to go with this?" he asked finally, looking more at Tasco than Corley.

Corley looked at Tasco before answering. He hadn't told Tasco anything. "We want to talk to the pickpocket again, the employees again. We've got some names from the audience, the paper had some more. We want them to see the tapes, see if they recognize somebody coming out of the other theaters. Ray wants to do more with Mr. Bussey's movements, see if there's some connection we don't know about."

"Okay," said the captain. "You've both got plenty of other work, but you can keep this one warm for a couple of days. Check the gangs. Maybe something there, initiation ritual, something. If it's some kind of hit, or if it's a user, it won't go far."

"I think it's a serial," said Corley.

"You mean you hope it's a serial," said the captain. "Otherwise you're not going to get him. That it?"

"Yessir," said Tasco.

"Oh, and Corley," the captain said as Corley was halfway through the door, "welcome back. Back to stay?"

They followed up with the employees and what members of the audience they could find, asked if they'd known anybody else in the theater, seen anything unusual, remembered someone walking around near the end of the movie. They showed them pictures of the pickpocket and Mr. Bussey's driver's license, the tapes of the other audiences, asked if anybody looked familiar.

Corley tried to make himself ask the questions as if they were new, as if he'd never even thought of them before. Same questions, same answers, and if you didn't listen because it all seemed the same, you missed something. Tasco always asked the questions right and was somehow not dulled by the routine, by the everlasting sameness. Tasco hunkered down and did his job, would see the waste and the stupidity of it all, say, "Jeez, why do they do that, we got to get the SOB that did this, aren't people horrible." Tasco's saving grace was that he didn't think about it. Corley didn't mean that in a mean way. It was a quality he envied, maybe even admired. Welcome back, back to stay? Sometimes he wondered why he didn't just walk away from it all.

They got Maggie to draw a seating chart and they put little pins in the squares, red for Mr. Bussey, yellow for the people they questioned, blue in seats that yellows remembered being occupied. The media played the story and boosted ratings and circulation, and more people from the audience came forward, and others who claimed to have been there but who Tasco said were probably on Mars at the time. The number of pins increased, but that was all.

"They sat all around him," said Corley, "and they didn't see anything."

"So who in this city ever sees anything?"

"Yeah, well, they should have seen something. Maybe they were watchng the movie. Maybe we should see it."

They used their shields to get into the seven o'clock show. The ticket girl told them that the crowd was down, especially in *Deathdancer.* Tasco bought a big tub of popcorn and two Cokes, and they sat in the middle, about halfway to the screen.

The horror flicks that had scared Corley as a kid played with the dark, the uncertain, the unknown, where you might not even see the killer clearly, where you were never sure if the clicking in the night outside was the antenna wire slapping in the wind or the sound of the giant crabs moving. One thing might be another, and there was no way to tell, and you never really knew if you were safe.

But this wasn't the same. Here the only unknowns were when the next kid was going to get it and how gross it would be. A series of bright red brutalities, each more bizarre than the last, more grotesque, more unreal. Corley couldn't take it seriously. But maybe the audience could. Unless they were cops or medics, maybe this was what it was like. Corley started watching them.

They were mostly under forty, sat in couples or groups, boys close to the screen or all the way to the wall and the corners, girls in the middle, turning their heads away and looking sideways; dates close, touching, copping feels; marrieds a married distance apart. They all talked and laughed too loud. On the screen the killer stalked the victim and the audience got quiet and focused on the movie. Corley could feel muscles stiffen, tension build as the sequence drew the moment out, the moment you knew would come, was coming, came, and they screamed at the killing, and after the killing sank back spent, then started laughing nervously, talking, wisecracking at the screen, at each other. Corley watched three boys sneak up behind a row of girls and grab at their throats, the girls shrieking, leaping, the boys collapsing in laughter. A girl chanted, "Esther wet her panties," and the whole audience broke up. On the screen, the killer started stalking his next victim and the cycle began again.

"What do you think?" asked Corley, lighting a cigarette as soon as they hit the lobby. People in line for the next show stared at their faces as if trying to see if they would be scared or bored or disgusted. Corley thought they all looked hopeful somehow.

Tasco shrugged, placid as ever. "It was a horror flick."

"Was it any good?"

"Who can tell? You'll have to ask my kids."

The summer wind was warm and filled with exhaust fumes.

"You wanta come up for a beer or something?" Corley asked.

Tasco looked at his watch. "Nah, better get back. Evelyn. See you tomorrow."

Corley thought about rephrasing it, asking if he wanted to stop in for a beer somewhere, but Tasco had already made his excuse. Used to be they'd have a beer once or twice a week before Tasco started his thirty-minute drive back to Evelyn and the kids and the postage-stamp yard he was so proud of, but that was before Corley had moved across town, out of his decent apartment, with the courtyard and the pool, into what he lived in now. Tasco had been to the new place once only. He'd looked around and popped his gum and looked surprised and amused and inhaled his beer and left. Corley was relieved that Tasco hadn't asked him why he'd moved. He asked himself the same thing.

After he fed the cat, Corley put on the tape of the audience leaving the other screens. At first they ignored the camera, looked away, pretended not to see it, nudged a companion, pointed discreetly. Some made faces and more people saw it, and more made faces or shot birds or mouthed "Hi, Mom" or walked straight at the camera so that their faces filled the pictures, stuck hands or popcorn boxes in front of the lens, waved, mugged, danced, pretended to strip, to moon the camera, to kiss Corley through the TV screen.

They had taped three audiences. They acted about the same.

Before he went to bed, Corley posted the newspaper articles and Franks's pictures on the cork wall, with a shot of Mr. Bussey in the center.

The heat woke him. He lay sweating, disoriented, fingers knotted in sheets. The night light threw a yellow oval on the wall opposite, gave the room a focus, showed him right where he was. He hated the panic that came from not being sure. He took three or four deep, slow breaths.

He hadn't always had the night light. He hadn't always strapped an extra gun to his leg or carried two speedloaders in his coat pockets every time he went out. He hadn't always spent so much time in his apartment, in front of the TV, asleep in front of the TV, in bed. He tried not to think about it. He tried not to think.

It was too early to be up, too late to go back to sleep, too hot to stay in the apartment. He could make coffee and go to the roof before the sun hit the tar, could catch the breeze off the river, let the cat stalk pigeons.

While the coffee dripped he sat on the couch and looked at the pictures on the wall. In the central picture Mr. Bussey sat with head up and eyes open like he was watching the movie, the wound like a big smile. Death in black and white. Not like the deaths in the movie. Real was more . . . something. Casual. Anticlimactic. Prosaic. Unaccompanied by soundtrack. Maybe Bussey wasn't really dead. Maybe it was just special effects. In the picture his hands held Mr. Bussey's head just above the ears. He wiped his palms on his shorts.

Mr. Gianelli's peephole darkened as Corley shut his door and the cat slid up the stairs. He was halfway to the landing when the door opened the width of the chain and Gianelli's face pressed into the crack, cheeks bulging around the wood. Over his shoulder a room was lit by a television's multicolored glow.

"I know what you're doing, young man," Gianelli called in a rasping voice.

"Sorry if I woke you," Corley said, kept climbing, smiled. Maybe thirty-eight seemed young to Gianelli.

"You leave my antenna alone," Gianelli said. "The one on the chimney. I been seventeen years in this building. I got rights. You hear me, young man? Next time my picture goes I'm calling a cop." He slammed his door and it echoed in the stairwell like a gunshot.

Corley beat Tasco to work.

"Whoa," said Franks on his way to the coffee pot. "On time and everything. You must have figured it out."

"Figured what out?" said Corley.

Franks smiled. "That you won't get fired for being late. You want out, you got to quit."

"So who wants out?"

"Who doesn't?"

Tasco had never said anything about Corley's being late. When Tasco came in, he didn't say anything about Corley's being early.

Another homicide came in and they spent the morning and most of the afternoon down by the river and the warehouses, Tasco and Corley and Maggie and Joe and the smells of creosote and fish and gasoline. Some punk had taken a twelve-gauge to the gut, sawed-off, Maggie said, because of the spread and the powder burns, another drug hit as the new champions of free enterprise tried to corner the market. It wasn't going to get solved unless somebody rolled over. A crowd gathered at the yellow police line ribbons. Lopez and Greengills came in for crowd control. The paramedics bitched about hauling corpses. Greengills didn't seem to be bothered by the body.

It was late when they got back to the station.

"I'm going to the movie," said Corley. "I'm going to take our pickpocket. Want to come?"

"What for ?"

"Like you said, maybe something in the movie freaked this guy. Maybe we can find something."

"I don't think we're going to get anywhere on this one."

"So you want to come, or not?" Tasco said no.

The pickpocket didn't want to go either. "My treat," Corley told him, not smiling.

Corley sat in Mr. Bussey's seat and told the pickpocket to reconstruct exactly what he had done, when he had done it. He got popcorn and grape soda like Bussey, put the empties into the next seat like Bussey, concentrated on the movie, tried not to see the pickpocket in the corner of his eye, tried to ignore the feeling that his back was to the door, tried to control his breathing. He hated this, hated the dark, the people around him, the long empty aisle on his left, he felt full of energy demanding use, fought to sit still. Finally on the screen the killer reached for the last survivor and the background music shrieked, and Corley slumped left and lowered his head and sat, and on the screen the girl fought off the killer, and they rescued her just in time, and they killed the killer and comforted the girl, and they discovered that the killer wasn't dead and had escaped, and then Corley felt the pickpocket fall across him, heard his "Sorry," felt the wallet slide out of his coat only because he was waiting for it. He sat slumped over while the audience filed out, giggling or groaning or silent. He sat until a nervous usher shook him and asked him to wake up.

He found the pickpocket throwing up in the men's room.

"We're just going to leave this open for a while," said the captain. "Put the river thing on warm."

Tasco nodded, popping his gum. Corley said nothing.

"Problem, Devin?"

"I'd like to stay on this awhile."

"Got something to sell? New leads? Anything?"

Corley shook his head. "Not really."

"Okay, then."

They went back to their desks.

"Learn anything last night?" asked Tasco.

Corley shrugged, remembering the dark, palpable and pressing; the icy air pushing not his lungs as he sat and waited, the effort to exhale; trying to concentrate on the movie, on what might have snapped somebody; and after, trying to help the pickpocket out of the stall, embarrassed for him now, and sorry, and the pickpocket twisting his elbow out of Corley's grip and tearing in half the twenty that Corley had stuffed into his shirt pocket, bloody money maybe, something, he wouldn't have it. "Not much," he said. "Bussey must have gotten it in that last sequence, like we thought."

"Funny, isn't it, all that stuff up there on the screen, and out in the audience some dude flicks out a blade and that's that."

"Yeah," said Corley. "That's that."

Corley found himself at a movie again that night, a horror flick near the university. He sat on the aisle, last row, back to the wall. The movie looked the same as the other, felt the same, same rhythms, same victims, same bright gore. The audience was younger, more the age of the characters on the screen, and louder, maybe, but still much the same as the others, shouting at the screen, groaning, cracking jokes, laughing in the wrong places, trying to scare each other, strange responses, inappropriate somehow. They had come for the audience as much as the movie. They had come to be in a group.

He found himself the next night in another movie, on the aisle, last row, back to the wall, fingering the speedloader in his pocket, trying to remember why he was wasting his time there.

Near the end of the show, he saw a silhouette down front rise and edge toward the aisle, stop, and his guts iced as he saw it reach out its left hand and pull back someone's head, heard a scream, saw it slash across the throat with its right hand and turn and run up the aisle for the exit, coming right for him, too perfect. He braced, tightening his grips on the armrests, fought to sit, sit, as the silhouette ran toward him, then he stuck out a leg and the man went down hard and Corley was on him with his knee in the back and his gun behind the right ear. He yelled for an ambulance, ordered the man to open his fist. The man was slow. Corley brought a gun butt down on the back of his hand. The fingers opened, and something bright rolled onto the carpet. Corley stared at it for a few seconds before he saw it was a tube of lipstick.

"It's only a game, man," said a voice above him, quavering. Corley looked up. The owner of the voice was pointing with a shaking finger to the bright red lipstick slash along his throat. "Only a game."

Corley cuffed them to each other and took them in. He was not gentle with them.

The papers had fun with the story. "Off-duty Detective Nabs Lipstick Slasher," said one headline. Corley posted the stories on the corkboard.

They gave him a hard time when he got to work, asked if he'd been wounded, if the stain would come out, warned him about the chapstick chopper. He didn't let it get to him.

What got to him was how much fun the slasher and his victim had. He tried to tell Tasco about it. He'd almost lost it, he said. He'd been shaking with rage, wanted to push them around, run them in hard, give them a dose of the fear of God, but it didn't sink in. They just kept replaying it all the way into the station.

"You really· didn't know for sure, did you?" the slasher had asked.

"Thought I was *gone,*" said the victim. "For a second there I thought this was it." He laid his head back on the seat, his face suddenly blue fading to black as the unit passed under a street light. "Oh, wow," he said.

"Shut up," Corley had snarled. "Just shut the hell up." They had gone silent, then looked at each other and giggled.

"Drugs," said Tasco.

"They weren't looped. It was like they were, but they weren't. This guy, the victim—for all he knew it was the killer. He was scared shitless, Ray, and he loved it."

Tasco shrugged. "It's a cheap high. Love that rush, maybe. Or maybe it's like they're in the flick. Makes 'em movie stars. Everybody wants to be a movie star. Put a Walkman on your head and your *life's* a fucking movie."

"I just wish I knew what the hell was going on." Corley

rocked back in his chair. "I'm going to a movie tonight. Want to come?"

Tasco stared at Corley for a second or two. "This on your own time?"

"You want to come, or not?"

"The river's on warm, remember? We're not going to get this one. It was a one-shot." He paused a second. "You okay?"

Corley rocked forward. "What the hell is that supposed to mean?"

"It's not supposed to mean anything. I only wanted . . ."

"All I did was ask if you wanted to go to a flick."

"Keep your voice down. Jesus. For six months you've been a walking burnout. I've been like partnered with a zombie . . ."

"I do my job, nobody can say I don't do my job."

". . . now suddenly you're doing overtime. I'm your partner. I just want to know if you're okay, that's all."

"I'm fine," Corley snapped.

"Okay, great. I'm just asking."

Corley got up and crossed the squad room and refilled his coffee cup and sat back down. He took a sip, burned his tongue. "Yeah, well," he said, "thanks for asking. You want to come?"

Tasco shook his head. "It's going to be a long day without that."

It was a long day, but Corley made the nine o'clock at the Majestic. The ticket girl let him in on his shield again, said the numbers were up, really up. The lobby was crowded, people two deep at the candy counter, clumped around video games, whooping over electronic explosions as someone blasted something on the screen. There were no seats left at the back or on the aisle, and Corley had to sit between two people. He kept his elbows off the armrests. During the movie the audience seemed more tense, everybody wide-eyed and alert, but he caught himself with knotted muscles more than once and thought the tension maybe was in him.

The lipstick game spread like bad news, and every night Corley ran in one or two slashers for questioning, and for anger, because it wasn't a game when he saw a head snap back or heard a scream, wasn't a game when the man moving down his row or running up the aisle might have a razor tucked in his fist. The games got elaborate, became contests with teams, slashers and victims alternating roles and tallying points in the lobby between shows. Sometimes someone would slash a stranger, and Corley broke up the fights at first, but later didn't bother, didn't waste time to risk injury for a pair of idiots. He went to movies every night that week, and every night he saw more people than the night before, and felt more alert and tense, and left more exhausted. His ulcer flared like sulfur; he was smoking again.

On Friday night near the end of the movie his beeper went off and half the audience screamed and jumped and clutched in their seats, then sank back as a wave of relief swept over them and they gave themselves to laughter and curses and groans and chatter, ignoring the movie.

Corley phoned in from the lobby. They had found a body after the last show at the Astro. He had been slashed.

Corley was strangely pleased.

"Could be some frigging copycat," said Tasco the next day, yawning.

Corley wasn't sleepy. "No way," he said. "Exactly the same."

"The paper had the details."

"It's the same guy, Ray."

"Okay, okay," said Tasco, palms up. "Same guy."

The routine began again, interviews, hunting up the audience, blue and yellow pins, lack of a good witness. Tasco asked where they'd sat, what they'd seen, who they'd known. Corley asked them why they'd gone, whether they'd like it, if they went to horror flicks often, if they'd played the assassin games. They didn't know how to answer him. He made them uncomfortable, sometimes angry, and they addressed their answers to Tasco, who looked amused and popped his gum and wrote it all down.

Corley posted the new pictures on the corkboard, and the articles and the editorials, and the movie ads. Various groups blasted the lipstick game, called for theaters to quit showing horror movies, called for theaters to close completely. Corley's theater owner wrote a guest editorial calling on readers not to be made prisoners by one maniac, not to give in to the creatures of the night. The Moviola ads promised armed guards; the Majestic dared people to come to the late show. The corkboard was covered by the end of the week, a vast montage filling the wall behind the blank television.

Tasco went with him to the movies now. There were lines at every ticket window, longer lines every night. The Moviola's security guards roamed the lobby and aisles; the Majestic installed airport metal detectors at the door; the Astro frisked its patrons, who laughed nervously, or cracked wise like Cagney or Bogart, and the guards made a big production when they found tubes of lipstick, asked if they had a license, were told it was for protection only or that they were collectors or with the FBI. They were all having a great time. The ticket girl said they gave her the creeps.

"That's two of us," Corley said.

Corley and Tasco sat on opposite sides of the theater, on the aisle, backs to the wall, linked with lapel mikes and earphones. Fewer and fewer played the lipstick game, but the audiences seemed electric and intense; Corley felt sharp and coiled, felt he could see everything, felt he was waiting for something.

After the movies, when he came home drained and sagged down on the couch, Corley found himself staring at the wall, at the picture of T. O. Bussey looking out at him from the aisle seat, his hands holding up the head, and he felt like he didn't know anything at all.

Corley turned off his electric razor and turned up the radio. An early morning DJ was interviewing a psychiatrist about the slasher. Corley knew he'd give the standard whacko profile, a quiet, polite, boy-next-door type who repressed sex and hated Daddy, and that everybody who knew him would be surprised and say what a nice guy he was and how they could hardly believe it. He got his notebook to write it down so he could quote it to Tasco.

"Said he was 'quiet, withdrawn, suffers repressed sexuality and sexual expression, experiences intense emotional build-up and achieves orgasm at climax of movie and murder, cycle of build-up and release, release of life, fluids, satisfaction.' " He flipped the notebook shut.

"Jeez, I hate that," said Tasco. "I hate the hell out of that. That doesn't mean squat. That's just words. Who is he, gets paid to say crap like that? He doesn't know anything."

"I want to talk to this guy," said Corley. "I just want to sit down and talk to him, you know? I just want to buy him a drink or something and ask him what the hell is going on."

"You mean the shrink?" Tasco was squinting.

"Our guy," said Corley. "The slasher."

Tasco didn't say anything.

"He knows something," said Corley.

Tasco looked angry again. "He doesn't know anything. What are you talking about?"

Corley tried to say what he meant, couldn't find it, couldn't make it concrete. Why was it so important to get this guy, see him, find out what he looked like, why he did it, not why, exactly, but how, maybe, how in the sense of giving people a chance to maybe have their throats cut, and having them line up like it was a raffle? What would that tell him about what was driving him off the street, what kept drawing him back down, why he was carrying an extra piece, what kept him in that lousy apartment in the middle of all of this tar and pavement when he could just walk away? What did he want?

"He knows something about people," Corley said finally.

Tasco waved his hand like he was fanning flies. "What could he know? He's just a sicko. . . ."

"Come on, Ray, we've seen sickos. They don't slash in public, not like this."

Anger was in both voices now.

"Maybe they do. Maybe he just wanted to see if he could. Ever think of that? Maybe it's the thrill of offing somebody in front of a live audience. Maybe that's all."

"Yeah, that's all, and all those people out there know he's out there, too, and they can't stay away. Why can't they stay away, Tasco?"

"We can't just keep going to movies, Devin. We got lives, you know."

"We're not going get him unless we get him in the act."

"That's just stupid. That won't happen. That's a stupid thing to say."

"Watch it, sergeant."

"Oh, kiss it, Corley. Jesus."

They were silent again, avoiding each other's eyes.

"I just want to bust this guy," said Corley.

"Yeah, well," said Tasco, looking out of the window, "what I want is to go home, see my wife and kids, maybe watch a ball game." He looked back to Corley. "So, we going out again tonight or what?"

They went again that night and the next night and the next. They always sat on the aisle at opposite ends of the last row so that they could cover both rear exits. Tasco would sit through only one show; Corley sat through both. He felt better when Tasco was at the other end, when he could hear him clear his throat, or mutter something to himself, or even snore when he nodded off as he sometimes did, which amazed Corley. Corley stayed braced in his seat.

When Tasco left, Corley felt naked on the aisle, so he'd move in one seat and drape a raincoat across the aisle seat so it looked occupied, so no one would sit there. The nine o'clock show was usually a sell-out, the audience filling every seat and pressing in on him, a single vague mass in the dark at a horror flick, hiding a man with a razor, maybe even inviting him, desiring him, seeking him. After five nights Corley was ragged and jumpy.

"I'm going to sit in the projection booth," he told Tasco. "Better view."

Tasco shrugged. "End of the week and that's it, okay?"

"We'll see."

"That's got to be it, Devlin."

The booth gave Corley a broader view, and gave him distance, height, a thick glass wall. At first he felt conspicuous whenever a pale face lifted his way as the audience waited for the movie to start. The manager showed him how to override the automatics and turn up the house lights, otherwise hands off. The projector looked like a giant Tommy gun sighted on the screen through a little rectangle outlined on the glass in masking tape. He had expected something more sophisticated.

Tasco was just out of sight below him, left aisle, last row,

back to the wall. Through his earphone, Corley could hear the
audience from Tasco's lapel mike, a general murmur, a burst of
high-pitched laughter, the crying of a baby who shouldn't even
be there. Corley wiped his glasses on his tie. Hundreds of
people out there, could be any one of them, and what the hell
were the rest of them doing out there, and what the hell was
he doing up here?

The lights dimmed and the projector lit up, commercials,
previews, the main feature. A little out-of-focus movie danced
in the rectangle on the glass, blobs of color and movement
bleeding out onto the masking tape; the soundtrack was thin
and tinny from the booth speaker and just half a beat behind in
the earphone, disconcerting. Beyond the glass, on exhibition,
the audience stirred and rippled; beyond them the huge and
distorted images filled the screen. He watched, and when
someone stood and moved toward the aisle, he warned Tasco
and felt adrenaline heat arms and legs and the figure reached
the aisle and turned and walked toward restroom or candy
counter, and Corley tried to relax again. It was easier to relax
up here, above it all.

The movie dragged on. Corley found by staring at a central
point in the audience and unfocusing his eyes, he could see all
movement instantly, and everybody was moving, scratching
ears and noses and scalps, lifting hands to mouths to cover
coughs or to feed, rocking, putting arms around dates, leaning
forward, leaning back, covering eyes with fingers. Again he saw
the patterns emerge around the on-screen killings, movements
ebbing as the killing neared, freezing at the death itself, melting
after, and flowing across the audience again, strong and choppy,
then quieter and smooth. He had to concentrate, breathe slowly
and carefully, to keep himself from narrowing his vision, focusing on one person. He didn't see the movie.

A flicker in the corner of his eye, flick of light on steel. He
swung eyes right, locked on movement, saw the head pulled
back, the blade flicker again, realized it was happening, that he
hadn't seen the killer move down the row because he was
sitting right behind his victim, it was happening now, all the
way across the theater from Tasco. He radioed Tasco as he
turned for the stairs and punched the lights, heard Tasco yell

for the man to stop, knew they were too late for the victim, but they had him now, they had him now, they had him now. He took the stairs three at a time, slipped, skidded down, arms flailing, wrenched his shoulder as he tried to break the fall, then on his feet and bursting through the door behind the concession stand, drawing his pistol as he ran, putting out his left arm and vaulting over the counter, popcorn and patron flying. He stopped in front of the double doors, pistol leveled, waiting for the maniac to run into his arms.

Nobody came. Corley crouched, frozen, pistol extended in two hands, and in his left ear the theater, voices and screams and music, and Tasco maybe, Tasco shouting something, and still nobody came. He moved forward, gun still extended, and jerked open a door with his left hand.

Lights still brightening, movie running, and the screams and shouts and music in the earphone echoed, echoed in his right ear and for an instant he lost where he was. Then he heard Tasco calling him in his earphone and saw him trying to hammer his way into a knot of people below the screen, the rest of the audience in their seats, watching the movie or those down front attacking the slasher.

Corley ran down the aisle, yelling for Tasco. The earphone went dead and Tasco was gone. Corley reached the mass, started pulling people out of his way, stepping on them, pushing. Some pushed back and turned on him, and he knocked one down and another man grabbed him, and he hit the man in the face, and backed toward the wall, gun leveled. The man changed his mind, backed away. Corley called Tasco, heard nothing through the earphone. He tried to elbow his way in the crowd, started clubbing with both hands around the pistol, fighting the urge to just start pulling the trigger and have done with it. A huge man turned and started to swing; Corley watched the fist come around in slow motion, easily deflected the blow, put a knee in the solar plexus, watched the man fall like a great tree, cuffed him across the jaw as he went down, felt that he could count the pores in the potato nose. They were right beneath the speakers, the music pounding his bones. He reached for the next one in his way.

He heard a shot, saw Tasco cornered by four or five, his gun pointed toward the ceiling but lowering. The next one wouldn't be a warning shot and those guys knew it and they weren't backing off. Corley tried to shout above the music, raised his pistol and fired toward the ceiling, fired again, heard Tasco's gun answer, fired a third time, and the crowd started breaking at the edges, some hurt, some bloody. Corley tried to hold them back, grabbed at one who twisted away, and they pushed past, ignoring him, laughing or shouting, and the others were leaving their seats now, mixing with them, and some in their seats were applauding and cheering.

There were people lying all around them, some groaning, some bleeding. The slasher's victim sprawled across an aisle seat, throat opened to the stars painted on the ceiling. "Help me, Jesus," someone was saying over and over. "Jesus, help me." He heard someone calling his name, saying something. It was Tasco.

"I couldn't stop them," Tasco was saying. Corley looked down. They had used the slasher's blade, and whatever else was handy. The slasher's features were unrecognizable, the head almost severed from the body. A sudden fury flashed through Corley, and he kicked the person lying nearest to him. "Couldn't stop them," Tasco repeated, his voice trembling.

"Is this him, do you think?" asked Corley.

Tasco didn't say anything.

"Maybe Maggie can tell us," said Corley. "Maybe the M.E." He could hear the desperation in his voice.

"It could be anybody," said Tasco.

When he used the phone in the ticket office to call it all in, he heard people demanding a refund because they hadn't gotten to see the end of the movie.

Corley didn't get home until late the next afternoon. He'd made it through the last eighteen hours by thinking about the crummy little apartment high above the street, with the couch and the double locks and the television. He heard the cat yowling before he even put the key in the first lock.

He fed the cat and opened a beer, and turned on his television, but the pictures were wrong, fuzzy, filled with snow. He tried to fix the image, but nothing worked, and he grew angry. Finally he checked the roof and found his antenna bent over.

"Gianelli," he shouted, pounding, standing to one side of the door, seeing an image of Gianelli spinning in slow motion toward pavement four floors down. "Come out of there, Gianelli." No answer. He spread the name out, kicking on the door once for each syllable. *"Gi—a—nel—li!"*

"You go away now," came a voice from inside. "You go away. I'm calling the cops."

"I *am* a cop," Corley shouted, dragging out his shield and holding it to the peephole.

"You go away now," Gianelli said after a moment of silence.

Corley gave the door one last kick.

He tried to salvage the antenna, but Gianelli had done a job on it, twisting the cross-pieces, cutting the wires into a dozen pieces.

Before he went to sleep, he took down the pictures and clippings about Mr. Bussey, and he dug around until he found the pictures of the previous occupant, and he pinned them all up. He crossed the room and sat on the couch to look at them. They were all black and white, blonde and pale eyes, and he wondered if she had walked away from whatever brought her here. He thought she was very beautiful. But who could tell from pictures?

He locked the doors and put on the night light.

LOREN D. ESTLEMAN

THE CROOKED WAY

*During 1988 Loren D. Estleman's Detroit private eye,
Amos Walker, appeared in his first collection of short
stories,* General Murders, *published by Houghton Mifflin.
The ten stories were even more impressive when gathered
together than they had been upon original magazine and
anthology publication. This Amos Walker story, the first
new one to appear since that collection, further cements
Estleman's position as one of the most deserving succes-
sors to Hammett and Chandler.*

You couldn't miss the Indian if you'd wanted to. He was sitting
all alone in a corner booth, which was probably his idea, but he
hadn't much choice because there was barely enough room in
it for him. He had shoulders going into the next county and a
head the size of a basketball, and he was holding a beer mug
that looked like a shot glass between his calloused palms. As I
approached the booth he looked up at me—not very far up—
through slits in a face made up of bunched ovals with a nose
like the corner of a building. His skin was the color of old brick.

"Mr. Frechette?" I asked.

"Amos Walker?"

I said I was. Coming from him my name sounded like two
stones dropping into deep water. He made no move to shake
hands, but he inclined his head a fraction of an inch and I
borrowed a chair from a nearby table and joined him. He had
on a blue shirt bottoned to the neck, and his hair, parted on
one side and plastered down, was blue-black without a trace of
gray. Nevertheless he was about fifty.

"Charlie Stoat says you track like an Osage," he said. "I hope
you're better than that. I couldn't track a train."

"How is Charlie? I haven't seen him since that insurance
thing."

"Going under. The construction boom went bust in Houston just when he was expanding his operation."

"What's that do to yours?" He'd told me over the telephone he was in construction.

"Nothing worth mentioning. I've been running on a shoe-string for years. You can't break a poor man."

I signaled the bartender for a beer and he brought one over. It was a workingman's hangout across the street from the Ford plant in Highland Park. The shift wasn't due to change for an hour and we had the place to ourselves. "You said your daughter ran away," I said, when the bartender had left. "What makes you think she's in Detroit?"

He drank off half his beer and belched dramatically. "When does client privilege start?"

"It never stops."

I watched him make up his mind. Indians aren't nearly as hard to read as they appear in books. He picked up a folded newspaper from the seat beside him and spread it out on the table facing me. It was yesterday's *Houston Chronicle*, with a banner:

BOYD MANHUNT MOVES NORTHEAST
Bandit's Van Found Abandoned in Detroit

I had read a related wire story in that morning's *Detroit Free Press*. Following the unassisted shotgun robberies of two savings and loan offices near Houston, concerned citizens had reported seeing twenty-two-year-old Virgil Boyd in Mexico and Okla-homa, but his green van with Texas plates had turned up in a city lot five minutes from where we were sitting. As of that morning, Detroit Police Headquarters was paved with Feds and sun-crinkled out-of-state cops chewing toothpicks.

I refolded the paper and gave it back. "Your daughter's taken up with Boyd?"

"They were high school sweethearts," Frechette said. "That was before Texas Federal foreclosed on his family's ranch and his father shot himself. She disappeared from home after the first robbery. I guess that makes her an accomplice to the second."

"Legally speaking," I agreed, "if she's with him and it's her idea. A smart DA would knock it down to harboring if she turned herself in. She'd probably get probation."

"She wouldn't do that. She's got some crazy idea she's in love with Boyd."

"I'm surprised I haven't heard about her."

"No one knows. I didn't report her missing. If I had, the police would have put two and two together and there'd be a warrant out for her as well."

I swallowed some beer. "I don't know what you think I can do that the cops and the FBI can't."

"I know where she is."

I waited. He rotated his mug. "My sister lives in Southgate. We don't speak. She has a white mother, not like me, and she takes after her in looks. She's ashamed of being half Osage. First chance she had, she married a white man and got out of Oklahoma. That was before I left for Texas, where nobody knows about her. Anyway she got a big settlement in her divorce."

"You think Boyd and your daughter will go to her for a getaway stake?"

"They won't get it from me, and he didn't take enough out of Texas Federal to keep a dog alive. Why else would they come here?"

"So if you know where they're headed, what do you need me for?"

"Because I'm being followed and you're not."

The bartender came around to offer Frechette a refill. The big Indian shook his head and he went away.

"Cops?" I said.

"One cop. J. P. Ahearn."

He spaced out the name as if spelling a blasphemy. I said I'd never heard of him.

"He'd be surprised. He's a commander with the Texas State Police, but he thinks he's the last of the Texas Rangers. He wants Boyd bad. The man's a bloodhound. He doesn't know about my sister, but he did his homework and found out about Suzie and that she's gone, not that he could get me to admit she isn't away visiting friends. I didn't see him on the plane from Houston. I spotted him in the airport here when I was getting my luggage."

"Is he alone?"

"He wouldn't share credit with Jesus for saving a sinner." He drained his mug. "When you find Suzie I want you to set up a meeting. Maybe I can talk sense into her."

"How old is she?"

"Nineteen."

"Good luck."

"Tell me about it. My old man fell off a girder in Tulsa when I was sixteen. Then I was fifty. Well, maybe one meeting can't make up for all the years of not talking after my wife died, but I can't let her throw her life away for not trying."

"I can't promise Boyd won't sit in on it."

"I like Virgil. Some of us cheered when he took on those bloodsuckers. He'd have gotten away with a lot more from that second job if he'd shot this stubborn cashier they had, but he didn't. He wouldn't hurt a horse or a man."

"That's not the way the cops are playing it. If I find him and don't report it I'll go down as an accomplice. At the very least I'll lose my license."

"All I ask is that you call me before you call the police." He gave me a high-school graduation picture of a pretty brunette he said was Suzie. She looked more Asian than American Indian. Then he pulled a checkbook out of his hip pocket and made out a check to me for fifteen hundred dollars.

"Too much," I said.

"You haven't met J. P. Ahearn yet. My sister's name is Harriett Lord." He gave me an address on Eureka. "I'm at the Holiday Inn down the street, room 716."

He called for another beer then and I left. Again he didn't offer his hand. I'd driven three blocks from the place when I spotted the tail.

The guy knew what he was doing. In a late-model tan Buick he gave me a full block and didn't try to close up until we hit Woodward, where traffic was heavier. I finally lost him in the grand circle downtown, which confused him just as it does most people from the greater planet Earth. The Indians who settled Detroit were being farsighted when they named it the Crooked Way. From there I took Lafayette to I-75 and headed downriver.

Harriett Lord lived in a tall, white frame house with blue shutters and a large lawn fenced by cedars that someone had bullied into cone shape. I parked in the driveway, but before leaving the car I got out the unlicensed Lugar I keep in a pocket under the dash and stuck it in my pants, buttoning my coat over it. When you're meeting someone they tell you wouldn't hurt a horse or a man, arm yourself.

The bell was answered by a tall woman around forty, dressed in a khaki shirt and corduroy slacks and sandals. She had high cheekbones and slightly olive coloring that looked more like sun than heritage and her short hair was frosted, further reducing the Indian effect. When she confirmed that she was Harriett Lord I gave her a card and said I was working for her brother.

Her face shut down. "I don't have a brother. I have a half-brother, Howard Frechette. If that's who you're working for, tell him I'm unavailable." She started to close the door.

"It's about your niece Suzie. And Virgil Boyd."

"I thought it would be."

I looked at the door and got out a cigarette and lit it. I was about to knock again when the door opened six inches and she stuck her face through the gap. "You're not with the police?"

"We tolerate each other on the good days, but that's it."

She glanced down. Her blue mascara gave her eyelids a translucent look. Then she opened the door the rest of the way and stepped aside. I entered a living room done all in beige and white and sat in a chair upholstered in eggshell chintz. I was glad I'd had my suit cleaned.

"How'd you know about Suzie and Boyd?" I used a big glass ashtray on the Lucite coffee table.

"They were here last night." I said nothing. She sat on the beige sofa with her knees together. "I recognized him before I did her. I haven't seen her since she was four, but I take a Texas paper and I've seen his picture. They wanted money. I thought at first I was being robbed."

"Did you give it to them?"

"Aid a fugitive? Family responsibility doesn't cover that even if I felt any. I left home because I got sick of hearing about our proud heritage. Howard wore his Indianness like a suit of armor, and all the time he resented me because I could pass for white. He accused me of being ashamed of my ancestry because I didn't wear my hair in braids and hang turquoise all over me."

"He isn't like that now."

"Maybe he's mellowed. Not toward me, though, I bet. Now his daughter comes here asking for money so she and her desperado boyfriend can go on running. I showed them the door."

"I'm surprised Boyd went."

"He tried to get tough, but he's not very big and he wasn't armed. He took a step toward me and I took two steps toward him and he grabbed Suzie and left. Some Jesse James."

"I heard his shotgun was found in the van. I thought he'd have something else."

"If he did, he didn't have it last night. I'd have noticed, just as I notice you have one."

I unbuttoned my coat and resettled the Luger. I was getting a different picture of "Mad Dog" Boyd from the one the press was painting. "The cops would call not reporting an incident like that being an accessory," I said, squashing out my butt.

"Just because I don't want anything to do with Howard doesn't mean I want to see my niece shot up by a SWAT team."

"I don't suppose they said where they were going."

"You're a good supposer."

I got up. "How did Suzie look?"

"Like an Indian."

I thanked her and went out.

I had a customer in my waiting room. A small angular party crowding sixty wearing a tight gray three-button suit, steel-rimmed glasses, and a tan snap-brim hat squared over the frames. His crisp gray hair was cut close around large ears that stuck out, and he had a long sharp jaw with a sour mouth slashing straight across. He stood up when I entered. "Walker?" It was one of those bitter pioneer voices.

"Depends on who you are," I said.

"I'm the man who ought to arrest you for obstructing justice."

"I'll guess. J. P. Ahearn."

"*Commander* Ahearn."

"You're about four feet short of what I had pictured."

"You've heard of me." His chest came out a little.

"Who hasn't?" I unlocked the inner office door. He marched in, slung a look around, and took possession of the customer's chair. I sat down behind the desk and reached for a cigarette without asking permission. He glared at me through the spectacles.

"What you did downtown today constitutes fleeing and eluding."

"In Texas, maybe. In Michigan there has to be a warrant out first. What you did constitutes harassment in this state."

"I don't have official status here. I can follow anybody for any reason or none at all."

"Is this what you folks call a Mexican standoff?"

"I don't approve of smoking," he snapped.

"Neither do I, but some of it always leaks out of my lungs." I blew some at the ceiling and got rid of the match. "Why don't let's stop circling each other and get down to why you're here?"

"I want to know what you and the Indian talked about."

"I'd show you, but we don't need the rain."

He bared a perfect set of dentures, turning his face into a skull. "I ran your plate with the Detroit Police. I have their complete cooperation in this investigation. The Indian hired you to take money to Boyd to get him and his little Osage slut to Canada. You delivered it after you left the bar and lost me. That's aiding and abetting and accessory after the fact of armed robbery. Maybe I can't prove it, but I can make a call and tank you for forty-eight hours on suspicion."

"Eleven."

He covered up his store-boughts. "What?"

"That's eleven times I've been threatened with jail," I said. "Three of those times I wound up there. My license has been swiped at fourteen times, actually taken away once. Bodily harm—you don't count bodily harm. I'm still here, six feet something and one hundred eighty pounds of incorruptible PI with a will of iron and a skull to match. You hard guys come and go like phases of the moon."

"Don't twist my tail, son. I don't always rattle before I bite."

"What's got you so hot on Boyd?"

You could have cut yourself on his jaw. "My daddy helped run Parker and Barrow to ground in '34. *His* daddy fought Geronimo and chased John Wesley Hardin out of Texas. My son's a Dallas city patrolman, and so far I don't have a story to hand him that's a blister on any of those. I'm retiring next year."

"Last I heard Austin was offering twenty thousand for Boyd's arrest and conviction."

"Texas Federal has matched it. Alive *or* dead. Naturally, as a duly sworn officer of the law I can't collect. But you being a private citizen—"

"What's the split?"

"Fifty-fifty."

"No good."

"Do you know what the pension is for a retired state police commander in Texas? A man needs a nest egg."

"I meant it's too generous. You know as well as I do those rewards are never paid. You just didn't know I knew."

He sprang out of his chair. There was no special animosity in his move; that would be the way he always got up.

"Boyd won't get out of this country even if you did give him money," he snapped. "He'll never get past the border guards."

"So go back home."

"Boyd's *mine.*"

The last word ricocheted. I said, "Talk is he felt he had a good reason to stick up those savings and loans. The company was responsible for his father's suicide."

"If he's got the brains God gave a mad dog he'll turn himself in to me before he gets shot down in the street or kills someone and winds up getting the needle in Huntsville. And his squaw right along with him." He took a shabby wallet out of his coat and gave me a card. "That's my number at the Houston post. They'll route your call here. If you're so concerned for Boyd you'll tell me where he is before the locals gun him down."

"Better you than some stranger, that it?"

"Just keep on twisting, son. I ain't in the pasture yet."

After he left, making as much noise in his two-inch cowboy

heels as a cruiserweight, I called Barry Stackpole at the Detroit *News.*

"Guy I'm after is wanted for robbery, armed," I said, once the small talk was put away. "He ditched his gun and then his stake didn't come through and now he'll have to cowboy a job for case dough. Where would he deal a weapon if he didn't know anybody in town?"

"Emma Chaney."

"Ma? I thought she'd be dead by now."

"She can't die. The Detroit cops are third in line behind Interpol and Customs for her scalp and they won't let her until they've had their crack." He sounded pleased, which he probably was. Barry made his living writing about crime and when it prospered he did, too.

"How can I reach her?"

"Are you suggesting I'd know where she is and not tell the authorities? Got a pencil?"

"I tried the number as soon as he was off the line. On the ninth ring I got someone with a smoker's wheeze. "Uh-huh."

"The name's Walker," I said. "Barry Stackpole gave me this number."

The voice told me not to go away and hung up. Five minutes later the telephone rang.

"Barry says you're okay. What do you want?"

"Just talk. It isn't cheap like they say."

After a moment the voice gave me directions. I hung up not knowing if it was male or female.

It belonged to Ma Chaney, who greeted me at the door of her house in rural Macomb County wearing a red Japanese kimono with green parrots all over it. The kimono could have covered a Toyota. She was a five-by-five chunk with marcelled orange hair and round black eyes embedded in her face like nail heads in soft wax. A cigarette teetered on her lower lip. I followed her into a parlor full of flowered chairs and sofas and pregnant lamps with fringed shades. A long strip of pimply blond youth in overalls and no shirt took his brogans off the coffee table and stood up when she barked at him. He gaped at me, chewing gum with his mouth open.

"Mr. Walker, Leo," Ma wheezed. "Leo knew my Wilbur in Ypsi. He's like another son to me."

Ma Chaney had one son in the criminal ward at the Forensic Psychiatry Center in Ypsilanti and another on Florida's Death Row. The FBI was looking for the youngest in connection with an armored car robbery in Kansas City. The whole brood had come up from Kentucky when Old Man Chaney got a job on the line at River Rouge and stayed on after he was killed in a propane tank explosion. Now Ma, the daughter of a Hawkins County gunsmith, made her living off the domestic weapons market.

"You said talk ain't cheap," she said, when she was sitting in a big overstuffed rocker. "How cheap ain't it?"

I perched on the edge of a hard upright with doilies on the arms. Leo remained standing, scratching himself. "Depends on whether we talk about Virgil Boyd," I said.

"What if we don't?"

"Then I won't take up any more of your time."

"What if we do?"

"I'll double what he's paying."

She coughed. The cigarette bobbed. "I got a business to run. I go around scratching at rewards I won't have no customers."

"Does that mean Boyd's a customer?"

"Now, why'd that Texas boy want to come to Ma? He can deal hisself a shotgun at any K mart."

"He can't show his face in the legal places and being new in town he doesn't know the illegal ones. But he wouldn't have to ask around too much to come up with your name. You're less selective than most."

"You don't have to pussyfoot around old Ma. I don't get a lot of second-timers on account of I talk for money. My boy Earl in Florida needs a new lawyer. But I only talk after, not before. I start setting up customers I won't get no first-timers."

"I'm not even interested in Boyd. It's his girlfriend I want to talk to. Suzie Frechette."

"Don't know her." She rocked back and forth. "What color's your money?"

Before leaving Detroit I'd cashed Howard Frechette's check. I laid fifteen hundred dollars on the coffee table in twenties and fifties. Leo straightened up a little to look at the bills. Ma resumed rocking. "It ain't enough."

"How much is enough?"

"If I was to talk to a fella named Boyd, and if I was to agree to sell him a brand new Ithaca pump shotgun and a P-38 still in the box, I wouldn't sell them for less than twenty-five hunnert. Double twenny-five hunnert is five thousand."

"Fifteen hundred now. Thirty-five hundred when I see the girl."

"I don't guarantee no girl."

"Boyd then. If he's come this far with her he won't leave her behind."

She went on rocking. "They's a white barn a mile north on this road. If I was to meet a fella named Boyd, there's where I might do it. I might pick eleven o'clock."

"Tonight?"

"I might pick tonight. If it don't rain."

I got up. She stopped rocking.

"Come alone," she said. "Ma won't."

On the way back to town I filled up at a corner station and used the pay telephone to call Howard Frechette's room at the Holiday Inn. When he started asking questions I gave him the number and told him to call back from a booth outside the motel.

"Ahearn's an anachronism," he said ten minutes later. "I doubt he taps phones."

"Maybe not, but motel operators have big ears."

"Did you talk to Suzie?"

"Minor setback," I said. "Your sister gave her and Boyd the boot and no money."

"Tight bitch."

"I know where they'll be tonight, though. There's an old auto court on Van Dyke between 21 and 22 Mile in Macomb County, the Log Cabin Inn. Looks like it sounds." I was staring at it across the road. "Midnight. Better give yourself an hour."

He repeated the information.

"I'm going to have to tap you for thirty-five hundred dollars," I said. "The education cost."

"I can manage it. Is that where they're headed?"

"I hope so. I haven't asked them yet."

I got to my bank just before closing and cleaned out my savings and all but eight dollars in my checking account. I hoped Frechette was good for it. After that I ate dinner in a restaurant and went to see a movie about a one-man army. I wondered if he was available.

The barn was just visible from the road, a moonlit square at the end of a pair of ruts cut through weeds two feet high. It was a chill night in early spring and I had on a light coat and the heater running. I entered a dip that cut off my view of the barn, then bucked up over a ridge and had to stand the Chevy on its nose when the lamps fell on a telephone pole lying across the path. A second later the passenger's door opened and Leo got in.

He had on a mackinaw over his overalls and a plaid cap. His right hand was wrapped around a large-bore revolver and he kept it on me, held tight to his stomach, while he felt under my coat and came up with the Lugar. "Drive." He pocketed it.

I swung around the end of the pole and braked in front of the barn, where Ma was standing with a Coleman lantern. She was wearing a man's felt hat and a corduroy coat with sleeves that came down to her fingers. She signaled a cranking motion and I rolled down the window.

"Well, park it around back," she said. "I got to think for you, too?"

I did that and Leo and I walked back. He handed Ma the Luger and she looked at it and put it in her pocket. She raised the lantern then and swung it from side to side twice.

We waited a few minutes, then were joined by six feet and two hundred and fifty pounds of red-bearded young man in faded denim jacket and jeans carrying a rifle with an infrared scope. He had come from the direction of the road.

"Anybody following, Mason?" asked Ma.

He shook his head and I stared at him in the lantern light. He had small black eyes like Ma's with no shine in them. This would be Mace Chaney, for whom the FBI was combing the western states for the Kansas armored car robbery.

"Go on in and warm yourself," Ma said. "We got some time."

He opened the barn door and went inside. It had just closed when two headlamps appeared down the road. We watched them approach and slow for the turn onto the path. Ma, lighting a cigarette off the lantern, grunted.

"Early. Young folks all got watches and they can't tell time."

Leo trotted out to intercept the car. A door slammed. After a pause the lamps swung around the fallen telephone pole and came up to the barn, washing us all in white. The driver killed the lamps and engine and got out. He was a small man in his early twenties with short brown hair and stubble on his face. His flannel shirt and khaki pants were both in need of cleaning. He had scant eyebrows that were almost invisible in that light, giving him a perennially surprised look. I'd seen that look in Frechette's *Houston Chronicle* and in both Detroit papers.

"Who's he?" He was looking at me.

I had a story for that, but Ma piped up. "You ain't paying to ask no questions. Got the money?"

"Not all of it. A thousand's all Suzie could get from the sharks."

"The deal's two thousand."

"Keep the P-38. The shotgun's all I need."

Ma had told me twenty-five hundred; but I was barely listening to the conversation. Leo had gotten out on the passenger's side, pulling with him the girl in the photograph in my pocket. Suzie Frechette had done up her black hair in braids and she'd lost weight, but her dark eyes and coloring were unmistakable. With that hairstyle and in a man's work shirt and jeans and boots with western heels she looked more like an Indian than she did in her picture.

Leo opened the door and we went inside. The barn hadn't been used for its original purpose for some time, but the smell of moldy hay would remain as long as it stood. It was lit by a bare bulb swinging from a frayed cord and heated by a barrel stove in a corner. Stacks of cardboard cartons reached almost to the rafters, below which Mace Chaney sat with his legs dangling over the edge of the empty loft, the rifle across his knees.

Ma reached into an open carton and lifted out a pump shotgun with the barrel cut back to the slide. Boyd stepped forward to take it. She swung the muzzle on him. "Show me some paper."

He hesitated, then drew a thick fold of bills from his shirt pocket and laid it on a stack of cartons. Then she moved to cover me. Boyd watched me add thirty-five hundred to the pile.

"What's *he* buying?"

Ma said, "You."

"Cop!" He lunged for the shotgun. Leo's revolver came out. Mace drew a bead on Boyd from the loft. He relaxed.

I was looking at Suzie. "I'm a private detective hired by your father. He wants to talk to you."

"He's here?" She touched Boyd's arm.

He tensed. "It's a damn cop trick!"

"You're smarter than that," I said. "You had to be, to pull those two jobs and make your way here with every cop between here and Texas looking for you. If I were one, would I be alone?"

"Do your jabbering outside," Ma reversed ends on the shotgun for Boyd to take. He did so and worked the slide.

"Where's the shells?"

"That's your headache. I don't keep ammo in this firetrap."

That was a lie, or some of those cartons wouldn't be labeled C-4 EXPLOSIVES. But you don't sell loaded guns to strangers.

Suzie said, "Virgil, you never load them anyway."

"Shut up."

"Your father's on his way," I said. "Ten minutes, that's all he wants."

"Come on." Boyd took her wrist.

"Stay put."

This was a new voice. Everyone looked at Leo, standing in front of the door with his gun still out.

"Leo, *what* in the *hell*—"

"Ma, the Luger."

She shut her mouth and took my gun out of her right coat pocket and put it on the carton with the money. Then she backed away.

"Throw 'er down, Mace." He covered the man in the loft, who froze in the act of raising the rifle. They were like that for a moment.

"Mason," Ma said.

His shoulders slumped. He snapped on the safety and dropped the rifle eight feet to the earthen floor.

"You, too, Mr. Forty Thousand Dollar *Re*ward," Leo said. "Even empty guns give me the jumps."

Boyd cast the shotgun onto the stack of cartons with a violent gesture.

"That's nice. I cut that money in half if I got to put a hole in you."

"That reward talk's just PR," I said. "Even if you get Boyd to the cops they'll probably arrest you, too, for dealing in unlicensed firearms."

"Like hell. I'm through getting bossed around by fat old ladies. Let's go, Mr. *Re*ward."

"No!" screamed Suzie.

An explosion slapped the walls. Leo's brows went up, his jaw dropping to expose the wad of pink gum in his mouth. He looked down at the spreading stain on the bib of his overalls and fell down on top of his gun. He kicked once.

Ma was standing with a hand to her left coat pocket. A finger of smoking metal poked out of a charred hole. "Dadgum it, Leo," she said, "this coat belonged to my Calvin, rest his soul."

I was standing in front of the Log Cabin Inn's deserted office when Frechette swung a rented Ford into the broken paved driveway. He unfolded himself from the seat and loomed over me.

"I don't think anyone followed me," he said. "I took a couple of wrong turns to make sure."

"There won't be any interruptions, then. The place has been closed a long time."

I led him to one of the log bungalows in back. Boyd's Plymouth, stolen from the same lot where he'd left the van, was parked alongside it facing out. We knocked before entering.

All of the furniture had been removed except a metal bedstand with sagging springs. The lantern we had borrowed from Ma Chaney hung hissing from one post. Suzie was standing next to it. "Papa." She didn't move. Boyd came out of the bathroom with the shotgun. The Indian took root.

"Man said you had money for us," Boyd said.

"It was the only way I could get him to bring Suzie here," I told Frechette.

"I won't pay to have my daughter killed in a shoot-out."

"Lying bastard!" Boyd swung the shotgun my way. Frechette backhanded him, knocking him back into the bathroom. I stepped forward and tore the shotgun from Boyd's weakened grip.

"Empty," I said. "But it makes a good club."

Suzie had come forward when Boyd fell. Frechette stopped her with an arm like a railroad gate. "Take Dillinger for a walk while I talk to my daughter," he said to me.

I stuck out a hand, but Boyd slapped it aside and got up. His right eye was swelling shut. He looked at the Indian towering a foot over him, then at Suzie, who said, "It's all right. I'll talk to him."

We went out. A porch ran the length of the bungalow. I leaned the shotgun against the wall and trusted my weight to the railing. "I hear you got a raw deal from Texas Federal."

"My old man did." He stood with his hands rammed deep in his pockets, watching the pair through the window. "He asked for a two-month extension on his mortgage payment, just till he brought in his crop. Everyone gets extensions. Except when Texas Federal wants to sell the ranch to a developer. He met the 'dozers with a shotgun. Then he used it on himself."

"That why you use one?"

"I can't kill a jackrabbit. It used to burn up my old man."

"You'd be out in three years if you turned yourself in."

"To you, right? Let you collect that reward." He was still looking through the window. Inside, father and daughter were gesturing at each other frantically.

"I didn't say to me. You're big enough to walk into a police station by yourself."

"You don't know Texas Federal. They'd hire their own prosecutor, see I got life, make an example. I'll die first."

"Probably, the rate you're going."

He whirled on me. The parked Plymouth caught his eye. "Just who the hell are you? And why'd you—" He jerked his chin toward the car.

I got out J. P. Ahearn's card and gave it to him. His face lost color.

"You work for that headhunter?"

"Not in this life. But in a little while I'm going to call that number from the telephone in that gas station across the road."

He lunged for the door. I was closer and got in his way. "I don't know how you got this far with a head that hot," I said. "For once in your young life listen. You might get to like it."

He listened.

"This is Commander Ahearn! I know you're in there, Boyd. I got a dozen men here and if you don't come out we'll shoot up the place!"

Neither of us had heard them coming, and with the moon behind a cloud the thin, bitter voice might have come from anywhere. This time Boyd won the race to the door. He had the reflexes of a deer.

"Kill the light!" I barked to Frechette. "Ahearn beat me to it. He must have followed you after all."

We were in darkness suddenly. Boyd and Suzie had their arms around each other. "We're cornered," he said. "Why didn't that old lady have shells for that gun?"

"We just have to move faster, that's all. Keep him talking. Give me a hand with this window." The last was for Frechette, who came over and worked his big fingers under the swollen frame.

"There's a woman in here!" Boyd shouted.

"Come on out and no one gets hurt!" Ahearn sounded wired.

The window gave with a squawking wrench.

"One minute, Boyd. Then we start blasting!"

I hoped it was enough. I slipped out over the sill.

"The car! Get it!"

The Plymouth's engine turned over twice in the cold before starting. The car rolled forward and began picking up speed down the incline toward the road. Just then the moon came out, illuminating the man behind the wheel, and the night came apart like mountain ice breaking up, cracking and splitting with the staccato rap of handgun fire and the deeper boom of riot guns. Orange flame scorched the darkness. Slugs whacked the car's sheet metal and shattered the windshield. Then a red glow started to spread inside the vehicle, and fists of yellow flame battered out the rest of the windows with a *whump* that shook the ground. The car rolled for a few more yards while the shooters, standing now and visible in the light of the blaze, went on pouring lead into it until it came to a stop against a road sign. The flame towered twenty feet above the crackling wreckage.

I approached Ahearn, standing in the overgrown grass with his shotgun dangling, watching the car burn. He jumped a little when I spoke. His glasses glowed orange.

"He made a dash, just like you wanted."

"If you think I wanted this you don't know me," he said.

"Save it for the six o'clock news."

"What the hell are you doing here, anyway?"

"Friend of the family. Can I take the Frechettes home or do you want to eat them here?"

He cradled the shotgun. "We'll just go inside together."

We found Suzie sobbing in her father's arms. The Indian glared at Ahearn. "Get the hell out of here."

"He was a desperate man," Ahearn said. "You're lucky that girl's alive."

"I said get out or I'll ram that shotgun down your throat."

He got out. Through the window I watched him rejoin his men. There were five, not a dozen as he'd claimed. Later I learned that three of them were off-duty Detroit cops and he'd hired the other two from a private security firm.

I waited until the fire engines came and Ahearn was busy talking to the firefighters, then went out the window again and crossed to the next bungalow, set farther back where the light of the flames didn't reach. I knocked twice and paused and knocked again. Boyd opened the door a crack.

"I'm taking Suzie and her father back to Frechette's motel for looks. Think you can lie low here until we come back in the morning for the rent car?"

"What if they search the cabins?"

"For what? You're dead. By the time they find out that's Leo in the car, if they ever do, you and Suzie will be in Canada. Customs won't be looking for a dead bandit. Give everyone a year or so to forget what you look like and then you can come

back. Not to Texas, though, and not under the name Virgil
Boyd."

"Lucky the gas tank blew."

"I've never had enough luck to trust to it. That's why I put a
box of C-4 in Leo's lap. Ma figured it was a small enough
donation to keep her clear of a charge of felony murder."

"I thought you were some kind of corpse freak." He still had
the surprised look. "You could've been killed starting that car.
Why'd you do it?"

"The world's not as complicated as it looks," I said. "There's
always a good and a bad side. I saw Ahearn's."

"You ever need anything," he said.

"If you do things right I won't be able to find you when I do."
I shook his hand and returned to the other bungalow.

A week later, after J. P. Ahearn's narrow, jug-eared features had
made the cover of *People,* I received an envelope from Houston
containing a bonus check for a thousand dollars signed by
Howard Frechette. He'd repaid the thirty-five hundred I'd given
Ma before going home. That was the last I heard from any of
them. I used the money to settle some old bills and had some
work done on my car so I could continue to ply my trade along
the Crooked Way.

EDWARD GORMAN

THE REASON WHY

Since his debut just a few years ago, Edward Gorman has produced five novels and numerous short stories. He has also become an increasingly important voice in the field through his editing of Mystery Scene, *a magazine of news and interviews that he copublishes with Bob Randisi. Three of Gorman's novels feature part-time private eye Jack Dwyer, who also appears in this nostalgic story of his twenty-fifth high school reunion.*

"I'm scared."

"This was your idea, Karen."

"You scared?"

"No."

"You bastard."

"Because I'm not scared I'm a bastard?"

"Your not being scared means you don't believe me."

"Well."

"See. I knew it."

"What?"

"Just the way you said 'Well.' You bastard."

I sighed and looked out at the big red brick building that sprawled over a quarter mile of spring grass turned silver by a fat June moon. Twenty-five years ago a 1950 Ford fastback had sat in the adjacent parking lot. Mine for two summers of grocery store work.

We were sitting in her car, a Volvo she'd cadged from her last marriage settlement, number four if you're interested, and sharing a pint of bourbon the way we used to in high school when we'd been more than friends but never quite lovers.

The occasion tonight was our twenty-fifth class reunion. But there was another occasion, too. In our senior year a boy named Michael Brandon had jumped off a steep clay cliff called Pierce

Point to his death on the winding river road below. Suicide.
That, anyway, had been the official version.

A month ago Karen Lane (she had gone back to her maiden
name these days, the Karen Lane-Cummings-Todd-Browne-
LeMay getting a tad too long) had called to see if I wanted to
go to dinner and I said yes, if I could bring Donna along, but
then Donna surprised me by saying she didn't care to go along,
that by now we should be at the point in our relationship where
we trusted each other ("God, Dwyer, I don't even look at other
men, not for very long anyway, you know?"), and Karen and I
had had dinner and she'd had many drinks, enough that I saw
she had a problem, and then she'd told me about something
that had troubled her for a long time. . . .

In senior year she'd gone to a party and gotten sick on wine
and stumbled out to somebody's backyard to throw up, and it
was there she'd overheard the three boys talking. They were
earnestly discussing what had happened to Michael Brandon
the previous week and they were even more earnestly discussing what would happen to them if "anybody ever really found
out the truth."

"It's bothered me all these years," she'd said over dinner a
month earlier. "They murdered him and they got away with it."

"Why didn't you tell the police?"

"I didn't think they'd believe me."

"Why not?"

She shrugged and put her lovely little face down, dark hair
covering her features. Whenever she put her face down that
way it meant that she didn't want to tell you a lie so she'd just
as soon talk about something else.

"Why not, Karen?"

"Because of where we came from. The Highlands."

The Highlands is an area that used to ring the iron foundries
and factories of this city. Way before pollution became a fashion-
able concern, you could stand on your front porch and see a
peculiarly beautiful orange haze on the sky every dusk. The
Highlands had bars where men lost ears, eyes, and fingers in
just garden-variety fights, and streets where nobody sane ever
walked after dark, not even cops unless they were in pairs. But
it wasn't the physical violence you remembered so much as the

emotional violence of poverty. You get tired of hearing your mother scream because there isn't enough money for food and hearing your father scream back because there's nothing he can do about it. Nothing.

Karen Lane and I had come from the Highlands, but we were smarter and, in her case, better looking than most of the people from the area, so when we went to Wilson High School—one of those nightmare conglomerates that shoves the poorest kids in a city in with the richest—we didn't do badly for ourselves. By senior year we found ourselves hanging out with the sons and daughters of bankers and doctors and city officials and lawyers and riding around in new Impala convertibles and attending an occasional party where you saw an actual maid. But wherever we went, we'd manage for at least a few minutes to get away from our dates and talk to each other. What we were doing, of course, was trying to comfort ourselves. We shared terrible and confusing feelings—pride that we were acceptable to those we saw as glamorous, shame that we felt disgrace for being from the Highlands and having fathers who worked in factories and mothers who went to Mass as often as nuns and brothers and sisters who were doomed to punching the clock and yelling at ragged kids in the cold factory dusk. (You never realize what a toll such shame takes till you see your father's waxen face there in the years-later casket.)

That was the big secret we shared, of course, Karen and I, that we were going to get out, leave the place once and for all. And her brown eyes never sparkled more Christmas-morning bright than at those moments when it all was ahead of us—money, sex, endless thrills, immortality. She had the kind of clean good looks brought out best by a blue cardigan with a line of white button-down shirt at the top and a brown suede car coat over her slender shoulders and moderately tight jeans displaying her quietly artful ass. Nothing splashy about her. She had the sort of face that snuck up on you. You had the impression you were talking to a pretty but in no way spectacular girl, and then all of a sudden you saw how the eyes burned with sad humor and how wry the mouth got at certain times and how absolutely perfect that straight little nose was and how the freckles enhanced rather than detracted from her beauty and by then of course you were hopelessly entangled. Hopelessly.

This wasn't just my opinion, either. I mentioned four divorce settlements. True facts. Karen was one of those prizes that powerful and rich men like to collect with the understanding that it's only something you hold in trust, like a yachting cup. So, in her time, she'd been an ornament for a professional football player (her college beau), an orthodontist ("I think he used to have sexual fantasies about Barry Goldwater"), the owner of a large commuter airline ("I slept with half his pilots; it was kind of a company benefit"), and a sixty-nine-year-old millionaire who was dying of heart disease ("He used to have me sit next to his bedside and just hold his hand—the weird thing was that of all of them, I loved him, I really did—and his eyes would be closed and then every once in a while tears would start streaming down his cheeks as if he was remembering something that really filled him with remorse; he was really a sweetie, but then cancer got him before the heart disease and I never did find out what he regretted so much, I mean if it was about his son or his wife or what"), and now she was comfortably fixed for the rest of her life and if the crow's feet were a little more pronounced around eyes and mouth and if the slenderness was just a trifle too slender (she weighed, at five-three, maybe ninety pounds and kept a variety of diet books in her big sunny kitchen), she was a damn good-looking woman nonetheless, the world's absurdity cataloged and evaluated in a gaze that managed to be both weary and impish, with a laugh that was knowing without being cynical.

So now she wanted to play detective.

I had some more bourbon from the pint—it burned beautifully—and said, "If I had your money, you know what I'd do?"

"Buy yourself a new shirt?"

"You don't like my shirt?"

"I didn't know you had this thing about Hawaii."

"If I had your money, I'd just forget about all this."

"I thought cops were sworn to uphold the right and the true."

"I'm an ex-cop."

"You wear a uniform."

"That's for the American Security Agency."

She sighed. "So I shouldn't have sent the letters?"

"No."

"Well, if they're guilty, they'll show up at Pierce Point to-night."

"Not necessarily."

"Why?"

"Maybe they'll know it's a trap. And not do anything."

She nodded to the school. "You hear that?"

"What?"

"The song."

It was Bobby Vinton's "Roses Are Red."

"I remember one party when we both hated our dates and we ended up dancing to that over and over again. Somebody's basement. You remember?"

"Sort of, I guess," I said.

"Good. Let's go in the gym and then we can dance to it again."

Donna, my lady friend, was out of town attending an advertising convention. I hoped she wasn't going to dance with anybody else because it would sure make me mad.

I started to open the door and she said, "I want to ask you a question."

"What?" I sensed what it was going to be so I kept my eyes on the parking lot.

"Turn around and look at me."

I turned around and looked at her. "Okay."

"Since the time we had dinner a month or so ago I've started receiving brochures from Alcoholics Anonymous in the mail. If you were having them sent to me, would you be honest enough to tell me?"

"Yes, I would."

"Are you having them sent to me?"

"Yes, I am."

"You think I'm a lush?"

"Don't you?"

"I asked you first."

So we went into the gym and danced.

*   *   *

Crepe of red and white, the school colors, draped the ceiling;
the stage was a cave of white light on which stood four balding
fat guys with spit curls and shimmery gold lamé dinner jackets
(could these be the illegitimate sons of Bill Haley?) playing
guitars, drum, and saxophone; on the dance floor couples who'd
lost hair, teeth, jaw lines, courage, and energy (everything, it
seemed, but weight) danced to lame cover versions of "Breaking Up Is Hard to Do" and "Sheila," "Runaround Sue" and
"Running Scared" (tonight's lead singer sensibly not even trying
Roy Orbison's beautiful falsetto) and then, while I got Karen
and myself some no-alcohol punch, they broke into a medley of
dance tunes—everything from "Locomotion" to "The Pepper-
mint Twist"—and the place went a little crazy, and I went right
along with it.

"Come on," I said.

"Great."

We went out there and we burned ass. We'd both agreed not
to dress up for the occasion so we were ready for this. I wore
the Hawaiian shirt she found so despicable plus a blue blazer,
white socks and cordovan penny-loafers. She wore a salmon-
colored Merikani shirt belted at the waist and tan cotton fatigue
pants and, sweet Christ, she was so adorable half the guys in the
place did the kind of double takes usually reserved for somebody outrageous or famous.

Over the blasting music, I shouted, "Everybody's watching
you!"

She shouted right back, "I know! Isn't it wonderful?"

The medley went twenty minutes and could easily have been
confused with an aerobics session. By the end I was sopping
and wishing I was carrying ten or fifteen pounds less and
sometimes feeling guilty because I was having too much fun (I
just hoped Donna, probably having too much fun, too, was
feeling equally guilty), and then finally it ended and mate fell
into the arms of mate, hanging on to stave off sheer collapse.

Then the head Bill Haley clone said, "Okay, now we're going
to do a ballad medley," so then we got everybody from Johnny
Mathis to Connie Francis and we couldn't resist that, so I moved
her around the floor with clumsy pleasure and she moved me

right back with equally clumsy pleasure. "You know something?" I said.

"We're both shitty dancers?"

"Right."

But we kept on, of course, laughing and whirling a few times, and then coming tighter together and just holding each other silently for a time, two human beings getting older and scared about getting older, remembering some things and trying to forget others and trying to make sense of an existence that ultimately made sense to nobody, and then she said, "There's one of them."

I didn't have to ask her what "them" referred to. Until now she'd refused to identify any of the three people she'd sent the letters to.

At first I didn't recognize him. He had almost white hair and a tan so dark it looked fake. He wore a black dinner jacket with a lacy shirt and a black bow tie. He didn't seem to have put on a pound in the quarter century since I'd last seen him.

"Ted Forester?"

"Forester," she said. "He's president of the same savings and loan his father was president of."

"Who are the other two?"

"Why don't we get some punch?"

"The kiddie kind?"

"You could really make me mad with all this lecturing about alcoholism."

"If you're not really a lush then you won't mind getting the kiddie kind."

"My friend, Sigmund Fraud."

We had a couple of pink punches and caught our respective breaths and squinted in the gloom at name tags to see who we were saying hello to and realized all the terrible things you realize at high school reunions, namely that people who thought they were better than you still think that way, and that all the sad little people you feared for—the ones with blackheads and low IQs and lame left legs and walleyes and lisps and every other sort of unfair infirmity people get stuck with—generally turned out to be deserving of your fear, for there was a sadness in their eyes tonight that spoke of failures of every sort, and you wanted to go up and say something to them (I wanted to go up to nervous Karl Carberry, who used to twitch—his whole body twitched—and throw my arm around him and tell him what a neat guy he was, tell him there was no reason whatsoever for his twitching, grant him peace and self-esteem and at least a modicum of hope; if he needed a woman, get him a woman, too), but of course you didn't do that, you didn't go up, you just made edgy jokes and nodded a lot and drifted on to the next piece of human carnage.

"There's number two," Karen whispered.

This one I remembered. And despised. The six-three blond movie-star looks had grown only slightly older. His blue dinner jacket just seemed to enhance his air of malicious superiority. Larry Price. His wife Sally was still perfect, too, though you could see in the lacquered blond hair and maybe a hint of face lift that she'd had to work at it a little harder. A year out of high school, at a bar that took teenage IDs checked by a guy who must have been legally blind, I'd gotten drunk and told Larry that he was essentially an asshole for beating up a friend of mine who hadn't had a chance against him. I had the street boy's secret belief that I could take anybody whose father was a surgeon and whose house included a swimming pool. I had hatred, bitterness, and rage going, right? Well, Larry and I went out into the parking lot, ringed by a lot of drunken spectators, and before I got off a single punch, Larry hit me with a shot that stood me straight up, giving him a great opportunity to hit me again. He hit me three times before I found his face and sent him a shot hard enough to push him back for a time. Before we could go at it again, the guy who checked IDs got himself between us. He was madder than either Larry or me. He ended the fight by taking us both by the ears (he must have trained with nuns) and dragging us out to the curb and telling neither of us to come back.

"You remember the night you fought him?"

"Yeah."

"You could have taken him, Dwyer. Those three punches he got in were just lucky."

"Yeah, that was my impression, too. Lucky."

She laughed. "I was afraid he was going to kill you."

I was going to say something smart, but then a new group of people came up and we gushed through a little social dance of nostalgia and lies and self-justifications. We talked success (at high school reunions, everybody sounds like Amway representatives at a pep rally) and the old days (nobody seems to remember all the kids who got treated like shit for reasons they had no control over) and didn't so-and-so look great (usually this meant they'd managed to keep their toupees on straight) and introducing new spouses (we all had to explain what happened to our original mates; I said mine had been eaten by alligators in the Amazon, but nobody seemed to find that especially believable) and in the midst of all this, Karen tugged my sleeve and said, "There's the third one."

Him I recognized, too. David Haskins. He didn't look any happier than he ever had. Parent trouble was always the explanation you got for his grief back in high school. His parents had been rich, truly so, his father an importer of some kind, and their arguments so violent that they were as eagerly discussed as who was or who was not pregnant. Apparently David's parents weren't getting along any better today because although the features of his face were open and friendly enough, there was still the sense of some terrible secret stooping his shoulders and keeping his smiles to furtive wretched imitations. He was a paunchy, balding little man who might have been a church usher with a sour stomach.

"The Duke of Earl" started up then and there was no way we were going to let that pass so we got out on the floor; but by now, of course, we both watched the three people she'd sent letters to. Her instructions had been to meet the anonymous letter writer at nine-thirty at Pierce Point. If they were going to be there on time, they'd be leaving soon.

"You think they're going to go?"

"I doubt it, Karen."

"You still don't believe that's what I heard them say that night?"

"It was a long time ago and you were drunk."

"It's a good thing I like you because otherwise you'd be a distinct pain in the ass."

Which is when I saw all three of them go stand under one of

the glowing red EXIT signs and open a fire door that led to the parking lot.

"They're going!" she said.

"Maybe they're just having a cigarette."

"You know better, Dwyer. You know better."

Her car was in the lot on the opposite side of the gym. "Well, it's worth a drive even if they don't show up. Pierce Point should be nice tonight."

She squeezed against me and said, "Thanks, Dwyer. Really."

So we went and got her Volvo and went out to Pierce Point where twenty-five years ago a shy kid named Michael Brandon had fallen or been pushed to his death.

Apparently we were about to find out which.

The river road wound along a high wall of clay cliffs on the left and a wide expanse of water on the right. The spring night was impossibly beautiful, one of those moments so rich with sweet odor and even sweeter sight you wanted to take your clothes off and run around in some kind of crazed animal circles out of sheer joy.

"You still like jazz," she said, nodding to the radio.

"I hope you didn't mind my turning the station."

"I'm kind of into Country."

"I didn't get the impression you were listening."

She looked over at me. "Actually, I wasn't. I was thinking about you sending me all those AA pamphlets."

"It was arrogant and presumptuous and I apologize."

"No, it wasn't. It was sweet and I appreciate it."

The rest of the ride I leaned my head back and smelled flowers and grass and river water and watched moonglow through the elms and oaks and birches of this new spring. There was a Dakota Staton song, "Street of Dreams," and I wondered as always where she was and what she was doing, she'd been so fine, maybe the most underappreciated jazz singer of the entire fifties.

Then we were going up a long, twisting gravel road. We pulled up next to a big park pavilion and got out and stood in the wet grass, and she came over and slid her arm around my waist and sort of hugged me in a half-serious way. 'This is all probably crazy, isn't it?"

I sort of hugged her back in a half-serious way. "Yeah, but it's a nice night for a walk so what the hell."

"You ready?"

"Yep."

"Let's go then."

So we went up the hill to the Point itself, and first we looked out at the far side of the river where white birches glowed in the gloom and where beyond you could see the horseshoe shape of the city lights. Then we looked down, straight down the drop of two hundred feet, to the road where Michael Brandon had died.

When I heard the car starting up the road to the east, I said, "Let's get in those bushes over there."

A thick line of shrubs and second-growth timber would give us a place to hide, to watch them.

By the time we were in place, ducked down behind a wide elm and a mulberry bush, a new yellow Mercedes sedan swung into sight and stopped several yards from the edge of the Point.

A car radio played loud in the night. A Top 40 song. Three men got out. Dignified Forester, matinee-idol Price, anxiety-tight Haskins.

Forester leaned back into the car and snapped the radio off. But he left the headlights on. Forester and Price each had cans of beer. Haskins bit his nails.

They looked around in the gloom. The headlights made the darkness beyond seem much darker and the grass in its illumination much greener. Price said harshly, "I told you this was just some goddamn prank. Nobody knows squat."

"He's right, he's probably right," Haskins said to Forester. Obviously he was hoping that was the case.

Forester said, "If somebody didn't know something, we would never have gotten those letters."

She moved then and I hadn't expected her to move at all. I'd been under the impression we would just sit there and listen and let them ramble and maybe in so doing reveal something useful.

But she had other ideas.

She pushed through the undergrowth and stumbled a little and got to her feet again and then walked right up to them.

"Karen!" Haskins said.

"So you did kill Michael," she said.

Price moved toward her abruptly, his hand raised. He was drunk and apparently hitting women was something he did without much trouble.

Then I stepped out from our hiding place and said, "Put your hand down, Price."

Forester said, "Dwyer."

"So," Price said, lowering his hand, "I was right, wasn't I?" He was speaking to Forester.

Forester shook his silver head. He seemed genuinely saddened. "Yes, Price, for once your cynicism is justified."

Price said, "Well, you two aren't getting a goddamn penny, do you know that?"

He lunged toward me, still a bully. But I was ready for him, wanted it. I also had the advantage of being sober. When he was two steps away, I hit him just once and very hard in his solar plexus. He backed away, eyes startled, and then he turned abruptly away.

We all stood looking at one another, pretending not to hear the sounds of violent vomiting on the other side of the splendid new Mercedes.

Forester said, "When I saw you there, Karen, I wondered if you could do it alone."

"Do what?"

"What?" Forester said. "What? Let's at least stop the games. You two want money."

"Christ," I said to Karen, who looked perplexed, "they think we're trying to shake them down."

"Shake them down?"

"Blackmail them."

"Exactly," Forester said.

Price had come back around. He was wiping his mouth with the back of his hand. In his other hand he carried a silver-plated .45, the sort of weapon professional gamblers favor.

Haskins said, "Larry, Jesus, what is that?"

"What does it look like?"

"Larry, that's how people get killed." Haskins sounded like Price's mother.

Price's eyes were on me. "Yeah, it would be terrible if Dwyer here got killed, wouldn't it?" He waved the gun at me. I didn't really think he'd shoot, but I sure was afraid he'd trip and the damn thing would go off accidentally. "You've been waiting since senior year to do that to me, haven't you, Dwyer?"

I shrugged. "I guess so, yeah."

"Well, why don't I give Forester here the gun and then you and I can try it again."

"Fine with me."

He handed Forester the .45. Forester took it all right, but what he did was toss it somewhere into the gloom surrounding the car. "Larry, if you don't straighten up here, I'll fight you myself. Do you understand me?" Forester had a certain dignity, and when he spoke his voice carried an easy authority. "There will be no more fighting, do you both understand that?"

"I agree with Ted," Karen said.

Forester, like a teacher tired of naughty children, decided to get on with the real business. "You wrote those letters, Dwyer?"

"No."

"No?"

"No. Karen wrote them."

A curious glance was exchanged by Forester and Karen. "I guess I should have known that," Forester said.

"Jesus, Ted," Karen said. "I'm not trying to blackmail you, no matter what you think."

"Then just what exactly are you trying to do?"

She shook her lovely little head. I sensed she regretted ever writing the letters, stirring it all up again. "I just want the truth to come out about what really happened to Michael Brandon that night."

"The truth," Price said. "Isn't that goddamn touching?"

"Shut up, Larry," Haskins said.

Forester said, "You know what happened to Michael Brandon?"

"I've got a good idea," Karen said. "I overheard you three talking at a party one night."

"What did we say?"

"What?"

"What did you overhear us say?"

Karen said, "You said that you hoped nobody looked into what really happened to Michael that night."

A smile touched Forester's lips. "So on that basis you concluded that we murdered him?"

"There wasn't much else to conclude."

Price said, weaving still, leaning on the fender support, "I don't goddamn believe this."

Forester nodded to me. "Dwyer, I'd like to have a talk with Price and Haskins here, if you don't mind. Just a few minutes." He pointed to the darkness beyond the car. "We'll walk over there. You know we won't try to get away because you'll have our car. All right?"

I looked at Karen.

She shrugged.

They left, back into the gloom, voices receding and fading into the sounds of crickets and a barn owl and a distant roaring train.

"You think they're up to something?"

"I don't know," I said.

We stood with our shoes getting soaked and looked at the green grass in the headlights.

"What do you think they're doing?" Karen asked.

"Deciding what they want to tell us."

"You're used to this kind of thing, aren't you?"

"I guess."

"It's sort of sad, isn't it?"

"Yeah. It is."

"Except for you getting the chance to punch out Larry Price after all these years."

"Christ, you really think I'm that petty?"

"I know you are. I know you are."

Then we both turned to look back to where they were. There'd been a cry and Forester shouted, "You hit him again, Larry, and I'll break your goddamn jaw." They were arguing about something and it had turned vicious.

I leaned back against the car. She leaned back against me. "You think we'll ever go to bed?"

"I'd sure like to, Karen, but I can't."

"Donna?"

"Yeah. I'm really trying to learn how to be faithful."

"That been a problem?"

"It cost me a marriage."

"Maybe I'll learn how someday, too."

Then they were back. Somebody, presumably Forester, had torn Price's shirt into shreds. Haskins looked miserable.

Forester said, "I'm going to tell you what happened that night."

I nodded.

"I've got some beer in the back seat. Would either of you like one?"

Karen said, "Yes, we would."

So he went and got a six-pack of Michelob and we all had a beer and just before he started talking he and Karen shared another one of those peculiar glances and then he said, "The four of us—myself, Price, Haskins, and Michael Brandon—had done something we were very ashamed of."

"Afraid of," Haskins said.

"Afraid that, if it came out, our lives would be ruined. Forever," Forester said.

Price said, "Just say it, Forester." He glared at me. "We raped a girl, the four of us."

"Brandon spent two months afterward seeing the girl, bringing her flowers, apologizing to her over and over again, telling her how sorry we were, that we'd been drunk and it wasn't like us to do that and   " Forester sighed, put his eyes to the ground. "In fact we had been drunk; in fact it wasn't like us to do such a thing—"

Haskins said, "It really wasn't. It really wasn't."

For a time there was just the barn owl and the crickets again, no talk, and then gently I said, "What happened to Brandon that night?"

"We were out as we usually were, drinking beer, talking about it, afraid the girl would finally turn us into the police, still trying to figure out why we'd ever done such a thing—"

The hatred was gone from Price's eyes. For the first time the matinee idol looked as melancholy as his friends. "No matter what you think of me, Dwyer, I don't rape women. But that night—" He shrugged, looked away.

"Brandon," I said. "You were going to tell me about Brandon."

"We came up here, had a case of beer or something, and talked about it some more, and that night," Forester said, "that night Brandon just snapped. He couldn't handle how ashamed he was or how afraid he was of being turned in. Right in the middle of talking—"

Haskins took over. "Right in the middle, he just got up and ran out to the Point." He indicated the cliff behind us. "And before we could stop him, he jumped."

"Jesus," Price said, "I can't forget his screaming on the way down, I can't ever forget it."

I looked at Karen. "So what she heard you three talking about outside the party that night was not that you'd killed Brandon but that you were afraid a serious investigation into his suicide might turn up the rape?"

Forester said, "Exactly." He stared at Karen. "We didn't kill Michael, Karen. We loved him. He was our friend."

But by then, completely without warning, she had started to cry and then she began literally sobbing, her entire body shaking with some grief I could neither understand nor assuage.

I nodded to Forester to get back in his car and leave. They stood and watched us a moment and then they got into the Mercedes and went away, taking the burden of years and guilt with them.

This time I drove. I went far out the river road, miles out, where you pick up the piney hills and the deer standing by the side of the road.

From the glove compartment she took a pint of J&B, and I knew better than to try and stop her.

I said, "You were the girl they raped, weren't you?"

"Yes."

"Why didn't you tell the police?"

She smiled at me. "The police weren't exactly going to believe a girl from the Highlands about the sons of rich men."

I sighed. She was right.

"Then Michael started coming around to see me. I can't say I

ever forgave him, but I started to feel sorry for him. His fear—"
She shook her head, looked out the window. She said, almost to
herself, "But I had to write those letters, get them there tonight,
know for sure if they killed him." She paused. "You believe
them?"

"That they didn't kill him?"

"Right."

"Yes, I believe them."

"So do I."

Then she went back to staring out the window, her small face
childlike there in silhouette against the moonsilver river. "Can
I ask you a question, Dwyer?"

"Sure."

"You think we're ever going to get out of the Highlands?"

"No," I said, and drove on faster in her fine new expensive
car. "No, I don't."

EDWARD D. HOCH

THE SPY AND THE GUY FAWKES BOMBING

This story deals with a crime committed nearly fifty years ago, at the height of the Battle of Britain. It is my favorite of those I published last year.

The nightly air raids over London began on 7 September 1940, when the first German bombers appeared at tea time out of a lazy afternoon sky. They were to continue for seventy-six nights, missing only the night of 2 November, when weather conditions were too poor for flying. The weather was better three nights later, on Guy Fawkes Day, and the planes did not need the traditional bonfires—banned during wartime—to guide them to their target. There were still fires burning in the East End of London from the previous nights' raids.

What was different about the Guy Fawkes bombing was that it wasn't limited to London and other large cities. It struck also at several top-secret RAF bases located in the South of England. Casualties and damage were high, and it wasn't until the following day that Military Intelligence succeeded in determining the source of the information that had guided the enemy planes. It was Colonel Rathbone himself who took the news to the underground War Rooms in Whitehall from which Churchill and other high officials were controlling the war in those dark days.

A pretty WAAF secretary showed Rathbone into Major Penrose's makeshift office beneath the Whitehall buildings. The older officer glanced around distastefully at the white wooden beams and said, "It's not pretty, but I suppose it's safer than up above."

"Indeed it is," Major Penrose agreed. He was a handsome man of about forty with sandy hair and pleasant blue eyes. Rathbone was certain the WAAF secretary enjoyed working for him, though Penrose kept a framed picture of his wife prominently on his desk. "We sometimes work through the night here with the raids going on above us." He lit a cigarette with a nervous hand. "What can we do for M.I.5 today?"

"The daily operations reports no doubt informed you of yesterday's multiple raids on RAF bases."

"Of course. Six were hit, and at least two sustained considerable damage."

"They were among the most secret in the South of England."

"How do you think the Germans learned their exact locations?"

Colonel Rathbone opened his briefcase. "This radio message was intercepted two nights ago and deciphered by the codebreaking unit at Bletchley Park. Unfortunately, by the time they completed their work, last night's raids were already under way."

Major Penrose gave a soft whistle. "This is serious."

"More serious than you may realize. The leak came from here."

"Let me have some coffee brought in and we'll look this over," the major said. "I'm sure you must be mistaken. The Cabinet War Rooms are quite secure."

The two men studied the message at some length over coffee, comparing the various numbers to certain other numbers contained in top-secret lists. "It's clear," Major Penrose said at last. "You're right, of course, Colonel. These numbers are the latitudes and longitudes of our RAF bases, including the six that were hit last night."

"The Germans obtained the locations from this coded message," Rathbone said, stabbing his finger at the document. "There is a spy in your midst."

"Anyone living nearby might know the location of one or two bases. But six? More than six, really. There are ten sets of coordinates listed here. What happened to the other four that weren't hit?"

"Three are too far north, out of range." Colonel Rathbone stirred some sugar into his coffee. "But the fourth one is quite interesting. The numbers are latitude 51 degrees 30 minutes, longitude 1 degree 17 minutes west. Oddly enough, several bombs were dropped last night at this exact location. They blew the hell out of a dairy farmer's fields and barns, killed seven head of cattle."

"The location was a mistake?"

"A typographical error," Rathbone confirmed. "The RAF base is some miles farther west, at 27 minutes rather than 17."

"Whose error was it? The spy's?"

"Actually it was our error." Rathbone picked up the copy of the top-secret list they'd been studying. It was headed: *Alphabetical List and Key to Locations of RAF Stations, etc., Shown on SD239.* Beneath the heading were four subheads: RAF Airfields, Latitude, Longitude, and Map Reference.

"What do you mean?" Penrose asked.

"A typographical error which we caught and corrected at the printing office." Rathbone raised his eyebrows at the other man. "Corrected in all copies but this one, Major Penrose."

Penrose actually laughed. "You insist there's a Nazi spy in these War Rooms. I told you we're quite secure, I handle it myself."

"Perhaps. I hope so, for your sake." Rathbone finished his coffee and stood up to leave. "This is to be kept strictly confidential, of course. You'll hear from me again shortly."

Major Penrose saw him to the door, and as he left Rathbone smiled at the WAAF. "Could you tell me the way to Colonel Cutler's office?"

"Straight down the corridor, sir."

"Thank you."

Colonel Cutler was huddled with Air Vice-Marshal Maynard in the mess when Rathbone finally tracked him down. Both were fairly young men, about Penrose's age. Maynard still flew some combat missions, though he was nearing forty. It was a young man's war, Rathbone thought, as they always were.

He sat. "I've been in to see Penrose," he told Cutler. "There's a situation you'll need to be briefed on when you're free."

Cutler glanced at his watch. "Can it wait until tomorrow? It's almost sundown and the Krauts will be coming over soon."

Colonel Rathbone nodded. "Tomorrow." He picked up a

biscuit as he got to his feet, said his good-byes, and left. He passed the closely guarded entrance to the War Rooms and went up the steps to the street level of Whitehall, past more guards. Rounding a barricade of sandbags, he had a perfect view of the blazing sun low in the afternoon sky. It would be a clear night, perfect for flying.

He headed down the street to where his staff car and driver waited and had almost reached it when the first sharp pain hit him.

Rand had never heard of Colonel Rathbone before the day forty-eight years later when Hastings summoned him to the offices of Concealed Communications. "Here's the perfect job for a re-tired department head like yourself," he told Rand. "This World War II material was recently declassified by the government and there are some interesting items here."

"You expect me to plow through all of that?" Rand asked, aghast.

"Only the material about Niles Rathbone. Ever heard of him?"

"Never."

"He was one of our top M.I.5 people during the first year of the war. He died in November of nineteen forty, apparently of a heart attack. These newly declassified papers show that he was actually poisoned."

"Poisoned! Why would they keep such a thing secret all these years?"

"For a very important reason. He died shortly after leaving a meeting at the underground War Rooms in Whitehall. It was presumed that he was poisoned by one of the officers on duty there—one of Churchill's inner circle."

"What possible motive could they have had?"

Hastings leaned back and lit his pipe. "It seems Colonel Rathbone thought one of them was a traitor in the pay of the Nazis. The locations of several RAF bases were pinpointed for German bombers, and the information could only have come from someone in the War Rooms."

Rand was beginning to understand. "They couldn't make this public until they knew the identity of the traitor."

"Exactly. After Rathbone's death, the investigation came to a dead end. No further evidence was uncovered, and the idea of a spy or traitor in the War Rooms was dismissed. The records were classified to prevent the spread of unfounded rumors. You can imagine the damage such rumors might have had at the height of the Battle of Britain."

"But this is nearly a half century later."

Hastings shrugged. "I suppose it was simply forgotten. But now that the records have been declassified, we'd like to get to the bottom of it. I thought of you at once. It's your sort of assignment, and without the least bit of danger. Most people connected with the War Rooms have been dead for years."

Rand stepped into the brisk October air carrying a large box of declassified wartime documents. He vaguely resented Hastings saying the job lacked danger. It was the sort of comment one made to an elderly employee no longer able to face the risks of a job. Rand was far from elderly, though he'd been retired from Double-C for more than a decade and was past his sixtieth birthday.

He took the train to Reading and drove home, surprised to find his wife Leila already back from her teaching day at the university. "Examinations this week," she reminded him. "I thought I'd use the time to rake up some of the leaves. What's in the box?"

"Hastings thought I'd like to look through some declassified files on a World War II case."

"He's getting you into it again, isn't he?"

"He assured me it wasn't dangerous," Rand grumbled.

He spent the rest of the week reading through the files, often finding himself sidetracked by some interesting bit of information. The intelligence and code-breaking unit at Bletchley Park, known to him only through legend, came alive in these documents. He read about the Guy Fawkes bombing, and about the coded message Bletchley Hall had cracked too late to counter the raids on the RAF bases. He read some of Colonel Rathbone's own notes, made the day he died, including his plan to question a Major Penrose who was in charge of the War Rooms security.

By the weekend, Rand was as convinced as Rathbone had

been. Someone in the Cabinet War Rooms had used the locations in a top-secret list to pinpoint targets for the Luftwaffe.

It had been forty-eight years ago almost to the day, he
realized, remembering that Guy Fawkes Day was due again the
following Saturday. Hastings was probably right. Anyone with
the rank to serve in the War Rooms would probably be dead by
now—if one of them *had* poisoned Colonel Rathbone, it was
too far in the past to do anything about it. Still, he felt he owed
something to this man he'd never known. He owed Niles
Rathbone a few more days of his time, at the very least. He
would take the morning train back into London on Monday.

They had it all on computers now. Rand merely asked for a
complete list of officers assigned to the War Rooms in November
1940 and it came up on the screen before his eyes. As an
afterthought he asked for civilians as well, and the computer
responded, leading off with CHURCHILL, WINSTON S., PRIME
MINISTER.

The bored-looking civil servant who operated the machine
shrugged. "That's it. Enlisted personnel would have been on
temporary duty and they're not listed."

"Can you tell me if any of these are still alive?"

"From November nineteen forty? There may be one or two."

The computer listed three:

        CUTLER, COLONEL MARCUS J.

        MAYNARD, AIR VICE-MARSHAL JAMES L.

        PENROSE, MAJOR HUGH B.

"You're in luck," the man told Rand. "There are three, and
they all have the same address if you want to visit them."

"The same address?"

"Waverly. It's a retirement home in the north for former
military officers. A great many World War II people are there."

"How far north?"

"Near York." He gave Rand a printout of the names and the
address.

That evening Rand told Leila he'd be going up to York at the
end of the week. "There are some people I want to see. Some
old soldiers."

* * *

He spent the next few days at home learning what he could about the three survivors. On Thursday he returned to London and visited the Cabinet War Rooms, which had recently been opened as an adjunct of the Imperial War Museum. He imagined Whitehall looking much as it had been in 1940 as he descended the steps and paid his admission.

The purpose of the underground rooms had been to protect Churchill, his cabinet, and chiefs of staff during any possible bombing of London by the Germans. The complex, ten feet underground, had been completed a week before war was declared in 1939 and was used during the Battle of Britain and the later German rocket attacks on the city. Rand walked down the long corridor beneath the reinforced concrete ceiling, looking in at the little rooms where the heads of government had worked and slept. The Cabinet Room itself was arranged exactly as it had been at 5:00 P.M. on 15 October 1940, at the height of the bombings.

In one of the glass display cases hanging on the wall, Rand found the top-secret list of RAF stations that had been the basis for Colonel Rathbone's deductions about a traitor in the War Rooms. Now it was only a historical momento. Forty-eight years ago it had cost countless lives.

He paused to study the office accommodations for the secretaries and typists, the facilities for making tea and coffee, the beds in a number of the offices. The map room and its annex held special fascination for him, as did the Prime Minister's office, with the bed in which Churchill had slept. Most of the officers assigned here had been generals or commanders, although a number of lesser ranks down to captain had served as support personnel at one time or another. Several civilians, male and female, had worked as private secretaries, along with occasional military personnel.

Rand's tour ended at the former mess room, now converted to a shop selling souvenirs and postcards. This was the most likely place for Colonel Rathbone to have been poisoned, but even the original layout of the room was now altered. It told him nothing. As hidden loudspeakers broadcast the sounds of a nighttime bombing of London, he went upstairs to the street level.

It was doubtful that the three remaining officers would know anything of value. Still, he felt he had to see them. Penrose, at least, had been specifically mentioned in Colonel Rathbone's notes. He may have been one of the last persons to see Rathbone alive.

On Friday he took an early train to York and rented a car to drive out to Waverly—a sprawling estate on a small rise of land that commanded a good view of the surrounding countryside. There were individual cottages grouped at the back for those former officers able to care for themselves, and Rand headed there first. A few of the men were gathering sticks and limbs from the nearby woods, piling them in a heap between the cottages and the main house. "What's all this?" Rand asked one grey-haired man. "Clean-up day?"

"It's for the Guy Fawkes bonfire tomorrow night."

Rand nodded. "Ah. I'd forgotten." He glanced toward the cottages. "Perhaps you can help me. I'm looking for Colonel Marcus Cutler."

"Old Cutler's in the main house now. After his wife died, it was too much for him out here alone. He's in the infirmary."

Rand thanked the man and went to the main house, deciding it was best to track down each of the three in turn. A pleasant nurse took him in charge. "Are you a relative of the colonel's or a friend?"

"Neither one, really. I'm engaged in a research project dealing with the Battle of Britain."

"I don't know how much help the colonel will be. He doesn't talk much about those days."

Marcus Cutler was a stooped old man in his eighties who supported himself shakily on canes. He peered at Rand through his glasses as if trying to remember who he was. "You don't know me," Rand quickly assured him. "I came up from London to talk with some of those who were assigned to the Cabinet War Rooms during the bombing."

Cutler motioned to a chair, then lowered himself slowly onto the bed. "I thought for a minute you were my son. He went to America and never came back, not even for his mother's funeral."

"I'm sorry to hear that. My name is Rand. I was in Intelligence work, with Concealed Communications, for a good many years."

"I don't know anything about codes. I worked on maps."

"I'm sure you were very good at it. You must have been, to be assigned to the War Rooms."

The old man shifted his body uncomfortably. "I barely remember those days."

"I was interested in one day in particular. It would have been November sixth, nineteen forty."

Cutler frowned. "The day after Guy Fawkes?"

"That's right."

Encouraged, Rand leaned closer. "Another colonel came to the War Rooms that day—an M.I.5 officer named Rathbone. Do you remember meeting him?"

"Yes."

"Did you speak with him?"

"Only a few minutes. I remember I was in the mess with another officer having a bite to eat before the bombers came. He wanted to speak with me and said he'd be back the following day. Then he went outside and had a heart attack before he reached his car. None of us could believe it."

"Did he eat anything while he was in the mess?"

"I don't remember that."

"The government has declassified the records from that period. An autopsy showed that Colonel Rathbone didn't die of a heart attack. He was poisoned."

"I don't know about that. What are you here for? What do you want?"

His cracking voice had risen alarmingly and the nurse hurried into the room. "What's the trouble here? You really should be lying down, Colonel Cutler." Then, to Rand, "I'm sorry, but you seem to be upsetting him—perhaps you could come back later."

Rand found the next man on the list, Air Vice-Marshal James Maynard, living alone in one of the cottages at the rear of the main house. He seemed younger than his eighty-odd years and still quite vigorous. After Rand explained his mission, Maynard stroked his shock of white hair. "I remember the Guy Fawkes raids," he said. "I was in charge of air operations, and the attacks on those bases was a terrible blow to us all. It pointed to a weakness in our security, for one thing."

"And Colonel Rathbone?"

"I remember being introduced to the man. In the mess, I believe. I don't recall anything else about it."

"Did he eat anything?"

"He may have taken a biscuit off the table but I can't really remember. I usually had tea at that time of day and never bothered with the biscuits. People often snitched them in passing. They still do it here."

"Did you know at the time that the information pinpointing the location of the RAF bases came from the War Rooms?"

"Certainly not—I never knew it until this instant! I'd swear everyone who worked there was loyal to the Crown. On what do you base your information?"

"On the fact that Colonel Rathbone was poisoned, apparently while conducting his investigation in the Cabinet War Rooms."

"My God! Why didn't we know about it?"

"The information has been classified until quite recently."

"You're saying we harbored not only a traitor but a murderer as well?"

"It's a possibility," Rand admitted. "Can you tell me anything, anything at all, about the people you worked with?"

"They were loyal," Maynard said firmly. "Of that much I'm certain."

"Do you have any idea how Colonel Rathbone might have been poisoned?"

"None."

"Well," Rand said, rising to leave, "thank you for your help, anyway, sir. It's been a pleasure chatting with you."

Maynard walked him to the door. "Who else have you come to see? There are others here from those days, you know."

"I've already spoken with Colonel Cutler."

"He talked to you? That surprises me. He usually doesn't like to be reminded of the past. He had a son who was killed in the war."

"He told me he went off to America."

"Sometimes I think he believes that. Who else are you seeing?"

"Major Penrose."

Maynard looked thoughtful for a moment. "Yes, of course, you'd be seeing Penrose. *He* was there, all right."

"Is there anything special I should ask him?"

"You might ask him why he never rose above the rank of major."

The nurse with the pleasant face had some bad news for Rand. "I'm afraid Major Penrose is out of sorts today. He's eighty-eight years old, you know, and not too well. I believe he's been sleeping all day. His daughter is with him now."

"Perhaps I could speak with her."

She smiled. "Let me see."

Presently a woman in her late sixties came into the waiting room with the nurse. "I'm Gwen Penrose. Gwen Penrose Forsyth, actually. Nurse said you wanted to see my father or me." She had been pretty once, Rand could see, and she carried herself with dignity.

"It's really your father I came to see. May we sit and talk?"

"Just for a moment. I don't want to leave him alone. He's beginning to wake up." She followed Rand to a sofa near the door.

"I was hoping to speak with him about his war experiences," Rand said as they sat.

"Did you serve under him?—but no, you're much too young for that."

"Only by a few years. I got into Intelligence work shortly after the war. Now I'm trying to piece together what happened in the Cabinet War Rooms during the Battle of Britain."

She nodded. "That was a terrible time. We could hear the bombers going over, bound for London. I was still a teenager."

"Do you know what your father did at the War Rooms?"

She nodded. "I helped him out for a few months when I was nineteen—during the rocket attacks late in the war. I don't know how they could work down there without ever seeing daylight. It drove me wild. Of course, during the Battle of Britain most of the attacks came at night. People were safe on the streets during the daylight hours. But you asked what my father did. He was the so-called Camp Commandant, responsible for security, domestic arrangements, and the day-to-day operations of the War Rooms."

Rand nodded, understanding now why Colonel Rathbone would come to a junior officer with his evidence. "Did you ever hear him mention an officer named Rathbone?"

"No, I don't believe so." She looked toward her father's room and got to her feet. "I really must be getting back."

"Let me come with you to see if he's awake."

"All right."

He followed her as far as the door and watched while she bent over the pale sleeping man. "His breathing's better," she whispered. "Perhaps you could see him tomorrow."

Rand had planned on catching an evening train back to London, but he was anxious to interview Penrose if it was at all possible. "I'll be back in the morning," he said.

He found a room for the night and phoned Leila to tell her he was staying over.

Saturday was a sunny day with unseasonably warm temperatures for this far north. Rand drove to Waverly in the late morning, after a leisurely breakfast. It wasn't until he spotted the large pile of brush for the bonfire that he remembered it was Guy Fawkes Day. Forty-eight years to the day since German bombers had flown their vapor trails across the Channel to hit six RAF bases and a farmer's barn.

The nurse greeted him in the reception area. "Major Penrose is much better this morning," she informed him with a smile. "You'll be able to visit him."

He found Penrose propped up in bed, awaiting his lunch. "My daughter told me you were here yesterday," the old man said. His voice had a certain vigor, and some color had returned to his wrinkled face. "What can I do for you?"

"I don't want to bother you if you're not feeling well—"

"Nonsense—I feel better than I did ten years ago. I just have a little trouble getting around. These old legs refuse to move."

"Your daughter tells me you were in charge of the Cabinet War Rooms."

"More or less. We had civilians helping with the management from time to time, but those were mainly housekeeping duties." He smiled. "I didn't order the Prime Minister about or anything like that."

"Security was one of your concerns?"

"In a sense. I made sure things were locked up when not in use."

"An Intelligence colonel named Rathbone came to visit you in nineteen forty."

"Ah, yes—Rathbone. I was questioned at the time, you know, but nothing ever came of the investigation."

"He believed there was a security leak in the War Rooms."

"If there was, it was never repeated. The incident with the airfields was the only time."

The nurse arrived with his tray of food. "Here you are, sir. Nice and hot. I can never remember—are you tea or coffee?"

"Coffee, please. I like it black."

She poured coffee from a Silex. "Just ring me when you're finished and I'll remove the tray."

When they were alone again, Rand said, "I've spoken to Cutler and Maynard."

"Have you? I've never been too friendly with them."

"You were older than both men, yet you remained a major. Was there any reason for that?" Rand tried to sound casual, inoffensive.

"The promotions went to officers with combat experience. I fought in the trenches at the end of the First War, but I didn't stay in uniform. I came home and married a wonderful girl. Gwen was born in 'twenty-one and our son Ralph in 'twenty-three. I was in the insurance business until the Second War seemed near, then I went back into the Army. They didn't want me for a combat post—I'd been an office manager at my firm and they felt I was better off in a management position in London. I was given a commission and promoted to major quickly enough, but that was as high as I ever went. Perhaps they put something in my file after that RAF business. I never tried to find out."

"Colonel Rathbone was poisoned the day he visited the War Rooms. Did you know that?"

The old man pushed the half-finished tray of food aside. "I suspected it from the questions they asked, but nobody ever said it. They questioned me more than the others because he'd come to see me."

"Did he eat anything while he was with you?"

Major Penrose shook his head. "Nothing. We had a cup of coffee, that was all. And we both drank from the same pot, so it had to be all right."

"He spoke to you about the list of RAF bases?"

"Yes. He was convinced the information transmitted to the Germans came from us because of a typographical error in only our copy."

Rand nodded. "Yes, I read about that in Rathbone's notes. Everything is declassified now, you know."

There was a tapping on the half-open door and Gwen Penrose came in, carrying a gift-wrapped basket of fruit. "Hello, Daddy. The Women's Auxiliary wants you to have this fruit basket. They said to tell you it was a Guy Fawkes gift. Hello, Mr. Rand. It's good to see you again."

Penrose looked distastefully at the fruit. "Not much there I can eat, but the nurses will be pleased to have it."

"You've had your lunch already. Is that all you ate?"

"It was enough. Mr. Rand and I were talking."

"They're getting ready for the bonfire tonight. Some of the men are making a Guy Fawkes dummy to burn on it."

"I'd like to see that," Penrose said.

"Perhaps we can take you out in the wheelchair." She glanced at Rand. "When will you be going back to London?"

"Soon. I'll leave you two alone while I look around the place. I'll come say good-bye before I catch the train."

He went up to Marcus Cutler's room on the floor above. The retired colonel was seated in a chair by the window. "You're Rand."

"That's right. You have a good memory."

"Memory's better than the eyesight, but I get by."

"I have one more question about that day Colonel Rathbone came to the War Rooms. He said he wanted to speak with you. Do you have any idea what it was about?"

"Maybe my son. Maybe he wanted to tell me how well my son was doing in the war. That was before he ran off to America. I never saw him after that."

"Did you ever see Rathbone again?"

"No. Rathbone died."

"You had a list of the RAF bases in the map room, didn't you?"

Cutler nodded.

"Who had access to it?"

"Everyone there. It was top secret, but we'd all been cleared by security."

"There were no copy machines in those days. Someone would have had to write down those locations by hand if they wanted to copy them. Wouldn't that have been noticed?"

"Not necessarily. The list was in a binder with a leather cover marked *Top Secret.* Someone could have slipped it out and taken it without anyone knowing it was gone."

Rand glanced at the dresser, where some framed family photographs stood. One was of some uniformed men and women squinting into the sun. He recognized some Whitehall buildings in the background. "Was this taken during the War Room days?"

"Yes, that's right. There I am, in the center. That's James Maynard next to me, and a cute little WAAF named Susan, who was his stenographer. This other chap's dead. A V-2 got him in 'forty-four."

"Major Penrose wasn't in the picture?"

"Penrose was gone by then. They shipped him up to a godforsaken base in Scotland where he couldn't do any harm."

"What sort of harm had he been doing?"

Cutler turned suddenly sullen, as he had the previous day. "Why are you asking all these questions? Who sent you? Did my son send you to spy on me?"

"No, I—"

But Cutler had lapsed into silent gloom.

James Maynard was around back near his cottage, putting the finishing touches on a life-sized Guy Fawkes dummy. "We'll have a blazer tonight, Mr. Rand—we'll light up the sky. Are you staying to see it?"

"I wasn't planning to."

"Stay and eat with me. You can see the bonfire and still catch an evening train back to London. It's dark here by four-thirty and the bonfire's at six."

"All right," Rand agreed.

He enjoyed a pleasant late-afternoon meal with the old man, and by the time they'd finished it was already dark. Walking back to his cottage from the main dining room, Maynard talked of the war and the people he'd served with. "I asked Penrose about his rank," Rand told him. "He said the promotions went to combat officers."

"Untrue, of course. Penrose was never promoted for the same reason they shipped him out of the War Rooms in 'forty-one. They thought he'd slipped up."

"On the Rathbone affair?"

"Yes. No one ever said it, and no charges were brought, but he was in charge of security and something went wrong. It was his responsibility."

"That's why you and Cutler aren't especially friendly with him?"

"You might say so."

"There was a sudden flash of fire in the darkness as a torch was lit. "They're a few minutes early," Rand commented.

"Like children. They can't wait."

"I'll be going now," Rand told him. "Thank you for your help."

"What help was I?"

The huge bonfire burst into flame and there was no need for a response. Rand listened to the cheering as he walked around the fire toward the house. On the terrace near the back door were a number of patients in wheelchairs, and as he drew closer he recognized Gwen Penrose standing behind her father's chair.

"You're still here," she said, surprised to see him.

"I said I'd say good-bye."

It was noisy on the terrace and Penrose told them, "Go down closer so you can see them throw the Guy on the fire."

"All right," his daughter agreed readily. When she and Rand were some distance away, she confided, "These old Army men use Guy Fawkes as an excuse to imbibe too much. I can't stand their noisy bragging anymore. Is that a sign I'm growing old, Mr. Rand?"

"Not at all. It's a normal reaction."

There was a great roar from the spectators as two men appeared carrying the stuffed effigy of Guy Fawkes. "Why did you come here?" she asked suddenly. "Are you trying to make trouble for my father?"

"No."

"Hasn't he been through enough already?"

"I don't know. What has he been through?"

"I know they always suspected him, that Colonel Rathbone suspected him and that others have since."

"That was all nearly fifty years ago," Rand reminded her.

The Guy went twisting, turning into the flames, igniting with a new burst of fire as the loudest cheer of all split the night air.

"Tell me one thing, Mr. Rand. Do you think my father betrayed his country and murdered Colonel Rathbone?"

"No," Rand answered quietly, feeling very old, feeling a bit of a chill even this close to the fire. "No, I think you did, Mrs. Forsyth."

It seemed like forever before she answered. "I was only a teenager at the time—you seem to have forgotten that."

"You told me you helped your father at the War Rooms for a few months when you were nineteen. You placed this at the time of the German rocket attacks in nineteen forty-four, but your father said you were born in nineteen twenty-one, so you would have been nineteen in nineteen forty, not nineteen forty-four—and both Cutler and Maynard said your father was transferred out of the War Rooms soon after the Rathbone business. Maynard specifically dated it as nineteen forty-one. If you helped him out for a few months while he was there, it must have been during nineteen forty. Cutler showed me a photograph of a group that included Maynard's WAAF stenographer. I imagine you were a WAAF, too, assigned to the War Rooms and working as your father's secretary. He told me he shared a pot of coffee with Colonel Rathbone that day. In the traditional manner, the coffee would have been made and brought into the office by you. Your father assured me it couldn't have been poisoned because both he and Rathbone drank it, but most people take sugar in their coffee and Rathbone probably did. Your father drinks his black to this day, I noticed at lunch. No one would know that fact better than a secretary who also happened to be his daughter. Some white powder mixed with the sugar would go unnoticed, and Rathbone would die while your father was unhurt. Naturally you disposed of the remaining sugar later."

"You're very good at surmises."

"You lied about when you worked there. Why, unless you had something to hide? You had the opportunity to copy the list of RAF base locations, and you had the motive and opportunity to poison Colonel Rathbone. I think you did both of those things."

She stared at the brightly burning fire for some time. "I'll tell you a story, Mr. Rand," she said at last. "I don't expect you to believe it, but it happens to be true.

"I enlisted in the WAAF when I was nineteen, and my father requested that I be assigned to the War Rooms to help him. You've guessed that much correctly. I was going with a young man at the time—the son of a French diplomat. We were very passionate for each other and I became pregnant in the late summer of nineteen forty. By October I was desperate. I couldn't tell my mother or my father, and pregnancy would mean my dismissal from the WAAF. Eric said he couldn't marry me, but he promised to arrange for a safe abortion if I would do one thing for him. He said his father needed the locations of the RAF bases in the South of England. I foolishly agreed to copy it for him. I knew it was wrong, but Free France was still our ally and to me it seemed only a technical crime. I couldn't believe it when I overheard Colonel Rathbone telling my father about the Guy Fawkes bombing of the bases. Worse than that, he seemed to be accusing my father of a breach of security."

"So you killed him."

"You have to believe this. It was a terrible, terrible accident. The poison wasn't meant for him."

"Who was it meant for?"

She took a deep breath. "Me."

"You'd better explain that."

"I had expected Eric to give me money for an abortion. Instead he presented me with a vial of white powder. He said it would make me ill and induce a miscarriage. He told me that was the safest way. I hadn't used it yet on the sixth of November. I suppose I was trying to work up my courage. When I heard Colonel Rathbone questioning my father, I knew I had to do something quickly. Either my father would be accused or the truth would come out about my part in it. I couldn't allow either to happen. I took the vial from my purse and mixed the white powder with the sugar. I figured it would make the colonel ill and delay the investigation—even a day's respite would give me time to think. I never imagined the powder would kill him. In fact, it was a full day before the terrible truth dawned on me—Eric had meant it to kill me!"

"What happened after that?"

"There was an intense investigation of my father, but nothing could be proven. The poisoning was hushed up, as you know, and he was simply transferred out of the War Rooms to a base in Scotland. I left when he did, reassigned to one of the very RAF bases the Germans had bombed. I think that was my worst punishment of all."

"The baby?"

"The tension was too much for me. I had a natural miscarriage before Christmas and no one ever knew."

"What about your friend Eric?"

"I never saw him again. He disappeared after Guy Fawkes Day. Someone told me he'd been killed in one of the London bombings, but I never knew it for sure. I think I spent the next ten years fearful he might turn up again any day, but he never did. Finally I married a businessman here in York." She turned to search his face with her eyes. "Do you believe me?"

"Yes," Rand said.

"Will you tell my father? The police?"

"I won't tell anyone. What good would it do?"

"Thank you." She sighed. "I must be getting back to him now."

He watched her walk up the path to the terrace where the old man in the wheelchair waited, then he went out to his car and drove away. In the rearview mirror the dying flames of the bonfire looked like a city burning.

CLARK HOWARD

THE DAKAR RUN

This novelette is something different by the always popular Clark Howard. It is the suspenseful, fast-moving story of an auto race from Paris to Dakar. Readers of Ellery Queen's Mystery Magazine *voted this tale their favorite of the year, making Clark Howard a three-time winner of the EQMM Readers' Award.*

Jack Sheffield limped out of the little Theatre Americain with John Garfield's defiant words still fresh in his mind. "What are you gonna do, kill me?" Garfield, as Charley Davis, the boxer, had asked Lloyd Gough, the crooked promoter, at the end of *Body and Soul.* Then, challengingly, smugly, with the Garfield arrogance, "Everybody dies!" And he had walked away, with Lilli Palmer on his arm.

Pausing outside to look at the *Body and Soul* poster next to the box office, Sheffield sighed wistfully. They were gone now, Garfield and Lilli Palmer, black-and-white films, the good numbers like Hazel Brooks singing "Am I Blue?" Even boxing—*real* boxing—was down the tubes. In the old days, hungry kids challenged seasoned pros. Now millionaires fought gold-medal winners.

Shaking his head at the pity of things changed, Sheffield turned up his collar against the chilly Paris night and limped up La Villette to the Place de Cluny. There was a cafe there called the Nubian, owned by a very tall Sundanese who mixed his own mustard, so hot it could etch cement. Every Tuesday night, the old-movie feature at the Theatre Americain changed and Jack Sheffield went to see it, whatever it was, and afterward he always walked to the Nubian for sausage and mustard and a double gin. Later, warm from the gin and the food, he would stroll, rain or fair, summer or winter, along the Rue de Rivoli next to the Tuileries, down to the Crazy Horse Saloon to wait for the chorus to do its last high kick so that Jane, the long-legged Englishwoman with whom he lived, could change and go home. Tuesdays never varied for Sheffield.

How many Tuesdays, he wondered as he entered the Nubian, had he been doing this exact same thing? As he pulled out a chair at the rickety little table for two at which he always sat, he tried to recall how long he had been with Jane. Was it three years or four? Catching the eye of the Sudanese, Sheffield raised his hand to signal that he was here, which was all he had to do; he never varied his order. The Sudanese nodded and walked with a camel-like gait toward the kitchen, and Sheffield was about to resume mentally backtracking his life when a young girl came in and walked directly to his table.

"Hi," she said.

He looked at her, tilting his head an inch, squinting slightly without his glasses. When he didn't respond at once, the girl gave him a wry, not totally amused look.

"I'm Chelsea," she said pointedly. "Chelsea Sheffield. Your daughter." She pulled out the opposite chair. "Don't bother to get up."

Sheffield stared at her incredulously, lips parted but no words being generated by his surprised brain.

"Mother," she explained, "said all I had to do to find you in Paris was locate a theater that showed old American movies, wait until the bill changed, and stand outside after the first show. She said if you didn't walk out, you were either dead or had been banished from France."

"Your mother was always right," he said, adding dryly, "about everything."

"She also said you might be limping, after smashing up your ankle at Le Mans two years ago. Is the limp permanent?"

"More or less." He quickly changed the subject. "Your mother's well, I presume."

"Very. Like a Main Line Philadelphia doctor's wife should be. Her picture was on the society page five times last year."

"And your sister?"

"Perfect," Chelsea replied, "just as she's always been. Married to a proper young stockbroker, mother of two proper little girls, residing in a proper two-story Colonial, driving a proper

Chrysler station wagon. Julie has *always* been proper. I was the foul-mouthed little girl who was too much like my race-car-driver daddy, remember?"

Sheffield didn't know whether to smile or frown. "What are you doing in Paris?" he asked.

"I came over with my boyfriend. We're going to enter the Paris-to-Dakar race."

Now it was Sheffield who made a wry face. "Are you serious?"

"You better believe it," Chelsea assured him.

"Who's your boyfriend—Parnelli Jones?"

"Funny, Father. His name is Austin Trowbridge. He's the son of Max Trowbridge."

Sheffield's eyebrows rose. Max Trowbridge had been one of the best race-car designers in the world before his untimely death in a plane crash. "Did your boyfriend learn anything from his father?" he asked Chelsea.

"He learned plenty. For two years he's been building a car for the Paris-Dakar Rally. It's finished now. You'd have to see it to believe it—part Land Rover, part Rolls-Royce, part Corvette. We've been test-driving it on the beach at Hilton Head. It'll do one hundred and ten on hard-packed sand, ninety on soft. The engine will cut sixty-six hundred RPMs."

"Where'd you learn about RPMs?" he asked, surprised.

Chelsea shrugged. "I started hanging out at dirt-bike tracks when I was fourteen. Gave mother fits. When I moved up to stock cars, she sent me away to boarding school. It didn't work. One summer at Daytona, I met Austin. We were both kind of lonely. His father had just been killed and mine—" she glanced away "—well, let's just say that Mother's new husband didn't quite know how to cope with Jack Sheffield's youngest."

And I wasn't around, Sheffield thought. He'd been off at Formula One tracks in Belgium and Italy and England, drinking champagne from racing helmets and Ferragamos with four-inch heels, looking for faster cars, getting older with younger women, sometimes crashing. Burning, bleeding, breaking—

"Don't get me wrong," Chelsea said, "I'm not being critical. Everybody's got to live his life the way he thinks best. I'm going my own way with Austin, so I can't fault you for going your own way without me."

But you do, Sheffield thought. He studied his daughter. She had to be nineteen now, maybe twenty—he couldn't even remember when her birthday was. She was plainer than she was pretty—her sister Julie had their mother's good looks, poor Chelsea favored him. Lifeless brown hair, imperfect complexion, a nose that didn't quite fit—yet there was something about her that he suspected could seize and hold a man, if he was the right man. Under the leather jacket she had unzipped was clearly the body of a woman, just as her direct grey eyes were obviously no longer the eyes of a child. There was no way, Sheffield knew, he could ever make up for the years he hadn't been there, but maybe he could do something to lessen the bad taste he'd left. Like talking her out of entering the Paris-Dakar Rally.

"You know, even with the best car in the world the Paris-Dakar run is the worst racing experience imaginable. Eight thousand miles across the Sahara Desert over the roughest terrain on the face of the earth, driving under the most brutal, dangerous, dreadful conditions. It shouldn't be called a rally, it's more like an endurance test. It's three weeks of hell."

"*You've* done it," she pointed out. "Twice."

"We already know I make mistakes. I didn't win either time, you know."

A touch of fierceness settled in her eyes. "I didn't look you up to get advice on whether to enter—Austin and I have already decided that. I came to ask if you'd go over the route map with us, maybe give us some pointers. but if you're too busy—"

"I'm not too busy," he said. Her words cut him easily.

Chelsea wrote down an address in Montmartre. "It's a rented garage. We've got two rooms above it. The car arrived in Marseilles by freighter this morning. Austin's driving it up tomorrow." She stood and zipped up her jacket. "When can we expect you?"

"Day after tomorrow okay?"

"Swell. See you then." She nodded briefly. "Good-night, Father."

"Good-night."

As she was walking out, Sheffield realized that he hadn't once spoken her name.

* * *

On Thursday, Sheffield took Jane with him to Montmarte, thinking at least he would have somebody on his side if Chelsea and Austin Trowbridge started making him feel guilty. It didn't work. Jane and Chelsea, who were only ten years apart in age, took to each other at once.

"Darling, you look just like him," Jane analyzed. "Same eyes, same chin. But I'm sure your disposition is much better. Jack has absolutely no sense of humor sometimes. If he wasn't so marvelous in bed, I'd leave him."

"He'll probably save you the trouble someday," Chelsea replied. "Father leaves everyone eventually."

"Why don't you two just talk about me like I'm not here?" Sheffield asked irritably.

Austin Trowbridge rescued him. "Like to take a look at the car, Mr. Sheffield?"

"Call me Jack. Yes, I would. I was a great admirer of your father, Austin. He was the best."

"Thanks. I hope I'll be half as good someday."

As soon as Sheffield saw the car, he knew Austin was already half as good, and more. It was an engineering work of art. The body was seamless, shaped not for velocity but for balance, with interchangeable balloon and radial wheels on the same axles, which had double suspension systems to lock in place for either. The steering was flexible from left-hand drive to right, the power train flexible from front to rear, side to side, corner to corner, even to individual wheels. The windshield displaced in one-eighth-inch increments to deflect glare in the daytime, while infrared sealed beams could outline night figures fifty yards distant. A primary petrol tank held one hundred liters of fuel and a backup tank carried two hundred additional liters. Everywhere Sheffield looked—carburetor, generator, distributor, voltage regulator, belt system, radiator, fuel lines—he saw imagination, innovation, improvement. The car was built for reliability and stability, power and pace. Sheffield couldn't have been more impressed.

"It's a beauty, Austin. Your dad would be proud."

"Thanks. I named it after him. I call it the 'Max One.'"

Nice kid, Sheffield thought. He'd probably been very close to his father before the tragedy. Not like Chelsea and himself.

After looking at the Max One, Sheffield took them all to lunch at a cafe on the Boulevard de la Chapelle. While they ate, he talked about the rally.

"There's no competition like it in the world," he said. "It's open to cars, trucks, motorcycles, anything on wheels. There's never any telling who'll be in—or on—the vehicle next to you: it might be a professional driver, a movie star, a millionaire, an Arab king. The run starts in Paris on New Year's Day, goes across France and Spain to Barcelona, crosses the Mediterranean by boat to Africa, then down the length of Algiers, around in a circle of sorts in Niger, across Mali, across Mauritania, up into the Spanish Sahara, then down along the Atlantic coast into Senegal to Dakar. The drivers spend fifteen to eighteen hours a day in their vehicles, then crawl into a sleeping bag for a short, badly needed rest at the end of each day's stage. From three to four hundred vehicles start the run each year. About one in ten will finish."

"We'll finish," Chelsea assured him. "We might even win."

Sheffield shook his head. "You won't win. No matter how good the car is, you don't have the experience to win."

"We don't have to win," Austin conceded. "We just have to finish well—respectably. There are some investors who financed my father from time to time. They've agreed to set me up in my own automotive-design center if I prove myself by building a vehicle that will survive Paris-Dakar. I realize, of course, that the car isn't everything—that's why I wanted to talk to you about the two rallies you ran, to get the benefit of your experience."

"You haven't been racing since you hurt your ankle," Chelsea said. "What have you been doing, Father?"

Sheffield shrugged. "Consulting, training other drivers, conducting track courses—"

"We're willing to pay you for your time to help us," she said.

Sheffield felt himself blush slightly. God, she knew how to cut.

"That won't be necessary," he said. "I'll help you all I can."

He wanted to add, "After all, you *are* my daughter," but he didn't.

As he and Jane walked home, she said, "That was nice, Jack, saying you'd help them for nothing."

"Nice, maybe, but not very practical. I could have used the money. I haven't made a franc in fourteen months."

Jane shrugged. "What does that matter? I earn enough for both of us."

It mattered to Sheffield. . . .

Sheffield began going to Montmartre every day. In addition to talking to Austin about the route and terrain of the rally, he also helped him make certain modifications on Max One.

"You've got to put locks on the doors, kid. There may be times when both of you have to be away from the car at once and there are places along the route where people will steal you blind."

Holes were drilled and locks placed.

"Paint a line on the steering wheel exactly where your front wheels are aligned straight. That way, when you hit a pothole and bounce, or when you speed off a dune, you can adjust the wheels and land straight. It'll keep you from flipping over. Use luminous paint so you can see the line after dark."

Luminous paint was secured and the line put on.

A lot of Sheffield's advice was practical rather than technical. "Get rid of those blankets. It gets down to twenty degrees in the Sahara at night. Buy lightweight sleeping bags. And stock up on unsalted nuts, granola bars, high-potency vitamins, caffeine tablets. You'll need a breathing aid, too, for when you land in somebody's dust wake. Those little gauze masks painters use worked fine for me."

Most times when Sheffield went to Montmartre, Chelsea wasn't around. Austin always explained that she was running errands or doing this or that, but Sheffield could tell that he was embarrassed by the excuses. His daughter, Sheffield realized, obviously didn't want to see him any more than necessary. He tried not to let it bother him. Becoming more friendly each visit with Austin helped. The young man didn't repeat Chelsea's offer to pay him for his time, seeming to understand that it was insulting, and for that Sheffield was grateful. No one, not even Jane, knew how serious Sheffield's financial predicament was.

No one except Marcel.

One afternoon when Sheffield got back from Montmartre, Marcel was waiting for him at a table in the cafe Sheffield had to pass through to get to his rooms. "Jack, my friend," he hailed, as if the encounter were mere chance, "come join me." Snapping his fingers at the waiter, he ordered, "Another glass here."

Sheffield sat down. At a nearby table were two thugs who accompanied the diminutive Marcel everywhere he went. One was white, with a neck like a bucket and a walk like a wrestler's. The other was café au lait, very slim, with obscene lips and a reputation for being deadly with a straight razor. After glancing at them, Sheffield drummed his fingers silently on the tablecloth and waited for the question Marcel invariably asked first.

"So, my friend, tell me, how are things with you?"

To which Sheffield, during the past fourteen months anyway, always answered, "The same, Marcel, the same."

Marcel assumed a sad expression. Which was not difficult since he had a serious face, anyway, and had not smiled, some said, since puberty. His round little countenance would have reminded Sheffield of Peter Lorre except that Marcel's eyes were narrow slits that, despite their owner's cordiality, clearly projected danger.

"I was going over my books last week, Jack," the Frenchman said as he poured Sheffield a Pernod, "and I must admit I was a little surprised to see how terrible your luck has run all year. I mean, horse races, dog races, prizefights, soccer matches—you seem to have forgotten what it is to pick a winner. Usually, of course, I don't let anyone run up a balance so large, but I've always had a soft spot for you, Jack."

"You know about the car in Montmartre, don't you?" Sheffield asked pointedly.

"Of course," Marcel replied at once, not at all surprised by the question. "I've known about it since it arrived in Marseilles." Putting a hand on Sheffield's arm, he asked confidentially, "What do you think of it, Jack?"

Sheffield moved his arm by raising the Pernod to his lips. "It's a fine car. One of the best I've ever seen."

"I'm glad you're being honest with me," Marcel said. "I've already had a man get into the garage at night to look at it for me. He was of the same opinion. He says it can win the rally."

Sheffield shook his head. "They're a couple of kids, Marcel. They may finish—they won't win."

Marcel looked at him curiously. "What is a young man like this Austin Trowbridge able to pay you, anyway?"

"I'm not being paid."

Marcel drew back his head incredulously. "A man in your financial situation? You work for nothing?"

"I used to know the kid's father," Sheffield said. Then he added, "I used to know his girlfriend's father, too."

Marcel studied the American for a moment. "Jack, let me be as candid with you as you are being with me. There are perhaps two dozen serious vehicles for which competition licenses have been secured for this year's rally. The car my associates and I are backing is a factory-built Peugeot driven by Georges Ferrand. A French driver in a French car. Call it national pride if you wish, call it practical economics—the fact is that we will have a great deal of money at risk on a Ferrand win. Of the two dozen or so vehicles that will seriously challenge Ferrand, we are convinced he will outdistance all but one of them. That one is the Trowbridge car. It is, as you said, a fine car. We have no statistics on it because it did not run in the optional trials at Cergy-Pontoise. And we know nothing about young Trowbridge himself as a driver—whether he's capable, has the stamina, whether he's *hungry*. The entire entry, car and driver, presents an unknown equation which troubles us."

"I've already told you, Marcel—the car can't win."

The Frenchman fixed him in an unblinking stare. "I want a guarantee of that, Jack." He produced a small leather notebook. "Your losses currently total forty-nine thousand francs. That's about eight thousand dollars. I'll draw a line through the entire amount for a guarantee that the Max One will not outrun Ferrand's Peugeot."

"You're not concerned whether it finishes?"

"Not in the least," Marcel waved away the consideration. "First place wins, everything else loses."

Sheffield pursed his lips in brief thought, then said, "All right, Marcel. It's a bargain."

Later, in their rooms, Jane said, "I saw you in the cafe with Marcel. You haven't started gambling again, have you?"

"Of course not." It wasn't a lie. He had never stopped.

"What did he want, then?"

"He and his friends are concerned about Austin's car. They know I'm helping the kid. They want a guarantee that the Max One won't ace out the car they're backing."

Jane shook her head in disgust. "What did you tell him?"

"That he had nothing to worry about. Austin's not trying to win, he only wants to finish."

"But you didn't agree to help Marcel in any way?"

"Of course not." Sheffield looked away. He hated lying to Jane, yet he did so regularly about his gambling. This time, though, he swore to himself, he was going to quit—when the slate was wiped clean with Marcel, he had made up his mind not to bet on anything again, not racing, not boxing, not soccer, not even whether the Eiffel Tower was still standing. And he was going to find work, too—some kind of normal job, maybe in an automobile factory, so he could bring in some money, settle down, plan for some kind of future. Jane, after all, was almost thirty; she wouldn't be able to kick her heels above her head in the Crazy Horse chorus line forever.

And his bargain with Marcel wouldn't matter to Austin and Chelsea, he emphasized to his conscience. All Austin had to do to get his design center was finish the race, not win it.

That night while Jane was at the club, Sheffield went to a bookstall on the Left Bank that specialized in racing publications. He purchased an edition of the special Paris-Dakar Rally newspaper that listed each vehicle and how it had performed in the optional trials at Cergy-Pontoise. Back home, he studied the figures on Ferrand's Peugeot and on several other cars which appeared to have the proper ratios of weight-to-speed necessary for a serious run. There was a Mitsubishi that looked very good, a factory-sponsored Mercedes, a Range Rover, a Majorette, a little Russian-built Lada, and a Belgian entry that looked like a VW but was called an Ostend.

For two hours he worked and reworked the stats on a pad of paper, dividing weights by distance, by average speeds, by days, by the hours of daylight which would be available, by the average wind velocity across the Sahara, by the number of stops necessary to adjust tire pressure, by a dozen other factors that a prudent driver needed to consider. When he finished, and compared his final figures with the figures he had estimated for Austin Trowbridge's car, Sheffield reached an unavoidable conclusion: The Max One might—just *might*—actually win the rally.

Sheffield put on his overcoat and went for a walk along the Champs-Elysees and on into the deserted Tuileries. The trees in the park were wintry and forlorn, the grass grey from its nightly frost, and the late-November air thin and cold. Sheffield limped along, his hands deep in his pockets, chin down, brow pinched. Marcel had used the word "guarantee"—and that's what Sheffield had agreed to: a guarantee that the Max One wouldn't win. But the car, Sheffield now knew, was even better than he'd thought: it *could* win. In order to secure his guarantee to Marcel, Sheffield was left with but one alternative. He had to tamper with the car.

Sheffield sat on a bench in the dark and brooded about the weaknesses of character that had brought him to his present point in life. He wondered how much courage it would take to remain on the bench all night and catch pneumonia and freeze to death. The longer he thought about it, the more inviting it seemed. He sat there until he became very cold. But eventually he rose and returned to the rooms above the cafe.

The following week, after conceiving and dismissing a number of plans, Sheffield asked Austin, "What are you going to do about oil?"

"The rally supply truck sells it at the end of every stage, doesn't it? I thought I'd buy it there every night."

"That's okay in the stages where everything goes right," Sheffield pointed out. "But the rally supply truck is only there for a couple of hours and then starts an overnight drive to the next stage. If you get lost or break down or even blow a tire, you could miss the truck and have to run on used oil the entire next day. You need to carry a dozen quarts of your own oil for emergencies."

"I hate to add the weight," Austin said reluctantly.

"I know of a garage that will seal it in plastic bags so you can eliminate the cans," Sheffield said. "That'll save you a couple of pounds."

"You really think it's necessary?"

"I'd do it," Sheffield assured him. Austin finally agreed. "Tell me the grade you want and I'll get it for you," Sheffield said.

Austin wrote down the viscosity numbers of an oil density that was perfect for the Max One's engine. On his way home, Sheffield stopped by the garage of which he had spoken. Before he ordered the bags of oil, he drew a line through some of Austin's numbers and replaced them with figures of his own—lower figures which designated less constancy in the oil's lubricating quality.

Several days later, the garage delivered to the rooms above the cafe a carton containing the bagged oil. Jane was home and accepted the delivery. The garageman gave her a message for Sheffield.

"Our mechanic said to tell Monsieur that if this oil is for a rally vehicle, it should be several grades lighter. This viscosity will reduce engine efficiency as the air temperature drops."

When the garageman left, Jane saw taped to the top bag the slip of paper with the viscosity numbers altered. When Sheffield returned from Montmartre, she asked him about it.

"Yes, I changed them," he said, his tone deliberately casual. "The oil Austin specified was too light."

"Does he know you changed his figures?"

"Sure."

"Are you lying to me, Jack?" She had been exercising and was in black leotards, hands on hips, concern wrinkling her brow.

"Why would I lie about a thing like motor oil?" Sheffield asked.

"I don't know. But I've had an uneasy feeling since I saw you with Marcel. If you're in some kind of trouble, Jack—"

"I'm not in any kind of trouble," he said, forcing a smile.

"You're not trying to get back at Chelsea for the way she's acting toward you, I hope."

"Of course not."

"Jack," she said, "I called Austin and said I thought the garage made a mistake. I read him your numbers and he said they were wrong."

"You *what?*" Sheffield stared at her. The color drained from his face. Jane sighed wearily and sat down.

"I knew it. I could feel it."

Sheffield felt a surge of relief. "You didn't call Austin."

She shook her head. "No." Her expression saddened. "Why are you doing it, Jack?"

Sheffield poured himself a drink and sat down and told her the truth. He told her about the lies of the past fourteen months, the money he'd bet and lost, the circle of desperation that had slowly been closing in on him. "I saw a way out," he pleaded.

"By hurting someone who trusts you?"

"No one will be hurt," he insisted. "Austin doesn't have to win, all he has to do—"

"Is finish," she completed the statement for him. "That's not the point, Jack. It's wrong and you know it."

"Look," he tried to explain, "when Austin uses this heavier oil, all it will do is make the Max One's engine cut down a few RPMs. He probably won't even notice it. The car will slow down maybe a mile an hour."

"It's wrong, Jack. Please don't do it."

"I've *got* to do it," Sheffield asserted. "I've got to get clear of Marcel."

"We can start paying Marcel. I have some savings."

"No." Sheffield stiffened. "I'm tired of being kept by you, Jane."

"*Kept* by me?"

"Yes, kept! You as much as said so yourself when you told my daughter I was marvelous in bed."

"Oh, Jack—surely you don't think Chelsea took me seriously!"

"*I* took you seriously."

Jane stared at him. "If you think you're going to shift onto me some of the responsibility for what you're doing, you're mistaken."

"I don't want you to take any of the responsibility," he made clear, "but I don't expect you to interfere, either. Just mind your own business."

Jane's eyes hardened. "I'll do that."

In the middle of December, the Crazy Horse closed for two weeks and Jane announced that she was going back to England for the holidays. "Dad's getting on," she said, "and I haven't seen my sister's children since they were toddlers. I'd invite you along but I'm afraid it would be awkward, our not being married and all."

"I understand," Sheffield said. "I'll spend Christmas with Chelsea and Austin."

"I rather thought you would." She hesitated. "Are you still determined to go through with your plan?"

"Yes, I am."

Jane shrugged and said no more.

After she was gone, Chelsea seemed to feel guilty about Sheffield being alone for Christmas. "You're welcome to come here," she said. "I'm not the greatest cook, but—"

"Actually, I'm going to England," he lied. "Jane telephoned last night and said she missed me. I'm taking the boat train on Christmas Eve."

What he actually took on Christmas Eve was a long, lonely walk around the gaily decorated Place de la Concorde, past the chic little shops staying open late along Rue Royale. All around him holiday music played, greetings were exchanged, and the usually dour faces of the Parisiennes softened a bit. When his ankle began to ache, Sheffield bought a quart of gin, a loaf of bread, and a small basket of cold meats and cheese, and trudged back to his rooms. The café downstairs was closed, so he had to walk around to the alley and go up the back way. A thin, cold drizzle started and he was glad it had waited until he was almost inside.

Putting his food away, he lighted a little space heater, opened the gin, and sat trying to imagine what the future held for him. The telephone rang that night and several times on Christmas

Day, but he did not answer it. He was too involved wondering about the rest of his life. And he was afraid it might be a wrong number.

Sheffield finally answered the telephone the following week when he came in one evening and found it ringing. It was Jane.

"I thought I ought to tell you, I'm staying over for a few days longer. There's a new cabaret opening in Piccadilly and they're auditioning dancers the day after New Year's. I'm going to try out. Actually, I've been thinking about working closer to home for a while. Dad's—"

"Yes, I know. Well, then. I wish you luck."

"No hard feelings?"

"Of course not. You?"

"Not anymore."

"Let me know how you make out."

"Sure."

After he hung up, Sheffield got the gin out again. He drank until he passed out. It was nearly twelve hours later when he heard an incessant pounding and imagined there was a little man inside his head trying to break out through his left eye with a mallet. When he forced himself to sit upright and engage his senses, he discovered that the pounding was on his door.

He opened the door and Chelsea burst in. "Austin's broken his arm!" she announced, distraught.

On their way to Montmartre, she gave him the details. "We decided to go out for dinner last night, to celebrate finishing the last of the work on the car. We went to a little café on Rue Lacaur—"

"That's a rough section."

"Tell me about it. On the way home, we were walking past these two guys and one of them made a comment about me. Austin said something back, and before I knew it both of them jumped him. They beat him up badly and one of them used his knee to break Austin's arm like a stick of wood. It was awful!"

In the rooms over the garage, Austin was in bed with an ice compress on his face and his right arm in a cast. "Two years of work down the tubes," he said morosely.

"It could have been worse," Sheffield told him. "People have been shot and stabbed on that street."

"I thought for a minute one of them was going to slice Austin with a razor," Chelsea said.

"A razor?" Sheffield frowned. "What kind of razor?"

"One of those barber's razors. The kind that unfolds like a pocket knife."

"A straight razor," Sheffield said quietly. An image of Marcel's two bodyguards came into focus. The thin one carried a straight razor, and the other one looked strong enough to break arms.

Sheffield managed to keep his anger under control while he tried to reconcile Austin and Chelsea to the fact that it wasn't the end of the rally for them. He gave Austin the names of four drivers he knew who weren't signed up for Paris-Dakar this year and might consider an offer to make the run. Two were here in Paris, one was in Zurich, and the other at his home in Parma. "Call them and see what you can do," he said. "I'll go back to my place and see if I can think of any others."

As soon as he left the garage, he went to a telephone kiosk around the corner and called Marcel's office.

"You son of a bitch," he said when the Frenchman came on the line. "We had an arrangement that *I* was to keep Austin Trowbridge from winning."

"That is not precisely correct," Marcel said. "You agreed to take care of the *car*. I decided, because of the amount of money at risk, that it would be best to protect your guarantee with an additional guarantee."

"That wasn't necessary, you son of a bitch!"

"That's twice you've called me that," Marcel said, his tone icing. "I've overlooked it up to now because I know you're angry. Please refrain from doing it again, however. For your information—" his voice broke slightly "—my mother was a saint."

"I don't think you had a mother," Sheffield said coldly. "I think you crawled up out of a sewer!" Slamming down the receiver, he left the kiosk and stalked across the street to a bar. He had a quick drink to calm himself down, then another, which he drank more slowly as he tried to decide what to do. There was no way he could turn in Marcel's thugs without admitting

his own complicity to Austin and Chelsea. And it was Marcel he
wanted to get even with. But Marcel was always protected. How
the hell did you take revenge on someone with the protection
he had?

As Sheffield worried it over, the bartender brought him
change from the banknote with which he'd paid for his drinks.
Sheffield stared at the francs on the bar and suddenly thought:
Of course. You didn't hurt a man like Marcel physically, you
hurt him financially.

Leaving the second drink unfinished, something Sheffield
hand't done in years, he left the bar and hurried back to the
rooms over the garage. Austin and Chelsea were at the telephone.

"The two drivers here turned us down," Austin said. "I'm
about to call the one in Zurich."

"Forget it," Sheffield said flatly. "I'm driving the Max One for
you. . . . "

It wasn't yet dawn in the Place d'Armes where the race was to
start, but a thousand portable spotlights created an artificial
daylight that illuminated the four lines of vehicles in eerie silver
light. A hundred thousand spectators jammed the early-morning
boulevard on each side, waving flags, signs, and balloons, cheering select cars and select drivers, the women throwing and
sometimes personally delivering kisses, the men reaching past
the lines of gendarmes to slap fenders and shout, "*Bon courage!*"

Young girls, the kind who pursue rock stars, walked the lines
seeking autographs and more while their younger brothers and
sisters followed them throwing confetti. Everyone had to shout
to be heard in the general din.

The Max One was in 182nd starting position, which put it in
the forty-sixth row, the second car from the inside. Chelsea, in
a racing suit, stood with Austin's good arm around her, both
looking with great concern at Jack as he wound extra last-
minute tape over the boot around his weak ankle.

"Are you absolutely sure about this, Jack?" the young designer
asked. "It's not worth further damage to your ankle."

"I'm positive," Sheffield said. "Anyway, we'll be using Chelsea's feet whenever we can." Looking up, he grinned. "You just be in Dakar to receive the trophy."

"That trophy will be yours, Jack."

"The prize money will be mine," Sheffield corrected. "The trophy will be yours."

There was a sudden roar from the crowd and a voice announced through static in the loudspeaker that the first row of four vehicles had been waved to a start. The rally had begun.

"Kiss him good-bye and get in," Sheffield said, shaking hands with Austin, then leaving the couple alone for the moments they had left.

Presently father and daughter were side by side, buckled and harnessed in, adrenaline rushing, their bodies vibrating from the revving engine, their eyes fixed on the white-coated officials who moved down the line and with a brusque nod and a wave started each row of four vehicles five seconds apart.

Sheffield grinned over at Chelsea. "I wonder what your mother would say if she could see us now?"

"I know exactly what she'd say—'Birds of a feather.' "

"Well, maybe we are," Sheffield said.

"Let's don't get sentimental, Father," Chelsea replied. "Driving together from Paris to Dakar doesn't make a relationship."

Looking at her determined young face, Sheffield nodded. "Whatever you say, kid."

A moment later, they were waved away from the starting line.

From Paris to Barcelona would have been 850 kilometers if the road had been straight. But it wasn't. It wound through Loiret, Cher, Creuse, Correze, Cantal, and more—as if the route had been designed by an aimless schoolboy on a bicycle. Nearly all the way, the roadsides were lined with cheering, waving, kiss-throwing well-wishers shouting, *"Bonne chance!"* From time to time, flowers were thrown into the cars as they bunched up in a village and were forced to slow down. Farther south, cups of *vin ordinaire*, slices of cheese, and hunks of bread were shared. The farther away from Paris one got, the more relaxed and cheerful were the French people.

Sheffield and Chelsea didn't talk much during the trip south. She was already missing Austin, and Sheffield was concentrating on finding ways to relieve pressure on his weak ankle by holding his foot in various positions. These preoccupations and the increasingly beautiful French countryside kept them both silently contemplative. The Paris-to-Barcelona stage of the rally was a liaison—a controlled section of the route in which all positions remained as they had started—so it wasn't necessary to speed or try to pass. A few vehicles invariably broke down the first day, but for the most part it was little more than a tourist outing. The real race would not begin until they reached Africa.

It was after dark when they crossed the Spanish border and well into the late Spanish dinner hour when they reached Barcelona. As the French had done, the Spaniards lined the streets to cheer on the smiling, still fresh drivers in their shiny, unbattered vehicles. Because of the crowds, and the absence of adequate crowd control, the great caterpillar of vehicles inched its way down to the dock, where the Spanish ferry that would take them to Algiers waited. It was midnight when Sheffield and Chelsea finally drove onto the quay, had their papers examined, and boarded the boat. The first day, eighteen and a half hours long, was over.

Crossing the Mediterranean, Sheffield and Chelsea got some rest and nourishment and met some of the other drivers. Sheffield was well known by most of them already. (He had asked Chelsea ahead of time how she wanted to be introduced. "I don't have to say I'm your father if you'd rather I didn't," he told her. She had shrugged. "It makes no difference to me. Everyone knows we don't choose our parents." "Or our children," Sheffield added.) He introduced her simply as Chelsea and told everyone she was the vehicle designer's girlfriend.

Ferrand, the French driver, Vera Kursk, a shapely but formidable-looking Russian woman, and Alf Zeebrug, a Belgian, all expressed great interest in the Max One's structural configuration. They were, Sheffield remembered from his computations, the three favorites to win the rally: Ferrand in his Peugeot, Vera Kursk in a Lada, Zeebrug in the Volkswagen look-alike called an Ostend.

As they studied the Max One, Ferrand winked at Sheffield and said, "So, you've brought in—what do you Americans call it, a ringer?"

Vera nodded her head knowingly. "I see why you passed up the trial races, Jack. Foxy."

"Let us look under the hood, Jack," pressed Zeebrug, knowing Sheffield wouldn't.

In the end, Ferrand spoke for them all when he said, "Welcome back, Jack. It's good to race with you again." Vera gave him a more-than-friendly kiss on the lips.

Later Chelsea said, "They all seem like nice people."

"They are," Sheffield said. "They're here for the race, nothing else—no politics, no nationalism, no petty jealousies. Just the race." Ferrand, Sheffield was convinced, knew nothing about Marcel's machinations in favor of the Peugeot. Had he known, Ferrand—an honorable man and an honest competitor—would have withdrawn and probably sought out Marcel for physical punishment.

Another comment Chelsea made just before they docked was, "They all seem to like and respect you, Father."

"There are some quarters in which I'm not a pariah," he replied. "Believe it or not."

In Africa, the first stage was Algiers to Ghardaia. Sheffield stuck a hand-printed list to the dashboard between them. It read:

> Ferrand–Peugeot
> Kursk–Lada
> Zeebrug–Ostend
> Sakai–Mitsubishi
> Gordon–Range Rover
> Smythe–Majorette

"These are the drivers and cars to beat," he told Chelsea. "I had a Mercedes on the list, too, but the driver was drinking too much on the ferry and bought a bottle of scotch to take with him when we docked. I don't think we'll have to worry about him."

Chelsea looked at him curiously. "I thought we were only in this to finish, so that Austin can get his design center."

Sheffield fixed her in a flat stare. "I'm a racer, kid. I enter races to *win.* This one is no exception. If you don't want to go along with that, you can get off here."

Chelsea shook her head determinedly. "Not on your life."

Sheffield had to look away so she wouldn't see his pleased smile.

During the first stage, it seemed to Chelsea that every car, truck, and motorcycle in the rally was passing them. "Why aren't we going faster?" she demanded.

"It's not necessary right now," Sheffield told her. "All these people passing us are the showboats—rich little boys and girls with expensive little toys. They run too fast too quickly. Most of them will burn up their engines before we get out of Algeria. Look over there—"

Chelsea looked where he indicated and saw Ferrand, Vera Kursk, and the other experienced drivers cruising along at a moderate speed just as Sheffield was doing. "I guess I've got a lot to learn," she said.

At Ghardaia, their sleeping bags spread like spokes around a desert campfire, the drivers discussed the day. "Let's see," Zeebrug calculated, "three hundred forty-four vehicles started and so far one hundred eighteen have dropped out."

"Good numbers," Ferrand said.

Vera Kursk smiled. "This could turn into a race instead of a herd."

Chelsea noticed that the Russian woman and Sheffield shared a little evening brandy from the same cup and that earlier, when the sleeping bags were spread, Vera had positioned hers fairly close to Sheffield's. Commie slut, she thought. When no one was paying any attention, Chelsea moved her own sleeping bag between them.

It took a week to get out of Algeria—a week in which Sheffield and the other experienced drivers continued to drive at reasonable, safe speeds that were easy on their engines, tires, and the bodies of both car and driver. All along the route, vehicles were dropping out—throwing pistons, getting stuck in sand, blowing too many tires, sliding off soft shoulders into gullies, dropping transmissions, or the exhausted drivers simply giving up. The Mercedes quit the second day—its driver, as Sheffield had

predicted, drinking too much liquor for the heat he had to
endure and the stamina required to drive. A surprise dropout
was the Mitsubishi. Driven by the Japanese speed-racer, Sakai, it
had hit a sand-concealed rock and broken its front axle. "One
down, five to go," Sheffield said, drawing a line through Sakai's
name on the dashboard list.

By the time they crossed into Niger, an additional sixty-three
vehicles had dropped out. "That leaves one hundred sixty-three
in," said Smythe, the Englishman driving the Majorette, when
they camped that night. He was feeling good about the drop-
outs. At noon the next day, he joined them when the Majorette
burned up its gearbox.

"Two down, four to go," Sheffield told Chelsea, and drew
another line.

After camping one night in Chirfa, Chelsea noticed the next
morning that Sheffield and Ferrand and the others shook hands
all around and wished each other good luck. "What was that all
about?" she asked.

"Everyone will be camping alone from now on," he said. "The
socializing is over." Sheffield pointed toward a band of haze on
the horizon. "We go into the Tenere Desert today. Now we start
racing."

The terrain they encountered that day was hell on a back
burner. The Max One was in ashlike sand up to its axles,
plowing along like a man walking against a gale wind. The stink
of the desert decay was unexpected and appalling to Chelsea.
She gagged repeatedly. Huge white rats the size of rabbits
leaped at the car windows. This stage of the rally that crossed
the Tenere was a nightmare in glaring daylight no newcomer
was ever prepared for.

Camped alone that night in some rocks above the desert
floor, Chelsea saw Sheffield massaging his foot. "How's the
ankle?" she asked.

"Just a little stiff. It'll be okay."

"Let's switch places tomorrow," she suggested. "I'll drive and
you relieve." Up to then, Sheffield had done eighty percent of
the driving. "Tomorrow," Sheffield told her, "we go over the
Azbine Plain. It's like driving across a huge corrugated roof."

"Let me drive," she said quietly. "I can manage it."

He let her drive—and she took them across the rough terrain like a pilgrim determined to get to Mecca. Along the way, they saw Zeebrug lying at the side of the road, a rally first-aid team inflating a splint on his leg. The Ostend was nearby, upside down in a ditch, one wheel gone.

"Three and three," Sheffield said. He handed Chelsea the marker and she crossed off Zeebrug's name.

Into the second week of the race, both Jack and Chelsea began to feel the strain of the collective pressures: the usually unheated, quickly eaten food that wreaked havoc with their digestion, the constant jarring and jolting of the car that pummeled their bodies, the freezing nights sleeping on the ground, the scorching, glaring sun by day, the sand and dirt in their mouths, ears, eyes, noses, the constant headaches and relentless fatigue that the short rests could not remedy. Depression set in, underscored by the begging of poverty-stricken Africans everywhere they stopped.

"*Cadeau*," the black children pleaded as Sheffield adjusted his tire pressure. "*Cadeau*," they whined as Chelsea filled the radiator from a village stream.

"We have no gifts," Sheffield told them in English, in French, and by a firm shaking of his head. "Try to ignore them," he advised Chelsea, and she did try, but her eyes remained moist. As did his.

Just over the border in Mali, their physical and mental distress was displaced in priority and urgency by problems the Max One began to develop. A fuel line cracked and split, and they lost considerable petrol before Chelsea noticed the trail it was leaving behind them and they stopped to repair it. The lost fuel had to be replaced at a township pump at exorbitant cost. Later the same day, for no apparent reason, a center section of the windshield bubbled and cracked. Sheffield patched it with some of the tape he had brought for his ankle. The very next day, the odometer cable snapped and they were unable to monitor their distance to the end of the stage.

"Austin's damned car," Chelsea seethed, "is falling apart."

"It's holding up better than most." Sheffield bobbed his chin at two cars, two trucks, and a motorcycle that had dropped out at the side of the road. By then, seventy-one more vehicles had quit the rally, leaving ninety-two still in.

Near Timbuktu, Sheffield and Chelsea happened on a small water pond that no one else seemed to notice. Behind a high rise, it had a few trees, some scrub, and even a patch of Gobi grass. "We've died and gone to heaven," Chelsea said when she was in the water. She began undressing. "I hope you're not modest."

"Not if you aren't."

They took their first bath in two weeks, and when they were clean they rubbed salve on their hips and shoulders where the Max One's seatbelts and harnesses had rubbed the skin raw.

"Mother never went with you when you raced, did she?" Chelsea asked reflectively.

"No."

"Who took care of you when you got hurt?"

"Whoever was around," Sheffield said. He looked off at the distance.

Chelsea patted his head maternally. "If you get hurt in this race, *I'll* take care of you," she assured him. Then she turned away to dress, as if her words embrassed her where her nakedness had not.

After Mali, they crossed into Mauritania. The topography of the route seemed to change every day. One stage would be a mazelike, twisting and turning trail along a dry riverbed, in turn sandy and dusty, then suddenly muddy where an unexpected patch of water appeared. Then they would encounter a long, miserable stage of deep ruts and vicious potholes, then a log-and-rock-strewn track that shook their teeth and vibrated agonizingly in Sheffield's weak ankle.

With each kilometer, his pain grew more intense. During the day he swallowed codeine tablets. At night Chelsea put wet compresses on his ankle and massaged his foot. Those days they came to a stage that was open, flat straightaway, Chelsea did the driving and Sheffield enjoyed temporary respite from the pain.

Nearly every day they caught glimpses of Ferrand, Vera Kursk, and the Australian Gordon in his Range Rover. There were no smiles, waves, or shouted greetings now—just grim nods that said, So you're still in it, are you? Well, so am I.

Into the third grueling week, the pain, fatigue, and depression evolved into recriminations. "How in hell did I let myself get into this mess anyway?" Sheffield asked as he untaped his swollen ankle one night. "I don't owe Austin Trowbridge *or* you anything."

"How did *you* get into it!" Chelsea shot back. "How did *I* get into it! I'm making the same damned mistake my mother made—getting mixed up with a man who thinks speed is some kind of religion."

"I could be back in Paris going to old movies," Sheffield lamented, "eating sausages with homemade mustard, drinking gin."

"And I could be in Philadelphia going to club meetings and playing tennis with your *other* daughter."

They caught each other's eyes in the light of the campfire and both smiled sheepishly. Chelsea came over and kneeled next to her father. "I'll do that," she said, and tended to his ankle.

Later, when he got into his sleeping bag and she was preparing to stand the first two-hour watch, flare gun at the ready, she looked very frankly at him. "You know," she said, her voice slightly hoarse from the dryness, "if we weren't blood relatives, I might find myself attracted to you."

Sheffield stayed awake most of the two hours he should have been sleeping. This was one race he would be very glad to have over—for more reasons than his swollen ankle.

From Mauritania, the route cut north across the border of the Spanish Sahara for a hundred or so kilometers of hot sand, between the wells of Tichia in the east and Bir Ganduz in the west. During that stage, with 71 vehicles of the original 344 still in the race, there was much jockeying for position, much cutting in, out, and around, much risky driving on soft shoulders, and much blind speeding as the dust wake of the vehicle in front reduced visibility to the length of your hood. It was a dangerous stage, driven with goggles and mouth masks, clenched jaws, white knuckles, tight sphincters, and the pedal to the metal, no quarter asked, none given.

In a one-on-one, side-by-side dash to be the first into a single lane between two enormous dunes, Chelsea at the wheel of the Max One and Gordon in his Range Rover were dead even on a thousand-yard straightaway, both pushing their vehicles to the limit, when Gordon glanced over at the Max One and smiled in his helmet at the sight of the girl, not the man, doing the driving. He had the audacity to take one hand off the wheel and wave good-bye as he inched ahead.

"You bastard," Chelsea muttered and juiced the Max One's engine by letting up on the accelerator two inches, then stomping down on it, jolting the automatic transmission into its highest gear and shooting the car forward as if catapulted. With inches to spare, she sliced in front of Gordon to the point where the dunes came together, surprising him so that he swerved, went up an embankment, and immediately slid back down, burying the Range Rover's rear end in five feet of what the nomad Arabs, translated, called "slip sand": grains that, although dry, held like wet quicksand. The Australian would, Sheffield knew, be stuck for hours, and was effectively out of the race as far as finishing up front was concerned.

"Nice work, kid," he said. Now they had only Ferrand and Vera Kursk with whom to contend.

That night they camped along with the other remaining drivers around the oasis well at Bir Ganduz. When the rally starts for the day were announced, they learned that seventeen more vehicles had fallen by the wayside on the Spanish Sahara stage, leaving fifty-four competitors: thirty-eight cars, ten trucks, and six motorcycles. Ferrand was in the lead position, one of the cyclists second, Vera Kursk third, and one of the trucks fourth, another cyclist fifth, and the Max One sixth.

"Are you disappointed we aren't doing better?" Chelsea asked as they changed oil and air filters.

Sheffield shook his head. "We can pass both cyclists and the truck anytime we want to. And probably will, tomorrow. It'll come down to Ferrand, Vera, and us."

"Do you think we can beat them?"

Sheffield smiled devilishly. "If we don't, we'll scare hell out of them." For a moment then he became very quiet. Presently he handed Chelsea a plastic jar. "Hustle over to the control truck and get us some distilled water."

"The battery wells aren't low—I just checked them."

"I want some extra, anyway, just in case. Go on."

As soon as she was out of sight, Sheffield reached into the car and got the flare gun. Turning to a stand of trees in deep shadows twenty feet from the car, he said, "Whoever's in there has got ten seconds to step out where I can see you or I'll light you up like the Arch of Triumph."

From out of the darkness stepped Marcel's two thugs. The one who carried a razor had a sneer on his gaunt brown face. The one with the bucket neck simply looked angry as usual. "We bring greetings from Marcel," said the thin one. "He said to tell you he is willing to be reasonable. Forget what has gone before. You and he will start fresh. He will cancel your debt and give you one hundred thousand francs if you do not overtake Ferrand."

"No deal," Sheffield replied flatly.

"I am authorized to go to a hundred and fifty thousand francs. That is twenty-five thousand dollars—"

"I can add. No deal."

The other man pointed a threatening finger. "To double-cross Marcel is not very smart—"

Sheffield cocked the flare gun. "You're the one who broke my friend's arm, aren't you? How'd you like to have a multicolored face?"

"No need for that," the thin one said quickly, holding up both hands. "We delivered Marcel's message, we have your answer. We'll go now."

"If I see you again," Sheffield warned them, "I'll tell the other drivers about you. They won't like what they hear. You'll end up either in a sandy grave or a Senegalese prison. I don't know which would be worse."

"Perhaps the young lady has an opinion," the thin man said, bobbing his chin toward the Max One, off to the side of Sheffield. It was the oldest ruse in the world, but Sheffield fell for it. He looked over to his left, and when he did the thin man leaped forward with enough speed and agility to knock the flare gun to the ground before Sheffield could resist. Then the man with the bucket neck was there, shoving him roughly until his back was against the car and driving a boot-toe hard against his painful ankle. Sheffield groaned and started to fall, but the other man held him up long enough to deliver a second brutal kick.

"That's all!" his partner said urgently. "Come on!"

They were gone, leaving Sheffield sitting on the sand clutching his ankle, tears of pain cutting lines on his dry cheeks, when Chelsea got back. She ran over to him. "My God, what happened?"

"I must have stepped in a hole. It's bad—"

The ankle swelled to thrice its normal size. For several hours, Chelsea made trips to and from the public well to draw cold water for compresses. They didn't help. By morning, Sheffield couldn't put any weight at all on the foot.

"That does it, I guess," he said resignedly. "Ferrand and Vera will have to fight it out. But at least Austin will get his design center; you can drive well enough for us to finish."

"I can drive well enough for us to win," Chelsea said. She was packing up their camp. "I proved that yesterday."

"Yesterday was on a flat desert straightaway. From here down the coast to Dakar are narrow, winding roads full of tricky curves, blind spots, loose gravel."

"I can handle it."

"You don't understand," Jack said, with the patience of a parent, "this is the final lap. This is for all the marbles—this is what the last twenty days of hell have been all about. These people still in the run are serious competitors—"

"I'm serious, too," Chelsea asserted. "I'm a racer, I'm in this run to win. If you can't accept that, if you don't want to drive with me, drop off here."

Sheffield stared incredulously at her. "You're crazy, kid. Ferrand, Vera, and the others will run you off a cliff into the Atlantic Ocean if they have to."

"They can try." She stowed their belongings on the rear deck and closed the hatchback. "You staying here?"

"Not on your life," Sheffield growled. He hopped over to the car. The passenger side.

* * *

The last lap into Dakar was a war on wheels. All caution was left behind on the Spanish Sahara. This was the heavyweight championship, the World Series, and the Kentucky Derby. No one who got this far would give an inch of track. Anything gained had to be taken.

As soon as the stage started, the Max One dropped back to eight, losing two positions as a pair of motorcycles outdistanced them. Chelsea cursed but Sheffield told her not to worry about it. "This is a good stretch for cycles. We'll probably be passed by a few more. They start falling back when we reach Akreidil; the track softens there and they can't maneuver well. Keep your speed at a steady ninety."

Chelsea glanced over. "I don't want advice on how to finish, just how to win."

"That's what you're going to get," Sheffield assured her. "You do the driving, I'll do the navigating. Deal?"

Chelsea nodded curtly. "Deal."

Sheffield tore the piece of paper from the dash and looked at the names of Ferrand and Vera Kursk. Crumbling it, he tossed it out the window.

"Litterbug," she said.

"Shut up and drive, Chelsea."

"Yes, Daddy."

They exchanged quick smiles, then grimly turned their attention back to the track.

By midmorning the Max One was back to eleventh, but Ferrand and Vera had also fallen behind, everyone being outrun by the six daredevil cyclists still in the rally. This was their moment of glory and they knew it. They would lead the last lap of the run for three magnificent hours, then—as Sheffield had predicted—start falling behind at Akreidil. From that point on, the four-wheeled vehicles overtook and passed them one by one. Ferrand moved back into first place, Vera pressed into second, and the Max One held fourth behind a modified Toyota truck. They were all sometimes mere feet apart on the dangerous track along the Mauritanian coast.

"Blind spot," Sheffield would say as they negotiated weird

hairpin turns. "Hug in," he instructed when he wanted Chelsea to keep tight to the inside of the track. "Let up," he said to slow down, "Punch it" to speed up, "Drop one" to go into a lower gear as he saw Ferrand's car suddenly nose up a grade ahead.

Two of the nine trucks behind them started crowding the track south of Mederdra, taking turns ramming into the Max One's rear bumper at ninety kph. "Get ready to brake," Sheffield said. Watching in a sideview mirror, he waited for exactly the right second, then yelled, "Brake!" Chelsea hit the brake and felt a jolt as one of the trucks ricocheted off the Max One's rear fender and shot across the rocky beach into the surf.

"The other one's passed us!" Chelsea shouted.

"I wanted it to," Sheffield said. "Watch."

The truck that had displaced them in fourth place quickly drew up and challenged the truck in third. For sixty kilometers they jockeyed and swerved and slammed sides trying to assert superiority. One kilometer in front of them, Ferrand and Vera held the two lead positions; behind them, Sheffield and Chelsea kept everyone else in back of the Max One to let the trucks fight it out. Finally, on the Senegal border, the crowding truck finally forced number three off the track and moved up to take its place.

"Okay!" Sheffield yelled at Chelsea. "His body's tired but his brain is happy because he just won. The two aren't working together right now. Punch it!"

Chelsea gunned the Max One and in seconds laid it right next to the victorious truck. The driver looked over, surprised. Sheffield smiled at him. Then Sheffield put his hand over Chelsea's and jerked the steering wheel sharply. The Max One leaped to the right, the truck swerved to avoid being hit, the Max One crossed the entire track, and the truck spun around and went backward into a ditch.

"Now let's go after Vera," Sheffield said.

"With pleasure," Chelsea replied.

It became a three-car race. For more than four hundred kilometers, speeding inland along Senegal's gently undulating sandy-clay plains, the Peugeot, the Lada, and the Max One vied for position. Along straightaways, it became clear that Austin Trowbridge's car was superior in speed to both the French and

Russian vehicles. Chelsea caught up with and passed them both.
"Yeeee*oh!*" she yelled as she sped into the lead.

"Don't open the champagne yet," Sheffield said.

When the straightaway ended and they once again encountered a stretch of the great continental dunes, the experienced
drivers again outmaneuvered and outdistanced the Max One.

"What am I doing wrong?" Chelsea pleaded.

"Hanging out with race-car drivers."

"That's not what I mean!" she stormed, her sense of humor
lost in the face of her frustration.

"We'll be on a sandstone flat when we cross the Saloum
River," Sheffield calmed her. "You'll have a chance to take the
lead again there."

When they reached the flat, Chelsea quickly caught up with
Vera Kursk and passed her, and was pressing Ferrand for first
place when the accident happened. A pack of hyenas, perhaps a
dozen, suddenly ran in front of the Peugeot. Seasoned professional that he was, Ferrand did not swerve an inch as he felt the
impact of his grille on the animals he hit and the rumble of his
tires on those he ran over. Then one of the hyenas was spun up
into the wheel well and, in a mangle of flesh and blood, jammed
the axle. Ferrand's front wheels locked and his vehicle flipped
end over end, landing a hundred feet out on the flats, bursting
into flames.

"Stop the car!" Sheffield ordered, and Chelsea skidded to a
halt on the shoulder. They unharnessed and leapt out, Sheffield
grabbing the portable fire extinguisher, Chelsea helping him to
balance upright on his swollen ankle. As they ran, hobbling,
toward the burning car, they became aware that the Lada had
also stopped and Vera Kursk was getting out.

At the fiery Peugeot, Sheffield handed Chelsea the extinguisher. "Start spraying the driver's door!" Chelsea pointed the
red cylinder and shot a burst of Halon up and down the door.
It immediately smothered the flames on that side and Sheffield
was able to reach through the window, unstrap Ferrand, and
drag him out of the car. Sheffield and Chelsea each took a hand
and, Sheffield limping agonizingly, dragged the unconscious

man far enough away so that when the Peugeot exploded none of them was hurt.

From overhead came the sound of a rotor. Looking up, Sheffield and Chelsea saw a rally control helicopter surveying a place to land. Paramedics wearing Red Cross armbands were in an open hatch waiting for touchdown.

"They'll take care of him," Sheffield said. He stood up, holding onto Chelsea for support, and they looked across at the Max One and the Lada parked side by side. Vera Kursk was beside the Lada, peering down the track, where several kilometers back came the surviving vehicles. Smiling, she threw Sheffield and Chelsea a wave and quickly got into her car. Chelsea started running, dragging Sheffield with her. "The bitch!" she said.

"I'd do the same thing in her place," Sheffield groaned.

By the time they were harnessed back into the Max One, the Lada was half a kilometer ahead and the rest of the pack was moving up behind them very quickly. "We're almost to Dakar," Sheffield told his daughter. "If you want to win, you'll have to catch her."

Chelsea got back on the track and shot the car forward like a bullet. Into the African farming communities she sped, watching for animals, people, other vehicles, always keeping the Lada in sight. "Am I gaining on her, do you think?" she asked.

"Not yet."

Through the farmland, into the nearer outskirts, past larger villages, a soap factory, a shoe factory. "Am I gaining?" she shouted.

"Not yet."

Past a power station, a cotton mill, small handicraft shops at the side of the road, a huge open-air market, increasing lines of spectators in marvelously colored native garb. "Am I gaining?"

"Not yet."

"God*damn!*"

Then into the city of Dakar itself and on to the far end of Gann Boulevard, a wide, tree-lined thoroughfare roped off a mere one hour earlier, when the control aircraft advised the city that the first of the rally vehicles was approaching. The boulevard led straight to the finish line in the Place de l'Independence. The Lada was still half a kilometer ahead. "Punch it!" Sheffield yelled. He beat his fist on the dashboard. "Punch it! Punch it!"

Chelsea punched it.

The Max One drew up dead even on the right side of the Lada. The two women exchanged quick, appraising glances, saw only unyielding determination in the other, and, as if choreographed, both leaned into their steering wheels and tried to punch their accelerators through the floorboards. "Come *on!*" Chelsea muttered through her clenched teeth.

The Max One pulled forward an inch. Then two. Then three. Vera Kursk glanced over again, desperation in her eyes. Sheffield yelled, "All right!"

The cars sped down to the finish line next to the war memorial in the great plaza. Thousands cheered them on from a vast crowd that was but a blur of color to the drivers. Stretched across the end of the boulevard, a great banner with FINIS lettered on it fluttered in the breeze. The Max One was less than a car length ahead, the Lada's windshield even with the American vehicle's rear bumper. Then Vera punched the Lada.

"She's pulling up!" Sheffield cried.

Chelsea saw Vera's face moving closer in the sideview mirror. In seconds, the Russian woman was next to her again. Biting down hard enough on her bottom lip to draw blood, Chelsea punched the Max One again.

The Max One crossed the finish line one and a half seconds ahead of the Lada.

At the banquet that night in the Saint Louis Hotel, Chelsea and Vera Kursk hugged each other and Austin Trowbridge read everyone a cable he had received congratulating him on the Max One and advising him that a bank account had been opened for one million dollars to start the Trowbridge Automotive Design Center. "I'd like you to come back to the States and be my partner," the young man told Sheffield. "Between the two of us, we can come up with cars nobody's ever imagined."

"I'll think about it, kid," Sheffield promised.

At midnight, Sheffield rode with Chelsea and Austin in a taxi out to Grand Dakar Airport, where they watched the Max One being rolled into the cargo hold of a Boeing 747 bound for Casablanca and New York. The young couple had seats in the passenger section of the same plane.

"Austin and I are going to be married when we get home," Chelsea told Sheffield. Austin had gone ahead, giving them time to say good-bye. "And we're going to start having babies. The first boy we have, I'm naming Jack. After a guy I recently met."

"Do yourself a favor," Sheffield said. "Raise him to be a doctor."

She shook her head. "Not on your life." She kissed him on the cheek. "Bye, Daddy."

"See you, kid."

Sheffield watched the plane rumble down the runway and climb into the starry African sky. Then he sighed and limped slowly off the observation deck and back into the terminal. When he reached the glass exit doors, he was met by the familiar face he'd been expecting.

"Hello, Marcel."

The Frenchman's two thugs were standing nearby.

"The Max One was pressing Ferrand when he crashed," Marcel accused. "You were racing to win."

"I always race to win," Sheffield replied evenly.

"Do you think you can get away with double-crossing me?" The Frenchman's eyes were narrowed and dangerous.

Sheffield merely shrugged. "What are you going to do, Marcel, kill me?" He cocked his head in the best John Garfield tradition. "Everybody dies," he said arrogantly. And pushing through the doors, he walked painfully out into the Senegalese night.

LINDA O. JOHNSTON
DIFFERENT DRUMMERS

This short-story is the first published fiction by Linda O. Johnston. It is remarkably professional in both concept and execution and definitely deserved the Robert L. Fish Memorial Award for Best First Short Story of 1988, presented to the author by the Mystery Writers of America.

They were the three supreme salespeople in all of the United States. The American Association of Super Sales Persons said so. And everyone knew the AASSP admitted only the elite of the country's sales force.

Each member had automatically been entered in AASSP's biennial sales contest. Four months before, the Association had sent its questionnaire to every member's employer requesting substantiating statistics: the product each member sold, its retail cost, the company's total yearly sales volume, and the sales volume achieved single-handedly by the member.

The results were tallied, digested, and evaluated, then kneaded together with a fudge factor to allow for the relative cost and utility of each company's product.

The first and second-place winners faced Sally Manhattan across the smudged glass-topped table of the isolated tropical lounge three miles inland from the Atlantic Ocean near Wilmington, North Carolina. Around them, palely thatched rattan chairs huddled defensively in empty clusters against the rain forest of the indoor jungle. Ferns strained toward the ceilings, fighting for root space with the shiny-leafed lianas spilling from wood planters and hanging baskets throughout the crannied room. Cool air spurted spasmodically from vents along the off-white wall, but the plucky air-conditioning unit was no match for the oppressively humid heat.

The AASSP grand champion, portly, proud Morton Sturdevant, was effusively gallant to Sally, barely blanketing an offensive male chauvinism in his gushy charm. "First woman ever to sit in the winners' circle of the AASSP contest," he said admiringly. "Miss Manhattan, let me be the first at this conference to congratulate you."

"Certainly, Morton," Sally said, extending her hand with no perceptible hesitation. She braced herself for a damp, flabby handshake but couldn't prevent herself from wincing when instead she felt the back of her hand dolloped with a damp, flabby kiss. She withdrew it, trying unobtrusively to wipe it on the napkin printed with an unclever insult that sat beneath her glass of chablis. What was this porcine obscenity going to do with the $500,000 first-place prize money? Use it to buy diamonds for his three fingers that remained bare?

"And let me be the second," piped Lester Grandsnelter. At least all he wanted was to shake her hand. Lester, quiet and wimpy, played Laurel to Morton's Hardy, Abbott to his Costello, for he was hardly more substantial than the candy-striped drinking straw he used to sip his gin and tonic. This was a super salesman? And he had won $200,000.

Her third prize was a paltry $100,000—barely half a year's earnings on commissions. Better than nothing, yes. But she should have won first place.

"Nice place, this," Lester said in his thin voice.

"Rather," Sally agreed. "It's one of my favorite haunts. In fact, it's owned by my brother. He's reserved the place for AASSP all weekend." She sighed. "It's no special thrill to be here, you know—I live just down the road about ten miles."

"You mean the old AASSP chose a resort in your own stomping grounds to hold its big conference?" Morton said. "That hardly seems fair."

Sally nodded.

"So a pretty girl like you's a super salesman," Morton continued. "Er, salesperson."

Sally stared studiously at her glass, not wanting to meet Morton's bright and beady eyes.

"Guess there's nothing to it for you. Just bat them long lashes, toss them dark curls, and give a come-hither look, and what man could refuse to buy from you?"

My looks are hardly what prompt people to buy my product, Sally thought, but again did not grace his comment with a reply.

"It was a good idea you had, Miss Manhattan, for the three of us winners to meet the evening before anyone else arrives for the conference," Lester said, turning a shy but lively smile on her. "Of course, we'll see each other all day tomorrow, then be awarded our prizes at the banquet tomorrow night, so I expect we'd get the chance to talk before getting up on the podium to be the guest panelists on Sunday, but I've always thought it's important for people leading discussions to have some kind of real rapport. And the only way to have it is to get to know each other a bit away from the others."

"Yes, that's what *I'd* hoped," Sally said.

The three remained in the almost deserted bar for a couple of hours. Sally listened silently while the men traded war stories and described sales conquests in foul detail. She watched them belt down one drink after another while she nursed two glasses of wine. (Lester had abandoned the drinking straw.) These were the big contest winners, a big blabbermouth and a mouse. It wasn't fair. If it weren't for them, she could have won half a million dollars instead of a mere hundred thousand.

When she'd had enough of their company, she decided it was time to wind up the evening. "Why, you gentlemen have nearly finished your drinks. Here, let me get you refills."

Without lingering long enough for them to protest, Sally rose and went to the bar at the far end of the empty room. It was late. Even the bartender had gone home.

A few minutes later, she returned to her companions with a small tray containing three drinks.

"So nice of you, Miss Manhattan," Morton Sturdevant effused, taking a long drink from the glass Sally placed before him. Belching slightly, he asked, "Do you two know what you're going to tell the audience was the secret of your success?"

"I've thought about it a lot," Lester said. "Of course, I'm not going to tell a whole conference full of people my real secret, but I think I can trust you two." He leaned over the small table conspiratorially.

Here it comes, Sally thought wearily. Another long-winded tale.

"You know," he said, "I found out I coulda won first prize in this contest if I'd sold just a dozen more of my product. Like I said, I sell window glass—'specially to stores that've been vandalized. And you know what?" He crooked his finger, drawing his companions closer over the table so that their heads nearly touched. "I, well, I sorta help my business along. Nights when things are quiet, I drive along some closed downtown areas shooting pellets through windows. Next day, well, there I am, ready to sell new plate glass, have it installed right away. Customers are grateful."

He rolled his eyes from Sally to Morton and back again, apparently failing to find the comradely tolerance he'd expected. "No one gets hurt," he said. "Insurance pays for it all."

Morton raised one piggish paw. "No, my man, I'm not condemning you. The fact is, I admire guts and ingenuity." He took another large swallow of his fresh drink, then, like Lester before him, he crooked his finger, drawing the band together over the table. "I work for an exterminator, like I told you. And when business is slow—well, I've got my own supply of roaches, fleas, even field mice. If I got to—to make a living, you know—I'll put a couple or more in a strategic spot—a big house, a restaurant, a laundry, wherever. In nothing flat, I've got a new sale. I use termites for long-term job security."

The two men leaned back in their chairs, staring at Sally, waiting for her to reveal her dirtiest secret, too, but she just sat staring at them.

"Miss Manhattan, you've not even told us what you *sell*," Lester finally cajoled.

"You know," Sally said, "when the president of AASSP told me I'd come in third in the contest, he let me know I'd only have had to sell two more of my product to beat you, Morton, since my product is high price, relatively low volume."

"That's a shame, Miss Manhattan," Morton said. "Maybe next time."

"No," Sally said. "In fact, I'm about to make those last two sales." She watched in satisfaction as both men began to clutch their windpipes and turn blue.

* * *

Sally hummed as she tidied the place for her brother—who'd swear she joined him hours earlier—washing and drying the glasses and wiping the table with a damp cloth.

She stopped before the inert forms at the table, sizing them up with her practiced eye. Fortunately, the company had extra wide funeral caskets in stock as well as extra narrow—top-of-the-line hand-carved mahogany, lined in gold lamé.

Strange that they should have thought they were so clever, she reflected as she headed for the door. Their sales-generating technique was not so novel. She'd been using it for years.

PETER LOVESEY

THE WASP

Peter Lovesey is always a pleasure to read, especially in a story as skillful as this one with its truly unique murder method. The story came in second for the EQMM Readers' Award. It was published almost simultaneously in England in Winter's Crimes 20 *under the title "Where Is Thy Sting?"*

The storm had passed, leaving a keen wind that whipped foam off the waves. Heaps of gleaming seaweed were strewn about the beach. Shells, bits of driftwood, and a few stranded jellyfish lay where the tide had deposited them. Paul Molloy, bucket in hand, was down there as he was every morning, alone and preoccupied.

His wife Gwynneth stood by the wooden steps that led off the beach through a garden of flowering trees to their property.

"Paul! Breakfast time!"

She had to shout it twice more before Paul's damaged brain registered anything. Then he turned and trudged awkwardly toward her.

The stroke last July, a few days before his sixty-first birthday, had turned him into a shambling parody of the fine man he had been. He was left with the physical coordination of a small child, except that he was slower. And dumb.

The loss of speech was the hardest for Gwynneth to bear. She hated being cut off from his thoughts. He was unable even to write, or draw pictures. She had to be content with scraps of communication. Each time he came up from the beach he handed her something he had found, a shell or a pebble. She received such gifts as graciously as she had once accepted roses.

They had said at the hospital that she ought to keep talking to him in an adult way even if he didn't appear to understand.

It was a mistake to give up. So she persevered, though inevitably it sounded as if she were addressing a child.

"Darling, what a beautiful shell! Is it for me? Oh, how sweet! I'll take it up to the house and put it on the shelf with all the other treasures you found for me—except that this one must stand in the center." She leaned forward to kiss him and made no contact with his face. He had moved his head to look at a gull.

She helped him up the steps and they started the short, laborious trek to the house. They had bought the land, a few miles north of Bundaberg on the Queensland coast, ten years before Paul retired from his Brisbane-based insurance company. As chairman, he could have carried on for years more, but he had always promised he would stop at sixty—before he got fat and feeble, as he used to say. They had built themselves this handsome retirement home and installed facilities they'd thought they would use: swimming pool, Jacuzzi, boat house, and tennis court. Only their guests used them now.

"Come on, love, step out quick," she urged Paul, "there's beautiful bacon waiting for you." And, tirelessly trying for a spark of interest, she added, "Cousin Haydn's still asleep by the look of it. I don't think he'll be joining you for your walks on the beach. Not before breakfast, anyway. Probably not at all. He doesn't care for the sea, does he?"

Gwynneth encouraged people to stay. She missed real conversation. Cousin Haydn was on a visit from Wales. He was a distant cousin she hadn't met before, but she didn't mind. She'd got to know him when she'd started delving into her family history for something to distract her. Years ago, her father had given her an old Bible with a family tree in the front. She'd brought it up to date. Then she had joined a family-history society and learned that a good way of tracking down ancestors was to write to local newspapers in the areas where they had lived. She had managed to get a letter published in a Swansea paper and Haydn had seen it and got in touch. He was an Evans also, and he'd done an immense amount of research. He'd discovered a branch of his family tree that linked up with hers, through Great-Grandfather Hugh Evans of Port Talbot.

Paul shuffled toward the house without even looking up at the drawn curtains.

"Mind you," Gwynneth continued, "I'm not surprised Haydn is used to staying indoors, what with the Welsh weather *I* remember. I expect he reads the Bible a lot, being a man of the cloth." She checked herself for speaking the obvious again and pushed open the kitchen door. "Come on, Paul. Just you and me for breakfast by the look of it."

Cousin Haydn eventually appeared in time for the midmorning coffee. On the first day after he'd arrived, he'd discarded the black suit and dog collar in favor of a pink T-shirt. Casual clothes made him look several years younger—say, forty-five— but they also revealed what Gwynneth would have called a beer gut had Haydn not been a minister.

"Feel better for your sleep?" she inquired.

"Infinitely better, thank you, Gwynneth." You couldn't mistake him for an Australian when he opened his mouth. "And most agreeably refreshed by a dip in your pool."

"Oh, you had a swim?"

"Hardly a swim. I was speaking of the small circular pool."

She smiled. "The Jacuzzi. Did you find the switch?"

"I was unaware that I needed to find it."

"It works the pumps that make the whirlpool effect. If you didn't switch on, you missed something."

"Then I shall certainly repeat the adventure."

"Paul used to like it. I'm afraid of him slipping, so he doesn't get in there now."

"Pity, if he enjoyed it."

"Perhaps I ought to take the risk. The specialist said he may begin to bring other muscles into use that aren't affected by the stroke—isn't that so, my darling?"

Paul gave no sign of comprehension.

"Does he understand much?" Haydn asked.

"I convince myself he does, even if he's unable to show it. If you don't mind, I don't really care to talk about him in this way, as if he's not one of us."

Cousin Haydn gave an understanding nod. "Let's talk about

something less depressing, then. I have good news for you, Gwynneth."

She responded with a murmur that didn't convey much enthusiasm. Sermons in church were one thing, her kitchen was another place altogether.

It emerged that Haydn's good news wasn't of an evangelical character. "One of the reasons for coming here—apart from following up our fascinating correspondence—is to tell you about a mutual ancestor, Sir Tudor Evans."

"*Sir* Tudor? We had a title in the family?"

"Back in the seventeenth century, yes."

"I don't recall seeing him on my family tree."

Haydn gave the slight smile of one who has a superior grasp of genealogy. "Yours started in the seventeen eighties, if I recall."

"Oh, yes."

"To say that it started then is, of course, misleading. Your eighteenth century forebears had parents, as did mine—and they in turn had parents. And so it goes back—first to Sir Tudor, and ultimately to Adam."

"Never mind Adam. Tell me about Sir Tudor." Gwynneth swung around to Paul, who was sucking the end of his thumb. "Bet you didn't know I came from titled stock, darling."

Haydn said, "A direct line. Planter Evans, they called him. He owned half of Barbados once, according to my research. Made himself a fortune in sugar cane."

"Really? A fortune. What happened to it?"

"Most of it went down with the *Gloriana* in 1683. One of the great tragedies of the sea. He'd sold the plantations to come back to the land of his fathers. He was almost home when a great storm blew up in the Bristol Channel and the ship was lost with all hands. Sir Tudor and his wife Eleanor were among those on board."

"How very sad!"

"God rest their souls, yes."

Gwynneth put her hand to her face. "I'm trying to remember. Last year was such a nightmare for us. A lot of things passed right over my head. The *Gloriana.* Isn't that the ship they found—those treasure hunters? I read about this somewhere."

"It was in all the papers," Haydn confirmed. "I have some of the cuttings with me, in my briefcase."

"I do remember. The divers were bringing up masses of stuff—coins by the bucketful, and silverware and the most exquisite jewelry. Oh, how exciting—can we make a claim?"

Cousin Haydn shook his head. "Out of the question, my dear. One would need to hire lawyers. Besides, it may be too late."

"Why?"

"As I understand it, when treasure is recovered from a wreck around the British coasts, it has to be handed over to the local receiver of wrecks or the Customs. The lawful owner then has a year and a day to make a claim. After that, the pieces are sold and the proceeds go to the salvager."

"A year and a day," said Gwynneth. "Oh, Haydn, this is too tantalizing. When did these treasure hunters start bringing up the stuff?"

"Last March."

"Eleven months! Then there's still time to make a claim. We must do it."

Haydn sighed heavily. "These things can be extremely costly."

"But we'd get it all back if we could prove our right to the treasure."

He put out his hand in a dissenting gesture. "*Your* right, my dear, not mine. Your connection is undeniable, mine is very tenuous. No, I have no personal interest here. Besides, a man of my calling cannot serve God and mammon."

"Do you really believe I have a claim?"

"The treasure hunters would dispute it, I'm sure."

"We're talking about millions of pounds, aren't we? Why should I sit back and let them take it all? I need to get hold of some lawyers—and fast."

Haydn coughed. "They charge astronomical fees."

"I know," said Gwynneth. "We can afford it—can't we, Paul?"

Paul made a blowing sound with his lips that probably had no bearing on the matter.

Gwynneth assumed so. "What is it they want—a down payment?"

"A retainer, I think is the expression."

"I can write a check tomorrow if you want. I look after all our personal finances now. There's more than enough in the deposit account. The thing is, how do I find a reliable lawyer?"

Haydn cupped his chin and his hands and looked thoughtful. "I wouldn't go to an Australian firm. Better find someone on the spot. Jones, Heap, and Jones of Cardiff are the best in Wales. I'm sure they could take on something like this."

"But is there time? We're almost into March now."

"It is rather urgent," Haydn agreed. "Look, I don't mind cutting my holiday short by a few days. If I got back to Wales at the weekend I could see them on Monday."

"I couldn't ask you to do that," said Gwynneth in a tone that betrayed the opposite.

"No trouble," said Haydn breezily.

"You're an angel. Would they accept a check in Australian pounds?"

"That might be difficult, but it's easily got around. Traveler's checks are the thing. I use them all the time. In fact, if you're serious about this—"

"Oh, yes."

"You could buy sterling traveler's checks in my name and I could pay the retainer for you."

"Would you really do that for me?"

"Anything to be of service."

She shivered with pleasure. "And now, if you've got them nearby, I'd love to have ten minutes with those press cuttings."

He left them with her, and she read them through several times during the afternoon when she was alone in her room and Paul had gone for one of his walks along the beach. Three pages cut from a color supplement had stunning pictures of the finds. She so adored the ruby necklace and the gold bracelets that she thought she would refuse to sell them. Cousin Haydn had also given her a much more detailed family tree than she had seen before. It proved beyond doubt that she was the only direct descendant of Sir Tudor Evans.

Was it all too good to be true?

One or two doubts crept into her mind later that afternoon. Presumably the treasure hunters had invested heavily in ships, divers, and equipment. They must have been confident that anything they brought up would belong to them. Maybe her claim wasn't valid under the law. She wondered also whether Cousin Haydn's research was entirely accurate. She didn't question his good faith—how could one in the circumstances?—but she knew from her own humble diggings in family history that it was all too easy to confuse one Evans with another.

On the other hand, she told herself, that's what I'm hiring the lawyers to find out. It's their business to establish whether my claim is lawful.

There was an unsettling incident toward evening. She walked down to the beach to collect Paul. The stretch where he liked to wander was never particularly crowded, even at weekends, and she soon spotted him kneeling on the sand. This time he didn't need calling. He got up, collected his bucket, and tottered toward her. Automatically she held out her hand for the gift he had chosen for her. He peered into the bucket and picked something out and placed it on her open palm.

A dead wasp.

She almost snatched her hand away and let the thing drop. She was glad she didn't, because it was obvious that he'd saved it for her and she would have hated to hurt his feelings.

She said, "Oh, a little wasp. Thank you, darling. So thoughtful. We'll take it home and put it with all my pretty pebbles and shells, shall we?"

She took a paper tissue from her pocket and folded the tiny corpse carefully between the layers.

In the house she unwrapped it and made a space on the shelf among the shells and stones. "There." She turned and smiled at Paul.

He put his thumb on the wasp and squashed it.

"Darling!"

The small act of violence shocked Gwynneth. She found herself quite stupidly reacting as if something precious had been destroyed. "You shouldn't have done that, Paul. You gave it to me. I treasure whatever you give me. You know that."

He shuffled out of the room.

*   *   *

That evening over dinner she told Cousin Haydn about the incident, once again breaking her own rule and discussing Paul while he was sitting with them. "I keep wondering if he meant anything by it," she said. "It's so unlike him."

"If you want my opinion," said Haydn, "he showed some intelligence. You don't want a wasp in the house, dead or alive. As a matter of fact, I've got quite a phobia about them. It's one of the reasons I avoid the beach. You can't sit for long on any beach without being troubled by them."

"Perhaps you were stung once."

"No, I've managed to avoid them, but one of my uncles was killed by one."

"Killed by a wasp?"

"He was only forty-four at the time. It happened on the front at Aberystwyth. He was stung here, on the right temple. His face went bright red and he fell down on the shingle. My aunt ran for a doctor, but all he could do was confirm that Uncle was dead."

Clearly the tragedy had made a profound impression on Haydn. His account of the incident, spoken in simple language instead of his usual florid style, carried conviction.

"Dreadful. It must have been a rare case."

"Not so uncommon as you'd think. I tell you, Gwynneth, the wasp is one of God's creatures I studiously avoid at all times." He turned to Paul and for the first time addressed him directly, trying to end on a less grave note. "So I say more power to your thumbs, boyo."

Paul looked at him blankly.

Toward the end of the meal Haydn announced he would be leaving in the morning. "I telephoned the airport. I am advised I can get something called a standby. They say it's better before the weekend, so I'm leaving tomorrow."

"*Tomorrow?*" said Gwynneth, her voice pitched high in alarm. "But you can't. We haven't bought those traveler's checks."

"That's all right, my dear. There's a place to purchase them at the airport. All you need to do is write me a check. In fact, you could write it now in case we forget in the morning."

"How much?"

"I don't know. I'm not too conversant with the scale of fees lawyers charge these days. Are you sure you want to get involved in this?"

"Absolutely. If I have no right to make a claim they'll let me know, won't they?"

"I'll let you know myself, my dear. How much can you spare without running up an overdraft? It's probably better for me to take more rather than less."

She wrote him a check for ten thousand Australian dollars.

"Then if you will excuse me, I'll go and pack my things and have a quiet hour before bedtime."

"Would you like an early breakfast tomorrow?"

Haydn smiled. "Early by my standards, yes. Say about eight? That gives me ample time to do something I promised myself— try the Jacuzzi with the switch on. Good-night and God bless you, my dear. And *you*, Paul, old fellow."

Gwynneth slept fitfully. At one stage in the night she noticed that Paul had his eyes open. She found his hand and gripped it tightly and talked to him as if he understood.

"I keep wondering if I've done the right thing, giving Haydn that check. It's not as if I don't trust him—I mean, you've got to trust a man of God, haven't you? I just wonder if you would have done what I did, my darling—giving him the check, I mean—and somehow I don't think so. In fact, I ask myself if you were trying to tell me something when you gave me the wasp. It was such an unusual thing for you to do. Then squashing it like that."

She must have drifted off soon after, because when she next opened her eyes the gray light of dawn was picking out the edges of the curtains. She sighed and turned toward Paul, but his side of the bed was empty. He must have gone down to the beach already.

She showered and dressed soon after, wanting to make an early start on cooking the breakfast. She would get everything ready first, she decided, and then fetch Paul from the beach before she started the cooking.

However, this was a morning of surprises.

For some unfathomable reason Paul had already come up from the beach without being called. He was seated in his usual place in the kitchen.

"Paul! You gave me quite a shock," Gwynneth told him. "What is it? Are you extra hungry this morning or something? I'll get this started presently. Would you like some bread while you're waiting? I'd better give Cousin Haydn a call first and make sure he's awake."

It crossed her mind as she went to tap on Haydn's door that Paul hadn't brought her anything from the beach. She wondered if she'd hurt his feelings by talking about the wasp as she had.

She didn't like knocking on Haydn's door in case she was interrupting his morning prayers, but it had to be done this morning in case he overslept.

He answered her call. "Thank you. Is there time for me to sample the Jacuzzi?"

"Of course. Shall we say twenty minutes?"

"That should be ample."

She returned to the kitchen and made a sandwich for Paul. The bucket he always took to the beach was beside him. Without being too obvious about it, Gwynneth glanced inside to see if the customary gift of a shell or a pebble was there. It was silly, but she was feeling quite neglected.

Empty.

She said nothing about it, simply busied herself setting the table for breakfast. Presently she started heating the frying pan.

Fifteen minutes later when everything was cooked and waiting in the oven, Haydn had not appeared. "He's really enjoying that Jacuzzi," she told Paul. "We'd better start, I think."

They finished.

"I'd better go and see," she said.

When she went to the door, the leg of Paul's chair was jammed against it, preventing her from opening it. "Do you mind, darling? I can't get out."

He made no move.

"Maybe you're right," Gwynneth said, always willing to assume that Paul's behavior was deliberate and intelligent. "I shouldn't fuss. It won't spoil for being left a few minutes more."

She allowed another quarter of an hour to pass. "Do you think something's happened to him? I'd better go and see, really I had. Come on, dear. Let me through."

As she took Paul by the arm and helped him to his feet, he reached out and drew her toward him, pressing his face against hers. She was surprised and delighted. He hadn't embraced her once since the stroke. She turned her face and kissed him before going to find Cousin Haydn.

Haydn was lying face down on the tile surround of the Jacuzzi, which was churning noisily. He was wearing black swimming trunks. He didn't move when she spoke his name.

"I think he may be dead," Gwynneth told the girl who took the emergency call.

The girl told her to try the kiss of life, an ambulance was on its way.

Gwynneth was still on her knees trying to breathe life into Cousin Haydn when the police arrived. They had come straight round the back of the house. "Let's have a look, lady," the sergeant said. Then, after a moment: "He's gone—no question. Who is he—your husband?"

She explained about Cousin Haydn.

"This is where you found him?"

"Well, yes. Was it an electric shock, do you think?"

"You tell me, lady. Was the Jacuzzi on when you found him?"

"Yes." Gwynneth suddenly realized it was no longer running. Paul must have switched it off while she was phoning for help. She didn't want Paul brought into this, "I don't know. I may be mistaken about that."

"There could be a fault," the sergeant speculated. "We'll get it checked. Is your husband about?"

"He was." She called Paul's name. "He must have gone down to the beach. That's where he goes." She told them about the stroke.

More policemen arrived, some in plainclothes. One introduced himself as Detective Inspector Perry. He talked to Gwynneth several times in the next two hours. He went into Cousin Haydn's room and opened the suitcase he had packed for the flight home. He turned to Gwynneth and smiled.

"You say you knew this man as Haydn Evans, your cousin from Wales?"

"That's who he was."

"A distant cousin?"

Gwynneth didn't care for his grin. "I can show you the family tree if you like.

"No need for that, Mrs. Molloy. His luggage is stuffed with family trees, all as bogus as his Welsh accent. He wasn't a minister of any church or chapel. His name was Brown. Michael Herbert Brown. An English con man we've been after for months. He was getting too well known for Scotland Yard, so he came out to Queensland this summer. He's been stinging people for thousands with the treasure-hunting story. Here's your check. Lucky escape, I'd say."

They finally took the body away in an ambulance.

Detective Inspector Perry phoned late in the afternoon. "I just thought I'd let you know that your Jacuzzi is safe to use, Mrs. Molloy. There's no electrical fault. I have the pathologist's report and I can tell you that Brown was not electrocuted."

"What killed him, then?"

He laughed. "Something rather appropriate. It was a sting."

Gwynneth frowned and put her hand to her throat. "A sting from a wasp?"

"In a manner of speaking." There was amusement in his voice. "Not the wasp you had in mind."

"I don't understand."

"No mystery in it, Mrs. Molloy. A sea-wasp got him. You know what a sea-wasp is?"

She knew. Everyone on the coast knew. "A jellyfish. An extremely poisonous jellyfish."

"Right, a killer."

"But the man didn't swim in the sea. He kept off the beach."

"That explains it, then."

"How?"

"He wouldn't have known about the sea-wasps. That storm washed quite a number onto the beaches. It looks as if Brown decided to take one look at the sea before he left this morning. He'd put on his swimming gear—and he must have waded in.

Didn't need to go far. There were sea-wasps stranded in the shallows. You and I know how deadly they are, but I reckon an Englishman wouldn't. He got bitten, staggered back to the house, and collapsed beside the Jacuzzi."

"I see." She knew it was nonsense.

"Try and remember, Mrs. Molloy. Did you see him walk down to the beach?"

"I was cooking breakfast."

"Pity. Where was your husband?"

"Paul?" She glanced over at Paul, now sitting in his usual armchair with his arms around his bucket. "He was with me in the kitchen." She was about to add that Paul had come up from the beach, but the inspector was already onto other possibilities.

"Maybe someone else saw Brown on the beach. I believe it's pretty deserted at that time."

"Yes."

"Be useful to have a witness for the inquest. All right, I heard what you said about him normally keeping off the beach, but it's a fact that he died from a sea-wasp sting. That's been established."

"I'm not questioning it."

"I ask you, Mrs. Molloy, how else could it have happened? There's only one other possibility I can think of. But how could a jellyfish get into a Jacuzzi, for Christ's sake?"

CARL MARTIN

FATHERLY LOVE

Carl Martin is the pseudonym of a writer who published his first story in 1967 and has been a contributor to the mystery magazines ever since, under his own and various other names. He started out as a tough crime writer, but his recent work has shown an increasing degree of compassion coupled with skillful plotting. This story is one of the best I've seen from him.

I walked through the casino slowly, listening to the buzz of conversation and the click of the roulette wheels. Now and then I paused to watch a hand of twenty-one being dealt or observe the throw of the dice at one of the crap tables.

The timeless quality of the big room always amazed me. Now, at eight in the morning, it looked much the same as it did at eight in the evening or any other hour in between. The hum of voices had an unchanging, hypnotic tone—the frenzy of the players was always identical. No matter what might be happening outside in Las Vegas or the rest of the world, within the casino time stood still. I couldn't count the number of times I'd stepped outside and been surprised to find it was raining, or the moon was high in the sky, or the sun was baking the pavement, or it was in some other way greatly different from when I had entered.

True, there were plenty of clues to indicate the passage of time for anyone who wanted to read them. The faces of the cocktail waitresses, dealers, and even the pit boss changed with each shift. The music coming from the lounge was either live or recorded, the players' clothing was a bit less crisp, collars were a bit more wilted, and more men needed shaves. I ignored these subtleties just as I ignored my wristwatch. Time wasn't important to me. Not anymore.

I'd made a lot of bad decisions and poor choices in my life.

Despite outward appearances, I didn't consider myself a success. Everything that might have mattered to me had been
abandoned and/or lost track of years before. Also, the results of
my latest physical examination had been ominous. The doctor
had diagnosed an inoperable terminal cancer. Now my life was
in a kind of holding pattern, revolving around the casino.

A few dealers gave me deferential nods as I passed, which I
returned. They recognized my face but didn't know who I was.
All they knew was that I was a man of importance—I repre-
sented the owners in some vague way. I might, for all they
knew, be one of the owners myself.

The barber shop was located off the wide corridor leading to
the hotel. I usually had a man shave me in my suite, but that
morning I felt restless. I wanted to get out and move around as
soon as my eyes opened. A walk through the casino to the
barber shop had seemed like a good way to begin the day.

Frank, the man who ran the shop, was the only one working
and he had someone in his chair. He looked over as I entered
and said, "Sorry, sir, I didn't know you was comin' in this
morning. I'll only be a couple of minutes."

I gave him a tight-lipped smile and waved my hand to show I
didn't mind the wait. Then, as he hurried to finish with the man
in the chair, I took a seat next to the magazine rack.

One of the periodicals, a fact-crime magazine with a particularly lurid cover, caught my eye. I picked it up and sat idly
turning the pages. The mingled odor of shaving soap, lotions,
and hair tonic was pleasant and the sound of the clicking shears
nearly lulled me to sleep. Then I saw the picture and read the
name. It came like a blow to the solar plexus, forcing me to
gasp for air. The article was about a series of grisly murders in
Los Angeles and the young man being charged with one of the
crimes.

I felt to blame for what I was reading and a wave of anger
laced with fear washed over me. Perhaps if I had been a better
father—a better husband! Perhaps if . . . My thoughts came in a
disorganized jumble of bits and pieces. Anger was something I
was used to controlling, focusing, making work for me. It was
easy to handle. But fear was an emotion I'd never felt before. I
had seen it often enough, but never felt it myself. Now my

hands were shaking. I was afraid I wouldn't have enough time left to do what had to be done. Time was suddenly very, very important to me.

"You okay, sir?"

I looked up. Frank was standing at my side, his face mirroring confusion and concern.

"Yeah, Frank, I'm okay," I said casually. I folded the magazine and slipped it into the side pocket of my suit coat as I got to my feet. "But I won't be able to wait, after all. I just remembered something I have to do."

I felt his eyes on me as I left the barber shop, but I didn't turn around.

I had one of the prized corner suites on the tenth floor of the hotel tower. From its picture windows I could look down on the Strip or watch the air traffic at McCarren Field. When I first came to Las Vegas, I had lived in a borrowed apartment near one of the small clubs in the northern end of town. I had come a long way in only a few miles.

I kept a suitcase packed and ready on the floor of the closet for such sudden trips as this. I got it out and checked its contents. Then I shaved, changed into a cheap off-the-rack suit, and called the airport to make sure I could get on the noon flight to Burbank.

Al Rossi, the man who managed the hotel and casino, wouldn't be in his office until ten, so I sprawled across the bed and read the magazine article again. It was no more palatable than the first time.

There had been a series of murders in and around Hollywood. All of the victims had been either prostitutes or suspected prostitutes. All had been attractive blondes between twenty-five and thirty-five. And all had been killed in the same way— strangled with a wire garrote, their bodies dumped on freeway off-ramps like so much garbage.

The killer claimed one or two fresh victims every month, and the police were certain it was all the work of one man—he apparently picked the women up on the street, and no one could remember seeing him. The newspapers put additional pressure on the police by printing stories about the Freeway

Strangler to build circulation. The stories sold newspapers, but they didn't bring the police any closer to catching the killer than they had been at the start.

At least that's how it was until murder number nineteen, Karen Simmons. This time the police were able to trace the dead woman's movements on the night she was killed. They found that she frequented a small bar on Melrose near Vine, and several patrons and the bartender remembered the man she left with. And they remembered the time. It was exactly fifteen minutes later that her nearly decapitated body was found.

Jon Mason was arrested two days later and identified as the man seen leaving the Melrose Avenue bar with Karen Simmons. A search of his car failed to turn up any useful evidence against him, but some interesting things were found in his apartment. First, there was a tweed sportcoat like the one witnesses described him wearing, and it had three long strands of blonde hair sticking to it. Laboratory analysis determined there was a ninety-eight percent probability that the hair came from the victim.

The light-blue slacks Mason was said to have worn that night couldn't be found, although his neighbors had seen him wearing them earlier in the week. The police interpreted this as damning negative evidence. "That wire garrote sliced into her neck like a knife. He got them all bloody and had to ditch them somewhere," a detective on the case theorized. "If not, where are they?"

His shoes provided the last bit of evidence. They had no idea what shoes he had worn that night, so they sent all three pairs of his shoes to the lab. A pair of oxblood cordovan wingtips tested positive. "Some effort was made to clean the blood off those shoes," the technician reported, "but they must have been drenched with it. I've never seen a case where so much blood seeped into the seams of a pair of shoes. And it was O-positive, the same as the victim's."

As soon as Jon Mason's picture appeared in the newspapers, a long line of women came forward to identify him as the man who had tried to lure them into his car. Some said he had flashed a phony police badge, others said he pretended to be lost and wanting directions. Neither ruse worked with these women because they were all too familiar with what genuine police credentials looked like, and none of them was in the business of doing favors for free.

"As soon as he stopped waving that badge and started waving a fifty-dollar bill, he had a lot more luck," one of the detectives speculated.

The phony police badge was never found—neither was the murder weapon. And no physical evidence was found to link him to the earlier murders. However, the prosecutor was convinced he had all the circumstantial evidence needed for a conviction in the Karen Simmons clase. What's more, he was certain in his own mind that they had the right man. "Jon Mason is just the kind of mad-at-the-world loner who ends up as a serial killer," he said. "And you'll notice that string of killings stopped as soon as we had him locked up."

Mason, twenty-four, was described as the product of a broken home. He had come to Hollywood from Chicago three years before to get into television. Back home, people had been telling the good-looking young man he should be in the movies. He believed them, quit his job as assistant manager in the produce department of a supermarket, and drove to California. His mother was dead and no one had seen or heard from his father since Jon was an infant. There was nothing holding him in Chicago.

But nothing happened in Los Angeles to fulfill his dreams. No agent was interested in representing an untrained, untested, would-be actor, and no producer would waste time or risk money on an actor who couldn't get an agent. He went from one dead-end job to another, and the months stretched into years. He took a few acting classes taught by aging actors who couldn't find work for themselves. The only time he was on a studio lot was when he paid to tour Universal Studios. Mason was bitter, disillusioned, and striking back at an unfair world in the only way he could think of. It made no difference to him that his victims were no better off than he was.

Judging from the photos in the magazine, he was taking his arrest quite well. He didn't cower and hide his face from the cameras, nor did he appear defiant. If anything, he seemed to be enjoying his new celebrity. It was exactly what he had come to Hollywood in search of, but any attention was apparently better than the total apathy he'd encountered before.

Now he was in jail awaiting trial. I glanced at the date on the magazine. It was the current issue. Perhaps I wasn't going on a fool's errand after all. If he hadn't been convicted, and I had enough time . . . I swung my legs off the bed and hurried to Al Rossi's office.

His secretary looked up and pushed the button, releasing the electric latch on the inner-office door without a word. I walked in and caught Rossi pouring a shot of bourbon into his morning coffee.

"Hitting the bottle kind of early, aren't you, Al?" I chided.

He shrugged. "I have to do something to get my heart started." Then he noticed the less-than-elegant suit I was wearing. "Is something wrong?"

"I'm taking the shuttle to Burbank," I said. "I'll need some cash."

"Yes, sir. How much?"

"Fifty to a hundred thousand now. In hundreds, old bills. I'll probably want you to send me the same amount in a few days. I'll call and tell you where I'm staying."

"Yes, sir," he said. There were no questions. I'd trained him well.

I prefer Burbank over LAX and try to schedule flights to Burbank whenever I travel to L.A. The Burbank airport is smaller and a bit closer to the places I usually want to go. The planes are usually crowded, but there is far less hassle once you're on the ground. There never seems to be a long wait for luggage, and there is always plenty of ground transportation available. Also, I am able to blend easily with the briefcase-carrying businessmen who seem to like it as much as I do.

While waiting for my suitcase to appear on the conveyer belt, I called the office of the court clerk in downtown L.A. I was given the name of Jon Mason's court-appointed attorney and the case number.

"Is that attorney with the Public Defender's Office?" I asked.

"Yes," she said.

Then I asked the woman to read me the last couple of docket

entries over the phone, something they never do—but she must have liked my voice because she did it, anyway. The entries weren't very interesting, but I did learn that the case was set for trial in two days.

Next I called Wilson Kesner's office. Kesner was a criminal lawyer who had come to my attention years before when he filed sixty-eight pretrial motions in a misdemeanor case. He had lost the case and the judge admonished him for wasting the court's time, but I had filed his name away for future use. He had impressed me as a fighter, and most lawyers don't know enough to be able to file sixty-eight motions about *anything*. Over the years I'd recommended him to people I knew and he had never disappointed.

Now he was well known and high priced. We had never met and he wouldn't have known my name, so I told his secretary I had been sent by a couple of names he would recognize. She gave me an appointment for later in the afternoon.

By then my suitcase was on the conveyer belt. I retrieved it and took a cab to the Hollywood Holiday Inn. I like to stay in Hollywood because of its central location, not because of its glamorous past or seedy present.

Once I'd checked in and was in my room, I called Al Rossi in Vegas to let him know where I was staying. Then I washed my face with cold water and sprawled out on the bed. I was feeling tired already. My energy level wasn't what it used to be. I used to stay up for two or three nights during a marathon card game and never lose my fine edge, but now I needed a rest after merely sitting for a couple of hours.

When it was almost time for my appointment, I took a cab to Kesner's office in downtown L.A. It didn't take long to get there. The Freeway moved swiftly, most of the traffic already heading out of the city by then. Kesner had a suite on the sixth floor of a building a few blocks from the courthouse. I was kept waiting a few minutes, then shown into a large corner room that contained a conference table but no desk. Kesner was sitting at the table. He wore a powder-blue single-breasted suit and a white shirt with a thin navy-blue stripe. His tie was also navy blue. His black loafers had the dull sheen of expensive leather. He was in his late thirties and starting to thicken around the middle, but not so much that he couldn't wear European styling for a few more years. His most riveting feature was his eyes. They were dark and luminous. Reptilian might describe them better. He seemed to look at me and through me at the same time. I imagine he used them to good effect on cross-examinations.

To make up for the delay, I took the seat across from him and got down to business right away. "I want you to represent Jon Mason in his upcoming trial," I said.

"The Freeway Strangler?"

"The man accused of being the Freeway Strangler," I corrected him mildly.

"Of course," he conceded. "The man accused." Then he frowned. "Doesn't he already have an attorney?"

"Yes. Court appointed. Someone from the Public Defender's Office. I want him to have you."

"I'm flattered," he said in a bored tone. "I'm also expensive. What's your interest in this case?"

From years of experience dealing with lawyers, I knew better than to lie, but I didn't tell the whole truth, either. "I just learned about this trouble he's in. I want to help him get out of it as quickly as possible. I guess you can call me a friend, if you have to give me a label."

As I spoke, he had been giving me an appraising look. When he reached my dime-thin wristwatch, he stopped. The platinum case with twelve tasteful diamonds on its face had his full attention. Not many men wear such expensive trinkets and those who do are seldom conscious of their value. Like yachts, if you have to ask the price, you can't afford them. His mental calculator clicked merrily away and his demeanor toward me changed.

"There could be a problem. You say he already has an attorney of record. He may be happy with his present representation and not want to change it."

"I imagine a visit from you will convince him," I said. "I'm sure he's heard of you and will consider you an answered prayer."

"Perhaps." Kesner made a show of considering my proposition. "Exactly what are your expectations? Are you looking for a miracle?"

"I don't think so. I simply want you to get him off," I said.

"Well, one thing in his favor—no one is more alone than a dead hooker. No friends or relatives of the victims are pressuring the prosecutor's office. If he does change attorneys, that would give us a good excuse for postponement and the motion should be unopposed."

"A postponement?"

"Yes. Delay is always in a defendant's favor. Witnesses disappear—they move away, die, or the police simply lose track of them. And key evidence can get lost."

"I'm not paying for delays. I want this to go forward as scheduled," I told him.

"In that case, perhaps I can negotiate a plea bargain. He's being charged with only the one murder. They might be willing to accept a plea to second or third degree to get the case out of the way. He'd have to serve some time, perhaps seven or eight years, but he wouldn't have to risk a first-degree murder conviction. That's pretty good, isn't it?"

"Yes, but not good enough. I want him out, not locked away in Folsom. Besides, your seven- or eight-year estimate isn't realistic. He's charged with only one killing, but the police are convinced he committed nineteen of them. Once locked away, he'd have to serve every minute of his maximum sentence. He wouldn't be receiving parole or any other early release."

Kesner knew all that, of course. He'd been testing me to see how much I knew. Now he leaned forward with his elbows on the table and built a steeple by touching the tips of his fingers together. "That brings us to my fee," he said.

Putting my briefcase on my lap and snapping the latches, I opened it far enough to remove two bundles of hundred-dollar bills, fifty in each. "Here's ten thousand," I said. "Talk to Jon Mason and get him to accept you as his attorney. As soon as that's accomplished, I'll give you another fifty thousand, also in cash, to handle the trial."

He put on his bargaining face. "This could be a long, long trial. I may lose other clients—"

I smiled. "It will be a three-day trial. That's how much time the court has already set aside for it," I said. "Of course, that was when the prosecutor thought he would be going up against a public defender, but I see no reason to change it. And when it's over, an innocent verdict will earn you a twenty-five-thousand-dollar bonus. Not bad for three days in court, is it?"

He had to agree it wasn't.

I sat in the rear of a small courtroom the first day while the jury selection was going on. Kesner handled it well. He asked all the right questions and seemed to know instinctively which prospective jurors might be trouble. Those he caused to make admissions that provoked the prosecutor into using a preemptory challenge, thereby saving his own for possible later use.

The prosecutor hadn't expected any problems, so he hadn't tried to stack the deck by calling a panel of retired postal employees or people who had been quick to vote guilty on juries in the past. It looked as though the names had been selected from the voting register without manipulation. As far as this jury was concerned, both sides were starting even.

I held a yellow legal-size pad across my knees. From time to time I made a note, for my own reference or to remind me to bring some minor point to Kesner's attention. A couple of newspaper reporters were the only other spectators who watched the entire proceeding. Other people, mostly court employees with time on their hands, came into the room, sat on the hard wooden benches for a few minutes, and then left. Jury selection was too boring to hold their attention for long.

The last juror was picked and the judge called a recess. The trial would begin after lunch. Jon Mason was walking between a pair of deputy sheriffs toward a side exit when he stopped, turned in my direction, and smiled. Kesner must have pointed me out to him.

Mason wasn't as good looking as his pictures. He was one of those people who photograph exceptionally well. In person, he had a hungry look, and his smile was about as sincere as a politician's promise. His jaw was weak and his lips soft and moist—sensuous is the way the newspapers described them, but they reminded me more of a baby's.

I acknowledged Mason's smile with a nod, and then he was gone.

Kesner came up to me. "The trial will be held in Section Fourteen. That's a much larger courtroom. They expect a lot of spectators. If you like, I'll get you a pass so you can be sure of a seat."

I shook my head. "Don't bother," I said. "I won't be attending the trial. I've seen all I want to see. I'll call you every evening and you can tell me how things are going."

Mason's defense was wholly dependent on the weakness of the prosecution's case, and the first day of the trial went as expected. There were no surprises. Kesner was able to shake almost every piece of testimony. He chuckled when he told me how his stare made witnesses squirm even though they were telling the truth, thereby lessening its impact. "The judge may even order a directed verdict of acquittal," he said with an uncharacteristic flood of optimism. "The prosecution is going to have to come up with more than this."

But near the end of the second day, the prosecutor did just that. He called a surprise witness—one who had just come forward. A truck driver had seen Jon Mason standing beside a car parked on the shoulder of the off-ramp where Karen Simmons's body was dumped and stopped to give assistance. Mason had waved him away, but not before the man had gotten a good look at him and the blood-spattered blue slacks he was wearing in the headlights. Worst of all, he had noted the time as he was driving away. It was exactly four minutes before another car had come along and spotted Karen Simmons's body beside the road.

That evening when I called Kesner, he was no longer filled with optimism. He was afraid the jury would make its decision without even leaving the box. "It doesn't look good," he said.

"I think you're painting too dark a picture," I said with far more confidence than I felt. I didn't want him giving up before the trial was over. "No one can predict with one-hundred-percent accuracy what any jury will do, you know that. Think of the times you've been surprised. I'll bet there have been a lot of them."

"Yes, but—"

"No buts. I have a good feeling about this case. I think that jury is going to surprise you," I said.

On the third day, I waited until the trial had resumed after lunch, then I made a telephone call to the clerk's office. "There's a bomb hidden somewhere in the building," I said. "A very large and powerful bomb." Then I hung up and walked two blocks to where I could watch the main entrance of the courthouse.

People came streaming out onto the sidewalk to stand in clusters, looking back at the building. As soon as the Mason jury appeared, I kept my eyes on them. After a while, someone made an announcement from the steps and the crowd began to drift away. It was clear that court had been recessed for the day.

I followed one of the jurors, a retired Army officer named Hauser. He usually had his wife pick him up at the end of the day, but now he had some unexpected time on his hands. He walked two blocks and entered a dimly lit saloon. I followed him inside and took the stool beside him at the bar. We were the only customers.

Hauser looked at me suspiciously. He was a ruddy-faced man with wide shoulders and heavy thighs. Being followed into a bar was a new experience for him.

"Good afternoon, Mr. Hauser," I said softly.

The bartender came over, we both ordered beer, were served, and he went away.

"Do I know you?" Hauser asked.

I ignored the question and placed my briefcase on the bar. I unsnapped the latches and positioned it so that the lid would screen its contents from the bartender's view. Then I lifted it.

Hauser had taken a sip of his beer. He almost choked.

"You're looking at one hundred thousand dollars," I said. "It can be yours." Then I closed the case and held it on my lap.

"How? What—?"

"If the jury you're on brings back a verdict of Not Guilty, the money is yours," I said.

"That guy's guilty as sin," Hauser said, speaking as softly as I was. "He was practically caught in the act. And I only have one vote. How can I—"

"You're a leader," I broke in. "You're almost certain to be chosen as foreman of the jury. You can exert a lot of influence on the others. In any case, you're a man used to taking charge. Do that in the jury room. Set an example for the others. It doesn't matter *why* they may decide to vote for acquittal, the only thing that matters is that they do it. Everyone can determine for himself what evidence to believe. I'm interested in the result, not in how it's arrived at."

Hauser was six thousand dollars in debt and living beyond his means with a wife twenty years his junior. I was sure that briefcase looked very good to him. I could practically hear the wheels turning in his head.

Finally I knew I had him. He shrugged. "Who cares about a dead hooker?" he said.

"Who indeed?" I answered.

I talked to two other jurors that afternoon, making each of them the same offer and speech. I could have had someone do it for me, but it was too personal a thing to delegate. I wanted to do it myself. When I went to sleep that evening, I was sure their greed would ensure the verdict I wanted.

The case was handed over to the jury the next afternoon. Kesner, expecting a quick verdict, hung around the courthouse for the first three hours. Then he went back to his office to wait. I spoke to him on the phone. "It's looking better with each passing minute," he said. "The longer they're out, the more chance there is of a Not Guilty verdict. I can't figure it. I thought they'd take one quick vote and be back. I wasn't able to shake that truck driver's testimony. This doesn't make any sense."

"I told you I had a good feeling," I said.

"Apparently you're not the only one expecting an acquittal. Word is getting around. I've had a call from a film producer who thinks there may be a movie in this. Two agents want to represent Jon Mason as soon as he's released. They say he has a big career as an actor ahead of him. And a New York publisher wants to do a book."

"That's great," I said, "but don't get so involved you forget to call me as soon as the verdict is in. Remember, I'll probably owe you a bonus and I'll be leaving the city as soon as I know."

"Don't worry, I trust you," he said, but I knew he'd call me before he did anything else—trust is never a lawyer's long suit.

Kesner called the next morning. "The jury just came back," he said.

"And?"

"The verdict is Not Guilty. You were right."

"What about Mason? Will he be released right away?"

"Yes. They're processing him out of jail now. He'll stop by my office as soon as he's free."

"Fine. I'll be there in a few minutes."

I packed everything into my suitcase, including all but the cash I had promised Kesner. The jurors, of course, would never see a nickel of the money they expected. It would be foolish to pay them. They couldn't take their votes back, and the prosecutor's office would be watching them for months. If any of them came into sudden wealth it would all come out.

I checked out of the Holiday Inn, put the suitcase into the trunk of the car I'd rented, and drove to Kesner's office.

Kesner was waiting for me at the conference table where I'd first met him. He watched me cross the room with his hooded eyes and smiled. "Someday I'm going to find out how you did it," he said.

"You give me too much credit," I said.

"I don't think so."

To change the subject, I opened my briefcase and paid him the bonus I'd promised. He kept busy fondling the bills until Jon Mason arrived.

Mason skipped to the center of the room, then leapt up and slapped the ceiling with a triumphant shout. "I'm *outa* that damned place! I can hardly believe it!" He stood in front of me. "I'll remember what you did for me as long as I live," he said.

"Probably," I agreed. Then I said, "Look, I've got a car downstairs. Let's take a ride. I'd like to talk to you."

His grin turned into a smirk, as though we shared some secret. "Sure," he said, "let's talk."

But we rode in silence until I had maneuvered the car onto the Santa Monica Freeway. Then I turned to him. "Do you have any idea why I wanted you out of jail?" I asked.

"Sure," he said. "I figured that out right away. You're my father."

I felt like howling with laughter. "Oh, no—I'm not your father. I don't have a son. But Karen Simmons was my daughter."

I left his body on the same off-ramp where he'd dumped Karen. It seemed like the thing to do.

JUDITH O'NEILL
BRIDEY'S CALLER

*Judith O'Neill published her first mystery short story in
1967, and has appeared all too infrequently over the past
twenty-two years. This fine memory of childhood's summer visits to grandparents won an Edgar nomination
from the Mystery Writers of America and shows O'Neill at
a high point in her writing career. We hope this will be
followed by many more stories—and soon!*

When the mail came this morning, I walked out to get it. The
letter from my cousin Nellie was full of chatty family news
about her children and grandchildren and questions about
mine. I smiled as I strolled back up to the house, reading. And
then she casually mentioned in current town happenings that
"old Bridey" had died. I had to sit down suddenly on the steps.

When I was very young, almost forty years ago now, I used
to go and stay with my grandparents in Helenwood, Kansas, for
long weeks in the summer. I loved it there. I was the oldest by
four years of all my cousins who lived in or around Helenwood.
So, during the time I was there, I was Miss Queen Bee. My
cousin Nellie and I were especially close. She lived on a farm
just outside the tiny town, and during my stays she would be
brought in to keep me company. She was an adoring little girl
with dark curly hair and big brown eyes. And because she was
so very gifted at worshipping, she was for years by far my
favorite cousin.

My grandparents did not live on a farm, but coming as I did
from the "big" city of St. Joseph just across the river, it seemed
very rural to me. These were my mother's parents—the sober,
honest, almost severe side of the family—as opposed to my
father's side, which is another story altogether.

The very order of everything in my grandparents' Helenwood
home appealed to me. All my remembering years I had been a

165

part of that old white house set back from the dusty street. Helenwood had only one paved street. Actually it was the highway that ran through town, but it was referred to as Main Street and had the post office, a grocery store, and farther along, the red brick school—kindergarten through twelfth grade. My grandparents' home was three blocks away from the highway, back where the houses were separated by huge tree-shaded flat lawns. There were no sidewalks anywhere in town. In winter when the snow melted or spring when the rains came and the river rose, you stayed indoors as much as you could.

Summers were dry and hot and my mother would drive me over the arched, narrow bridge from St. Joe and deliver me to my grandparents. Nellie would already be there and we would set about exploring. We did a lot of "exploring" because there wasn't much else to do. We walked everywhere, from the creek to the Missouri River, up to the highway and the post office, talking, talking.

But our favorite place, only four houses up the street from my grandparents' house was Bridey's. Bridget was her name, and I'm not sure we ever knew her last name; everyone referred to her as Bridey and so did we. She was a tall, thin woman with gray hair pulled back in a bun and gray eyes. I remember they were gray because she was one of the few people I ever knew whose eyes were exactly the same color as her hair. She had a small three-room house, and the front room she had set up as a country store. Straight back from that was her bedroom and then the kitchen at the back. The "bathroom" was out the back path, surrounded by vines and trees. It was all very neat and clean. She had a door shutting off her bedroom/sitting room, but in the summer all the doors stood open to let a breeze through, so when you walked into her store, you could look right back through the bedroom and kitchen to the back porch.

But Nellie and I were not very interested in what Bridey had in the back rooms. What she had in the front room was what we went for—that long, oval, zinc washtub set up on short sawhorses and filled with huge chunks of ice and floating bottles of soda pop. Leaning against that icy tub, fishing around for your favorite soda, was the coldest you could get in Helenwood in the summer. It is hard for people now to understand the effort and energy we had to put into keeping cool in those days. Nowadays it is just as hot in Kansas, but you can escape into air-conditioning. Then you couldn't escape it. Even at night, when breezes turn cool in other places, in Kansas a hot wind blows up across Texas and Oklahoma and fries you. It is a sweet-smelling wind, and if it doesn't blow you can poach in your own sweat, but it doesn't really cool you. No, in those days there was no way to escape it except to jump in the creek or the river, but there was always my grandmother's fear of polio. So mostly we tried to find ways to bear it and that led us to spending a lot of time in Bridey's, leaning against the soda tub. She was never short or impatient with us, she let us lean and play in the water. She didn't pay special attention to us and we in our turn were polite, not making a mess or noise. As "Emmitt and Louise's grandchildren," we were conscious of a certain amount of responsibility. We behaved ourselves so as not to reflect badly on our elders. I'm not sure how they managed that bit of psychological control, I don't think they ever *told* us that, it was something we just knew. Nellie loved grape soda above all else and I was overly fond of cream. Even then I appreciated that Bridey kept the tub well stocked. When my whole arm finally became numb I would fish one out and pop it open with the opener tied with a string onto the tub handle. Then I would lean my bare back against the tub and slug that first icy gulp down my hot, dry throat.

I always thought it was an oversized zinc washtub, but it was very long for that and when I thought about it later, and believe me I did think *a lot* about it later, I thought maybe it had been a trough for horses to drink out of at one time. I have seen them from time to time in antique shops since then, and they always make me a little sick at my stomach.

Bridey lived alone, and while there were all kinds of Sunday laws in Kansas in those days, she would open her door about ten in the morning on Sunday and if you went by, she would sell you what you wanted. But in our eyes Bridey had a fault. This was her Sunday caller. Every Sunday, about two P.M., Bridey's caller would come. He drove across the bridge from St. Joe and down onto the shaded streets of Helenwood and around to the back of Bridey's. He never parked in front, always in the back under the trees there. Why, I can't imagine, as everyone in town could see his car in back as well as if he had parked it in front. He would then get out of his car—a short, energetic, good-looking man in a dark suit and hat, and walk to the back door and go in. Shortly thereafter Bridey would close her front door and her back door and no longer be available for business. Somewhere about five P.M. her caller would depart the way he had come, out the back, into his car, down the streets, and out of Helenwood to the bridge, not to be seen again until the next Sunday. I had broodingly watched this coming and going from my grandfather's grape arbor countless Sundays.

Of course Nellie and I were affronted by this because Bridey's was *never* closed. If she was there, day or night, she was open and there was easy access to the soda tub. And it seemed the hottest and thirstiest we ever got was between two and five on Sunday afternoons. I was vaguely aware that my grandmother was affronted by this, too, but I could not fathom her giving a whit about the soda tub and she rarely ran out of things just as she needed them, so I couldn't put my finger on the cause of her displeasure. She liked Bridey, I knew; Grandma had known her all of her life. She would sometimes go and sit on Bridey's porch when she was passing on her way to or from the post office and they would talk. But when the Sunday closings came up she would frown and get testy. My grandfather got a big kick out of it. Once, as we sat at Sunday dinner, Nellie and I were again complaining, of course, and Nellie, being as blunt and repetitive as any six-year-old, asked for about the five hundredth time that summer, "Why does she close every Sunday like this?" and my grandmother snapped, "Because she has a caller, you know that, now eat those mashed potatoes."

I was a little perplexed by this behavior myself. We didn't go around closing all our doors and keeping people out when we had company. "But why does she close the doors?" I asked, musing. "It must be hot in there."

My grandfather laughed. "I bet," he said.

"Emmitt, Emmitt!" my grandmother warned sharply.

But my grandfather was enjoying himself now and teasing my red-faced grandmother. It was seldom I had seen her blush. "I think," he said, laughing at her, "that Bridey takes a little after-dinner nap."

My grandmother threw her fork down on the table and glared at him. "Emmitt, that's just about enough!"

He was laughing so hard now he had to take his glasses off and wipe his eyes with his napkin. And while he was doing this Nellie said in her self-righteous little way, "But isn't it rude of Bridey to take a nap while her caller is there?"

My grandfather started choking and had to leave the table, and my grandmother turned on Nellie and me and told us in no uncertain terms that other people's manners were not our business and we had plenty to do to mind our *own* manners and it was *very* bad manners to be so nosy about other people's lives and how they conducted them.

That was my tenth summer. It stands out clearly in my mind for many reasons. For one, it was the most incredibly hot summer I have ever lived through, everyone talked about nothing but the weather and the crops and the lack of rain, and Nellie and I consumed a prodigious amount of soda. Secondly, I was at my grandparents' all summer for the first time ever and the reason for that is the third but by far the most important reason I remember that summer. At the very beginning of it, just after school was out, my mother had a nervous breakdown. Up until the previous Christmas I had never suspected she had a nerve in her body. She was always a happy, fun person with laughing eyes. To this day, when I think of her, I remember those laughing brown eyes. Well, they weren't laughing that year. My father had fallen in love with someone else, she had told me just before Christmas. Just like that, my happy-go-lucky, handsome, generous father was gone. Gone with someone else. There's a lot about that Christmas I don't remember. I remember my mother sitting very still at the dining room table in our house in St. Joe, with the snow falling outside the window behind her, and telling me he had gone. I had never even heard them argue. We would get used to it, my mother said bleakly, we would go on with our lives and they would be different, but we would get used to it. Somewhere in that body I knew my mother must still reside, but I couldn't see her at all in the dead brown eyes and the bleached white face.

I went to my grandparents' the day school was out, and my mother went to the hospital.

My grandparents were sick with worry. They didn't talk about it to me much, but they talked *to* me a lot more. They seemed to go out of their way, both of them, to explain the whys of things and the idiosyncracies of the people in town. "Look at poor Cynthia Jenkins," my grandmother would say, "she lost both her parents in a flood when she was very young and she's turned out all right." That sort of thing. I learned a lot about people in Helenwood I hadn't previously known as my grandparents gently pointed out one survivor after another. And somewhere in that summer I learned that Bridget was one of these—her father dead when she was less than three years old. Her mother had married a man with four children, and it came out (from my grandfather, I'm sure) that the Sunday caller was one of these stepbrothers, a *married* stepbrother, my grandmother snorted.

We all suffered into August, one brilliant blazing day after another. We woke up drenched, unable to cheat nature out of even a few minutes' early morning coolness, moved sluggishly through the day, and sank exhausted into the already heated sheets at dusk. It was that kind of a day the Sunday I was hanging around the grape arbor waiting for Bridey to open up. It was about time for her caller to leave, so I strolled up through the three back yards separating ours from hers. Yes, the car was still there under the trees at the back of her yard. The back door was still shut. Standing well away from the trunk of the tree to catch even the hot wind and feeling it dry the perspiration on my face and bare arms and scorch my eyes, I waited impatiently for Bridey's caller to leave. And, waiting, I went to sit in the thick, green grass along the stone foundation of her little house where the breeze always seemed cooler.

And I heard Bridey crying. I don't think I purposely sat right under her bedroom window. I was just searching for the coolest spot around and that looked like it, on the shady side of the house, the grass deep and green and bending in the wind. But there I was, right under her open bedroom window. I should have crawled away, but the sobbing was so close I was afraid she would see me. She cried out in a low, strangled voice,

"Don't please don't, Ray, don't say you're going for good." She was crying so frantic and wild that I was mesmerized there, scrunched up against the rough stone of the foundation. I could hear his voice as he answered her, but not his words. She began to beg. I cannot, writing here, relay to you the utter desperation and grief in those low pleas, nor their effect on me. It was Bridey's voice, strangled and harsh in terror and hurt and desolation, begging, begging. It was my voice, and my mother's voice. And I, who had taken the news of my own father's departure stoically, and my mother's breakdown grimly but dry-eyed, rose from the grass sightlessly and ran along the side of the house and back into the trees and down into my grandfather's grape arbor.

I threw myself on the ground under the heavy green leaves and clutched the grass there in my hands and wrenched and tore it out of the ground and beat the earth with my fists. But none of it helped and just like an earthen dam gives way, so did I. I shut my eyes as tight as I could, but I could feel the flood coming, the terrible bitter tears of irreplaceable loss ripping out my heart, and then the dam gave way.

When the weeping was all over and I had rolled onto my back to stare up through the grape leaves at the bright sky, I marveled that there could have been that much water in me. And then I thought about Bridey. Now I know that he must have been everything to her. For twenty years, she must have lived for those short Sunday afternoons. Three precious hours of his time a week.

My grandfather was asleep on the recliner on the front porch, his iced tea sitting on the porch floor, all its ice long melted. My grandmother and Nellie were napping, too, when I went into the house. Nellie in her white, little girl cotton slip on the big bed we shared, her dark curls stuck wetly to her forehead. I went into the bathroom and washed my face and combed my hair and wandered down to join my grandfather on the porch.

And then the young people from the Baptist church came swinging down the street, led by the new minister. They had been calling on the sick and widowed and just plain backslidden. Dressed in their Sunday best they looked hot and bedraggled and sweaty. The girls' hair was all wet and hanging down

their faces. They frowned against the sun. The boys had on their
suit coats and looked like to die.

"We'll stop for a cool drink at Bridey's," the new minister
said. "We'll try to get her to open a little early."

So of course I tagged along. The minister, being new, had
obviously not caught on to the significance of the car's being
there yet, but everyone else in the group had, because they
craned their necks to glance toward the back. It was still there,
but the young people, looking uncomfortable as the new minister walked up onto the porch and banged on the door, weren't
about to tell him. I didn't have the words to tell him with. I
stood in the shade with the others while he knocked and called.
He came back shaking his head. "Guess she's not going to
open," he smiled apologetically. "Let's go back to the parsonage
for iced tea." And they went off.

I stood there, loath to put forth the effort to get myself back
to my grandparents' house, loath to put forth any effort at all,
and saw Sheriff Mills come out of his house three houses farther
down the road and start toward me. Sheriff Mills had company
every Sunday. Mrs. Mills had brothers all over the place and
they all gathered with wives and families every week. I knew
them, but they didn't have kids my age.

"Afternoon, missy," he said. He was a big, broad, older man
and he called all women under twenty "missy." "Miss Bridey
not open yet?" he asked, surprised, consulting his watch.

I shook my head. He glanced around at the back. "Hmm . . .,"
he said. Sheriff Mills was not new in town. He turned back to
look down the street toward his house. "Well," he said, "it's
getting on toward six and Mother needs milk to get supper on."
He glanced behind the house again, hesitated, and mounted the
steps.

I guess she had to open when she saw who it was. She didn't
look all that different from the way she had earlier that day.
Maybe her eyes were a little puffy, but that was all. Her hair was
in the bun, not a wisp escaping, her plain face pale but calm.

"I'm real sorry about this, Bridey," the sheriff said, stepping
into the store and explaining his quandary. We both of us
refrained from glancing into the back room. As Bridey was
getting the milk from the big white icebox, I scooted past the

sheriff and went to the soda tub. I was fishing around for a cream soda and I could hear her and Sheriff Mills talking, but I wasn't paying any attention really.

The water felt *so* good. I was barefooted and I remember there was a lot of cold water on the dark wood floor. I found my cream soda and clasped it as it bobbed among the huge chunks of ice and the other bottles and then the ice and the bottles floated apart and I looked down into the face of Bridey's caller. He had blue eyes, I remember, very blue. He seemed to be gazing up past me to the ceiling. Then the ice and the bottles floated together again and covered his face.

I thought for a second that I was having heatstroke. My grandmother had talked about it endlessly and warned us time and again to stay out of the sun. She had had it once, when she was young, and when we asked her what it was like, she said you get sick at your stomach and dizzy and disoriented. I thought disoriented must mean seeing things.

I clutched my cream soda and moved it slowly back and forth in the water to clear some space. The ice and the bottles slid apart again and there he was. He seemed to be lying on the bottom of the long tub staring up through the water, his curly hair gently waving over his forehead.

I took out my soda and let the chunks of ice float back together and I turned to look at Bridey. She was staring over the sheriff's shoulder as he dug into his pockets and rattled on. We looked at each other. Sheriff Mills turned and saw me and said, "I see you got your soda, missy," or something inane like that and went right on talking to Bridey. Bridey just stared at me. I think now of all the things I could have done. She must have been waiting for me to scream or faint or just say, "Look here, Sheriff Mills, at Bridey's caller in the soda tub."

I didn't do any of those things. I just walked across the small room, laid my dime on the linoleum-topped counter, and walked out. I remember the tough burnt grass on my bare feet as I crossed the yards. I remember my grandpa still asleep on the porch when I came up onto it. I remember going in and sitting on a chair at the kitchen table and drinking my cream soda while my grandmother moved slowly around in the heat,

starting to lay out things for a cold dinner. I don't remember at
all just when I started to breathe again.

I don't know what she finally did with him. I don't know how
she killed him or got him in the tub. Now that I'm older and
have thought of the details of it, one crazy question keeps
popping into my mind is, how did she keep him on the bottom
of the tub? Bodies float, don't they?

I don't know how she got rid of the car or how she explained
it all. They found the car way out by Krug Park in St. Joe across
the river, my grandmother told me. It was a big scandal in
Helenwood—how Bridey's caller had disappeared. And Bridey
went right on living there, running her little store. I can't say
that she was especially nice to me after that. She had never
been not nice to me. We were just more aware of each other.
She had to know that I knew. I wasn't four or five. I was ten.
She had seen me see him.

I wonder now at how she must have waited. Maybe she
thought I would tell my grandparents or my mother when she
finally got well or a school friend when school started. It's
strange that it never crossed my mind to fear her. I could have
easily disappeared down a well or in the river.

I didn't see a great deal of her after that summer. My mother
took me back home in time to start sixth grade in September.
My father moved up to Mound City, and I began to spend
summers with him and his new family. Two years later we
moved to St. Louis and my mother remarried. So when I was in
Helenwood, it was usually en route to my father's or just coming
back from his place, so I was there for only a few days at a time.
And then, of course, I grew up and had my own life.

Bridey lived there all the rest of her life in that little three-
room house. She never had another caller. She would sit out on
her porch in the evenings, and she didn't close anymore on
Sunday afternoons. Sometimes when Nellie and I were teen-
agers, before I could drive grandpa's car over to St. Joe, we
would stroll down to Bridey's.

Nellie would still get her grape pop, but I never drank another
bottle of cream soda. I had switched to ice cream bars, and if
anyone noticed, they thought it was more nutritional anyway.

Bridey would take our money and exchange pleasantries, asking me about St. Louis, how I liked school there, and how my mother was getting on. I answered politely. We kept our eyes neutral. I never saw anything in hers aside from the polite curiosity she had always had, and I kept mine bright and warm and empty.

Of all the questions I have pondered there is one I never had to ask myself. Why didn't I tell? Why didn't I run screaming out of the store to my grandmother and fall fainting against her, babbling and hysterical? You must know the answer to that one.

Any other summer maybe I would have. But that summer, after all, I knew all about men leaving you.

SARA PARETSKY

THE CASE OF THE PIETRO ANDROMACHE

We welcome Sara Paretsky to this annual with a novelette featuring her popular private eye V. I. Warshawski. Paretsky is increasingly praised by American critics and was winner of last year's Silver Dagger, awarded by the British Crime Writers' Association. Paretsky has chronicled only a few shorter V. I. Warshawski cases. This is the best so far.

"**Y**ou only agreed to hire him because of his art collection. Of that I'm sure." Lotty Herschel bent down to adjust her stockings. "And don't waggle your eyebrows like that—it makes you look like an adolescent Groucho Marx."

Max Loewenthal obediently smoothed his eyebrows, but said, "It's your legs, Lotty—they remind me of my youth. You know, going into the Underground to wait out the air raids, looking at the ladies as they came down the escalators. The updraft always made their skirts billow."

"You're making this up, Max. I was in those Underground stations, too, and as I remember the ladies were always bundled in coats and children."

Max moved from the doorway to put an arm around Lotty. "That's what keeps us together, *Lottchen*—I am a romantic and you are severely logical. And you know we didn't hire Caudwell because of his collection. Although I admit I am eager to see it. The board wants Beth Israel to develop a transplant program. It's the only way we're going to become competitive—"

"Don't deliver your publicity lecture to me," Lotty snapped. Her thick brows contracted to a solid black line across her forehead. "As far as I am concerned he is a cretin with the hands of a Caliban and the personality of Attila."

Lotty's intense commitment to medicine left no room for the

177

mundane consideration of money. But as the hospital's executive director, Max was on the spot with the trustees to see that
Beth Israel ran at a profit. Or at least at a smaller loss than
they'd achieved in recent years. They'd brought Caudwell in
part to attract more paying patients—and to help screen out
some of the indigents who made up twelve percent of Beth
Israel's patient load. Max wondered how long the hospital could
afford to support personalities as divergent as Lotty and Caudwell with their radically differing approaches to medicine.

He dropped his arm and smiled quizzically at her. "Why do
you hate him so much, Lotty?"

"*I* am the person who has to justify the patients I admit to
this—this troglodyte. Do you realize he tried to keep Mrs.
Mendes from the operating room when he learned she had
AIDS? He wasn't even being asked to sully his hands with her
blood, and he didn't want me performing surgery on her."

Lotty drew back from Max and pointed an accusing finger at
him. "You may tell the board that if he keeps questioning my
judgment they will find themselves looking for a new perinatologist. I am serious about this. You listen this afternoon, Max,
you hear whether or not he calls me 'our little baby doctor.' I
am fifty-eight years old, I am a Fellow of the Royal College of
Surgeons besides having enough credentials in this country to
support a whole hospital, and to him I am a 'little baby doctor.' "

Max sat on the daybed and pulled Lotty down next to him.
"No, no *Lottchen*, don't fight. Listen to me. Why haven't you
told me any of this before?"

"Don't be an idiot, Max. You are the director of the hospital.
I cannot use our special relationship to deal with problems I
have with the staff. I said my piece when Caudwell came for his
final interview. A number of the other physicians were not
happy with his attitude. If you remember, we asked the board
to bring him in as a cardiac surgeon first and promote him to
chief of staff after a year if everyone was satisfied with his
performance."

"We talked about doing it that way," Max admitted. "But he
wouldn't take the appointment except as chief of staff. That was
the only way we could offer him the kind of money he could
get at one of the university hospitals or Humana. And, Lotty,

even if you don't like his personality, you must agree that he is a first-class surgeon."

"I agree to nothing." Red lights danced in her black eyes. "If he patronizes me, a fellow physician, how do you imagine he treats his patients? You cannot practice medicine if—"

"Now it's my turn to ask to be spared a lecture," Max interrupted gently. "But if you feel so strongly about him, maybe you shouldn't go to his party this afternoon."

"And admit that he can beat me? Never."

"Very well then." Max got up and placed a heavily brocaded wool shawl over Lotty's shoulders. "But you must promise me to behave. This is a social function we are going to, remember, not a gladiator contest. Caudwell is trying to repay some hospitality this afternoon, not to belittle you."

"I don't need lessons in conduct from you. Herschels were attending the emperors of Austria while the Loewenthals were operating vegetable stalls on the Ring," Lotty said haughtily.

Max laughed and kissed her hand. "Then remember these regal Herschels and act like them, *Eure Hoheit.*"

II

Caudwell had bought an apartment sight unseen when he moved to Chicago. A divorced man whose children are in college only has to consult with his own taste in these matters. He asked the Beth Israel board to recommend a realtor, sent his requirements to them—twenties construction, near Lake Michigan, good security, modern plumbing—and dropped seven hundred and fifty thousand for an eight-room condo facing the lake at Scott Street.

Since Beth Israel had paid handsomely for the privilege of retaining Dr. Charlotte Herschel as their perinatologist, nothing required her to live in a five-room walkup on the fringes of Uptown, so it was a bit unfair of her to mutter "Parvenu" to Max when they walked into the lobby.

Max relinquished Lotty gratefully when they got off the elevator. Being her lover was like trying to be companion to a Bengal tiger: you never knew when she'd take a lethal swipe at you. Still, if Caudwell were insulting her—and her judgment—

maybe he needed to talk to the surgeon, explain how important Lotty was for the reputation of Beth Israel.

Caudwell's two children were making the obligatory Christmas visit. They were a boy and a girl, Deborah and Steve, within a year of the same age, both tall, both blond and poised, with a hearty sophistication born of a childhood spent on expensive ski slopes. Max wasn't very big, and as one took his coat and the other performed brisk introductions, he felt himself shrinking, losing in self-assurance. He accepted a glass of special *cuvee* from one of them—was it the boy or the girl, he wondered in confusion—and fled into the melee.

He landed next to one of Beth Israel's trustees, a woman in her sixties wearing a grey textured minidress whose black stripes were constructed of feathers. She commented brightly on Caudwell's art collection, but Max sensed an undercurrent of hostility: wealthy trustees don't like the idea that they can't out-buy the staff.

While he was frowning and nodding at appropriate intervals, it dawned on Max that Caudwell did know how much the hospital needed Lotty. Heart surgeons do not have the world's smallest egos: when you ask them to name the world's three leading practitioners, they never can remember the names of the other two. Lotty was at the top of her field, and she, too, was used to having things her way. Since her confrontational style was reminiscent more of the Battle of the Bulge than the Imperial Court of Vienna, he didn't blame Caudwell for trying to force her out of the hospital.

Max moved away from Martha Gildersleeve to admire some of the paintings and figurines she'd been discussing. A collector himself of Chinese procelains, Max raised his eyebrows and mouthed a soundless whistle at the pieces on display. A small Watteau and a Charles Demuth watercolor were worth as much as Beth Israel paid Caudwell in a year. No wonder Mrs. Gildersleeve had been so annoyed.

"Impressive, isn't it."

Max turned to see Arthur Gioia looming over him. Max was shorter than most of the Beth Israel staff, shorter than everyone but Lotty. But Gioia, a tall muscular immunologist, loomed over everyone. He had gone to the University of Arkansas on a football scholarship and had even spent a season playing tackle for Houston before starting medical school. It had been twenty years since he last lifted weights, but his neck still looked like a redwood stump.

Gioia had led the opposition to Caudwell's appointment. Max had suspected at the time that it was due more to a medicine man's not wanting a surgeon as his nominal boss than from any other cause, but after Lotty's outburst he wasn't so sure. He was debating whether to ask the doctor how he felt about Caudwell now that he'd worked with him for six months when their host surged over to him and shook his hand.

"Sorry I didn't see you when you came in, Loewenthal. You like the Watteau? It's one of my favorite pieces. Although a collector shouldn't play favorites any more than a father should, eh, sweetheart?" The last remark was addressed to the daughter, Deborah, who had come up behind Caudwell and slipped an arm around him.

Caudwell looked more like a Victorian seadog than a surgeon. He had a round red face under a shock of yellow-white hair, a hearty Santa Claus laugh, and a bluff, direct manner. Despite Lotty's vituperations, he was immensely popular with his patients. In the short time he'd been at the hospital, referrals to cardiac surgery had increased fifteen percent.

His daughter squeezed his shoulder playfully. "I know you don't play favorites with us, Dad, but you're lying to Mr. Loewenthal about your collection—come on, you know you are."

She turned to Max. "He has a piece he's so proud of he doesn't like to show it to people—he doesn't want them to see he's got vulnerable spots. But it's Christmas, Dad, relax, let people see how you feel for a change."

Max looked curiously at the surgeon, but Caudwell seemed pleased with his daughter's familiarity. The son came up and added his own jocular cajoling.

"This really is Dad's pride and joy. He stole it from Uncle Griffen when Grandfather died and kept Mother from getting her mitts on it when they split up."

Caudwell did bark out a mild reproof at that. "You'll be giving my colleagues the wrong impression of me, Steve. I didn't steal it from Grif. Told him he could have the rest of the estate if he'd leave me the Watteau and the Pietro."

"Of course he could've bought ten estates with what those two would fetch," Steve muttered to his sister over Max's head.

Deborah relinquished her father's arm to lean over Max and whisper back, "Mom, too."

Max moved away from the alarming pair to say to Caudwell, "A Pietro? You mean Pietro d'Alessandro? You have a model, or an actual sculpture?"

Caudwell gave his staccato admiral's laugh. "The real McCoy, Loewenthal. The real McCoy. An alabaster."

"An alabaster?" Max raised his eyebrows. "Surely not. I thought Pietro worked only in bronze and marble."

"Yes, yes," chuckled Caudwell, rubbing his hands together. "Everyone thinks so, but there were a few alabasters in private collections. I've had this one authenticated by experts. Come take a look at it—it'll knock your breath away. You come, too, Gioia," he barked at the immunologist. "You're Italian, you'll like to see what your ancestors were up to."

"A Pietro alabaster?" Lotty's clipped tones made Max start— he hadn't noticed her joining the little group. "I would very much like to see this piece."

"Then come along, Dr. Herschel, come along." Caudwell led them to a small hallway, exchanging genial greetings with his guests as he passed, pointing out a John William Hill miniature they might not have seen, picking up a few other people who for various reasons wanted to see his prize.

"By the way, Gioia, I was in New York last week, you know. Met an old friend of yours from Arkansas. Paul Nierman."

"Nierman?" Gioia seemed to be at a loss. "I'm afraid I don't remember him."

"Well, he remembered you pretty well. Sent you all kinds of messages—you'll have to stop by my office on Monday and get the full strength."

Caudwell opened a door on the right side of the hall and let them into his study. It was an octagonal room carved out of the corner of the building. Windows on two sides looked out on Lake Michigan. Caudwell drew salmon drapes as he talked about the room, why he'd chosen it for his study even though the view kept his mind from his work.

Lotty ignored him and walked over to a small pedestal which stood alone against the paneling on one of the far walls. Max followed her and gazed respectfully at the statue. He had seldom seen so fine a piece outside a museum. About a foot high, it depicted a woman in classical draperies hovering in anguish over the dead body of a soldier lying at her feet. The grief in her beautiful face was so poignant that it reminded you of every sorrow you had ever faced.

"Who is it meant to be?" Max asked curiously.

"Andromache," Lotty said in a strangled voice. "Andromache mourning Hector."

Max stared at Lotty, astonished equally by her emotion and her knowledge of the figure—Lotty was totally uninterested in sculpture.

Caudwell couldn't restrain the smug smile of a collector with a true coup. "Beautiful, isn't it? How do you know the subject?"

"I should know it." Lotty's voice was husky with emotion. "My grandmother had such a Pietro. An alabaster given her great-grandfather by the Emperor Joseph the Second himself for his help in consolidating imperial ties with Poland."

She swept the statue from its stand, ignoring the gasp from Max, and turned it over. "You can see the traces of the imperial stamp here still. And the chip on Hector's foot which made the Hapsburg wish to give the statue away to begin with. How came you to have this piece? Where did you find it?"

The small group that had joined Caudwell stood silent by the entrance, shocked at Lotty's outburst. Gioia looked more horrified than any of them, but he found Lotty overwhelming at the best of times—an elephant confronted by a hostile mouse.

"I think you're allowing your emotions to carry you away, doctor." Caudwell kept his tone light, making Lotty seem more gauche by contrast. "I inherited this piece from my father, who bought it—legitimately—in Europe. Perhaps from your—grandmother, was it? But I suspect you are confused about something you may have seen in a museum as a child."

Deborah gave a high-pitched laugh and called loudly to her

brother, "Dad may have stolen if from Uncle Grif, but it looks like Grandfather snatched it to begin with anyway."

"Be quiet, Deborah," Caudwell barked sternly.

His daughter paid no attention to him. She laughed again and joined her brother to look at the imperial seal on the bottom of the statue.

Lotty brushed them aside. "I am confused about the seal of Joseph the Second?" she hissed at Caudwell. "Or about this chip on Hector's foot? You can see the line where some Philistine filled in the missing piece. Some person who thought his touch would add value to Pietro's work. Was that you, *doctor*? Or your father?"

"Lotty." Max was at her side, gently prising the statue from her shaking hands to restore it to its pedestal. "Lotty, this is not the place or the manner to discuss such things."

Angry tears sparkled in her black eyes. "Are you doubting my word?"

Max shook his head. "I'm not doubting you. But I'm also not supporting you. I'm asking you not to talk about this matter in this way at this gathering."

"But, Max, either this man or his father is a thief!"

Caudwell strolled up to Lotty and pinched her chin. "You're working too hard, Dr. Herschel. You have too many things on your mind these days. I think the board would like to see you take a leave of absence for a few weeks, go someplace warm, get yourself relaxed. When you're this tense, you're no good to your patients. What do you say, Loewenthal?"

Max didn't say any of the things he wanted to—that Lotty was insufferable and Caudwell intolerable. He believed Lotty, believed that the piece had been her grandmother's. She knew too much about it, for one thing. And for another, a lot of artworks belonging to European Jews were now in museums or private collections around the world. It was only the most godawful coincidence that the Pietro had ended up with Caudwell's father.

But how dare she raise the matter in the way most likely to alienate everyone present? He couldn't possibly support her in such a situation. And at the same time, Caudwell's pinching her chin in that condescending way made him wish he were not chained to a courtesy that would have kept him from knocking the surgeon out even if he'd been ten years younger and ten inches taller.

"I don't think this is the place or the time to discuss such matters," he reiterated as calmly as he could. "Why don't we all cool down and get back together on Monday, eh?"

Lotty gasped involuntarily, then swept from the room without a backward glance.

Max refused to follow her. He was too angry with her to want to see her again that afternoon. When he got ready to leave the party an hour or so later, after a long conversation with Caudwell that taxed his sophisticated urbanity to the utmost, he heard with relief that Lotty was long gone. The tale of her outburst had of course spread through the gathering at something faster than the speed of sound; he wasn't up to defending her to Martha Gildersleeve who demanded an explanation of him in the elevator going down.

He went home for a solitary evening in his house in Evanston. Normally such time brought him pleasure, listening to music in his study, lying on the couch with his shoes off, reading history, letting the sounds of the lake wash over him.

Tonight, though, he could get no relief. Fury with Lotty merged into images of horror, the memories of his own disintegrated family, his search through Europe for his mother. He had never found anyone who was quite certain what became of her, although several people told him definitely of his father's suicide. And stamped over these wisps in his brain was the disturbing picture of Caudwell's children, their blond heads leaning backward at identical angles as they gleefully chanted, "Grandpa was a thief, Grandpa was a thief," while Caudwell edged his visitors out of the study.

By morning he would somehow have to reconstruct himself enough to face Lotty, to respond to the inevitable flood of calls from outraged trustees. He'd have to figure out a way of soothing Caudwell's vanity, bruised more by his children's behavior than anything Lotty had said. And find a way to keep both important doctors at Beth Israel.

Max rubbed his grey hair. Every week his job brought him less joy and more pain. Maybe it was time to step down, to let the board bring in a young MBA who would turn Beth Israel's finances around. Lotty would resign then, and it would be an end to the tension between her and Caudwell.

Max fell asleep on the couch. He awoke around five muttering, "By morning, by morning." His joints were stiff from cold, his eyes sticky with tears he's shed unknowingly in his sleep.

But in the morning things changed. When Max got to his office he found the place buzzing, not with news of Lotty's outburst but word that Caudwell had missed his early morning surgery. Work came almost completely to a halt at noon when his children phoned to say they'd found the surgeon strangled in his own study and the Pietro Andromache missing. And on Tuesday, the police arrested Dr. Charlotte Herschel for Lewis Caudwell's murder.

III

Lotty would not speak to anyone. She was out on two hundred fifty thousand dollars' bail, the money raised by Max, but she had gone directly to her apartment on Sheffield after two nights in county jail without stopping to thank him. She would not talk to reporters, she remained silent during all conversations with the police, and she emphatically refused to speak to the private investigator who had been her close friend for many years.

Max, too, stayed behind an impregnable shield of silence. While Lotty went on indefinite leave, turning her practice over to a series of colleagues, Max continued to go to the hospital every day. But he, too, would not speak to reporters; he wouldn't even say, "No comment." He talked to the police only after they threatened to lock him up as a material witness, and then every word had to be pried from him as if his mouth were stone and speech Excalibur. For three days V. I. Warshawski left messages which he refused to return.

On Friday, when no word came from the detective, when no reporter popped up from a nearby urinal in the men's room to try to trick him into speaking, when no more calls came from the state's attorney, Max felt a measure of relaxation as he drove home. As soon as the trial was over he would resign, retire to

London. If he could only keep going until then, everything would be—not all right, but bearable.

He used the remote release for the garage door and eased his car into the small space. As he got out he realized bitterly he'd been too optimistic in thinking he'd be left in peace. He hadn't seen the woman sitting on the stoop leading from the garage to the kitchen when he drove in, only as she uncoiled herself at his approach.

"I'm glad you're home—I was beginning to freeze out here."

"How did you get into the garage, Victoria?"

The detective grinned in a way he usually found engaging. Now it seemed merely predatory. "Trade secret, Max. I know you don't want to see me, but I need to talk to you."

He unlocked the door into the kitchen. "Why not just let yourself into the house if you were cold? If your scruples permit you into the garage, why not into the house?"

She bit her lip in momentary discomfort but said lightly, "I couldn't manage my picklocks with my fingers this cold."

The detective followed him into the house. Another tall monster; five foot eight, athletic, light on her feet behind him. Maybe American mothers put growth hormones or steroids in their children's cornflakes. He'd have to ask Lotty. His mind winced at the thought.

"I've talked to the police, of course," the light alto continued behind him steadily, oblivious to his studied rudeness as he poured himself a cognac, took his shoes off, found his waiting slippers, and padded down the hall to the front door for his mail.

"I understand why they arrested Lotty—Caudwell had been doped with a whole bunch of Xanax and then strangled while he was sleeping it off. And, of couse, she was back at the building Sunday night. She won't say why, but one of the tenants ID'd her as the woman who showed up around ten at the service entrance when he was walking his dog. She won't say if she talked to Caudwell, if he let her in, if he was still alive."

Max tried to ignore her clear voice. When that proved impossible he tried to read a journal which had come in the mail.

"And those kids, they're marvelous, aren't they? Like something out of the *Fabulous Furry Freak Brothers*. They won't talk to me but they gave a long interview to Murray Ryerson over at the *Star*.

"After Caudwell's guests left, they went to a flick at the Chestnut Street Station, had a pizza afterward, then took themselves dancing on Division Street. So they strolled in around two in the morning—confirmed by the doorman—saw the light on in the old man's study. But they were feeling no pain and he kind of overreacted—their term—if they were buzzed, so they didn't stop in to say goodnight. It was only when they got up around noon and went in that they found him."

V. I. had followed Max from the front hallway to the door of his study as she spoke. He stood there irresolutely, not wanting his private place desecrated with her insistent, air-hammer speech, and finally went on down the hall to a little-used living room. He sat stiffly on one of the brocade armchairs and looked at her remotely when she perched on the edge of its companion.

"The weak piece in the police story is the statue," V. I. continued.

She eyed the Persian rug doubtfully and unzipped her boots, sticking them on the bricks in front of the fireplace.

"Everyone who was at the party agrees that Lotty was beside herself. By now the story has spread so far that people who weren't even in the apartment when she looked at the statue swear they heard her threaten to kill him. But if that's the case, what happened to the statue?"

Max gave a slight shrug to indicate total lack of interest in the topic.

V. I. plowed on doggedly. "Now some people think she might have given it to a friend or a relation to keep for her until her name is cleared at the trial. And these people think it would be either her Uncle Stefan here in Chicago, her brother Hugo in Montreal, or you. So the Mounties searched Hugo's place and are keeping an eye on his mail. And the Chicago cops are doing the same for Stefan. And I presume someone got a warrant and went through here, right?"

Max said nothing, but he felt his heart beating faster. Police in his house, searching his things? But wouldn't they have to get his permission to enter? Or would they? Victoria would know, but he couldn't bring himself to ask. She waited for a few minutes, but when he still wouldn't speak, she plunged on. He could see it was becoming an effort for her to talk, but he wouldn't help her.

"But I don't agree with those people. Because I know that Lotty is innocent. And that's why I'm here. Not like a bird of prey, as you think, using your misery for carrion. But to get you to help me. Lotty won't speak to me, and if she's that miserable I won't force her to. But surely, Max, you won't sit idly by and let her be railroaded for something she never did."

Max looked away from her. He was surprised to find himself holding the brandy snifter and set it carefully on a table beside him.

"Max!" Her voice was shot with astonishment. "I don't believe this. You actually think she killed Caudwell."

Max flushed a little, but she'd finally stung him into a response. "And you are God who sees all and knows she didn't?"

"I see more than you do," V. I. snapped. "I haven't known Lotty as long as you have, but I know when she's telling the truth."

"So you are God." Max bowed in heavy irony. "You see beyond the facts to the innermost souls of men and women."

He expected another outburst from the young woman, but she gazed at him steadily without speaking. It was a look sympathetic enough that Max felt embarrassed by his sarcasm and burst out with what was on his mind.

"What else am I to think? She hasn't said anything, but there's no doubt that she returned to his apartment Sunday night."

It was V. I.'s turn for sarcasm. "With a little vial of Xanax that she somehow induced him to swallow? And then strangled him for good measure? Come on, Max, you know Lotty—honesty follows her around like a cloud. If she'd killed Caudwell, she'd say something like, 'Yes, I bashed the little vermin's brains in.' Instead she's not speaking at all."

Suddenly the detective's eyes widened with incredulity. "Of course. She thinks you killed Caudwell. You're doing the only thing you can to protect her—standing mute. And she's doing the same thing. What an admirable pair of archaic knights."

"No!" Max said sharply. "It's not possible. How could she think such a thing? She carried on so wildly that it was embarrassing to be near her. I didn't want to see her or talk to her. That's why I've felt so terrible. If only I hadn't been so obstinate, if only I'd called her Sunday night. How could she think I would kill someone on her behalf when I was so angry with her?"

"Why else isn't she saying anything to anyone?" Warshawski demanded.

"Shame, maybe," Max offered. "You didn't see her on Sunday. I did. That is why I think she killed him, not because some man let her into the building."

His brown eyes screwed shut at the memory. "I have seen Lotty in the grip of anger many times, more than is pleasant to remember, really. But never, never have I seen her in this kind of—uncontrolled rage. You could not talk to her. It was impossible."

The detective didn't respond to that. Instead she said, "Tell me about the statue. I heard a couple of garbled versions from people who were at the party, but I haven't found anyone yet who was in the study when Caudwell showed it to you. Was it really her grandmother's, do you think? And how did Caudwell come to have it if it was?"

Max nodded mournfully. "Oh, yes. It was really her family's, I'm convinced of that. She could not have known in advance about the details, the flaw in the foot, the imperial seal on the bottom. As to how Caudwell got it, I did a little looking into that myself yesterday. His father was with the Army of Occupation in Germany after the war. A surgeon attached to Patton's staff. Men in such positions had endless opportunities to acquire artworks after the war."

V. I. shook her head questioningly.

"You must know something of this, Victoria. Well, maybe not. You know the Nazis helped themselves liberally to artwork belonging to Jews everywhere they occupied in Europe. And not just to Jews—they plundered Eastern Europe on a grand scale. The best guess is that they stole sixteen million pieces— statues, paintings, altarpieces, tapestries, rare books. The list is beyond reckoning, really."

The detective gave a little gasp. "Sixteen million! You're joking."

"Not a joke, Victoria. I wish it were so, but it is not. The U.S. Army of Occupation took charge of as many works of art as they found in the occupied territories. In theory, they were to find the rightful owners and try to restore them. But in practice few pieces were ever traced, and many of them ended up on the black market.

"You only had to say that such-and-such a piece was worth less than five thousand dollars and you were allowed to buy it. For an officer on Patton's staff, the opportunities for fabulous acquisitions would have been endless. Caudwell said he had the statue authenticated, but of course he never bothered to establish its provenance. Anyway, how could he?" Max finished bitterly. "Lotty's family had a deed of gift from the emperor, but that would have disappeared long since with the dispersal of their possessions."

"And you really think Lotty would have killed a man just to get this statue back? She couldn't have expected to keep it. Not if she'd killed someone to get it, I mean."

"You are so practical, Victoria. You are too analytical, sometimes, to understand why people do what they do. That was not just a statue. True, it is a priceless artwork, but you know Lotty, you know she places no value on such possessions. No, it meant her family to her, her past, her history, everything that the war destroyed forever for her. You must not imagine that because she never discusses such matters that they do not weigh on her."

V. I. flushed at Max's accusation. "You should be glad I'm analytical. It convinces me that Lotty is innocent. And whether you believe it or not I'm going to prove it."

Max lifted his shoulders slightly in a manner wholly European. "We each support Lotty according to our lights. I saw that she met her bail, and I will see that she gets expert counsel. I am not convinced that she needs you making her innermost secrets public."

V. I.'s grey eyes turned dark with a sudden flash of temper. "You are dead wrong about Lotty. I'm sure the memory of the war is a pain that can never be cured, but Lotty lives in the present, she works in hope for the future. The past does not obsess and consume her as, perhaps, it does you."

Max said nothing. His wide mouth turned in on itself in a narrow line. The detective laid a contrite hand on his arm.

"I'm sorry Max. That was below the belt."

He forced a ghost of a smile to his mouth.

"Perhaps it's true. Perhaps it's why I love these ancient things so much. I wish I could believe you about Lotty. Ask me what you want to know. If you promise to leave as soon as I've answered and not to bother me again, I'll answer your questions."

IV

Max put in a dutiful appearance at the Michigan Avenue Presbyterian Church Monday afternoon for Lewis Caudwell's funeral. The surgeon's former wife came, flanked by her children and her husband's brother Griffen. Even after three decades in America Max found himself puzzled sometimes by the natives' behavior: since she and Caudwell were divorced, why had his ex-wife draped herself in black? She was even wearing a veiled hat reminiscent of Queen Victoria.

The children behaved in a moderately subdued fashion, but the girl was wearing a white dress shot with black lightning forks which looked as though it belonged at a disco or a resort. Maybe it was her only dress with black in it, Max thought, trying hard to look charitably at the blond Amazon—after all, she had been suddenly and horribly orphaned.

Even though she was a stranger both in the city and the church, Deborah had hired one of the church parlors and managed to find someone to cater coffee and light snacks. Max joined the rest of the congregation there after the service.

He felt absurd as he offered condolences to the divorced widow: did she really miss the dead man so much? She accepted his conventional words with graceful melancholy and leaned slightly against her son and daughter. They hovered near her with what struck Max as a stagey solicitude. Seen next to her daughter, Mrs. Caudwell looked so frail and undernourished that she seemed like a ghost. Or maybe it was just that her children had a hearty vitality that even a funeral couldn't quench.

Caudwell's brother Griffen stayed as close to the widow as the children would permit. The man was totally unlike the hearty seadog surgeon. Max thought if he'd met the brothers standing side by side he would never have guessed their relationship. He was tall, like his niece and nephew, but without their robustness. Caudwell had had a thick mop of yellow-white hair; Griffen's domed head was covered by thin wisps of grey. He seemed weak and nervous, and lacked Caudwell's outgoing *bonhomie*; no wonder the surgeon had found it easy to decide the disposition of their father's estate in his favor. Max wondered what Griffen had gotten in return.

Mrs. Caudwell's vague, disoriented conversation indicated that she was heavily sedated. That, too, seemed strange. A man she hadn't lived with for four years and she was so upset at his death that she could only manage the funeral on drugs? Or maybe it was the shame of coming as the divorced woman, not a true widow? But then why come at all?

To his annoyance, Max found himself wishing he could ask Victoria about it. She would have some cynical explanation— Caudwell's death meant the end of the widow's alimony and she knew she wasn't remembered in the will. Or she was having an affair with Griffen and was afraid she would betray herself without tranquilizers. Although it was hard to imagine the uncertain Griffen as the object of a stong passion.

Since he had told Victoria he didn't want to see her again when she left him on Friday, it was ridiculous of him to wonder what she was doing, whether she was really uncovering evidence that would clear Lotty. Ever since she had gone he had felt a little flicker of hope in the bottom of his stomach. He kept trying to drown it, but it wouldn't quite go away.

Lotty, of course, had not come to the funeral, but most of the rest of the Beth Israel staff was there, along with the trustees. Arthur Gioia, his giant body filling the small parlor to the bursting point, tried finding a tactful balance between honesty and courtesy with the bereaved family; he made heavy going of it.

A sable-clad Martha Gildersleeve appeared under Gioia's elbow, rather like a furry football he might have tucked away. She made bright, unseemly remarks to the bereaved family about the disposal of Caudwell's artworks.

"Of course, the famous statue is gone now. What a pity. You could have endowed a chair in his honor with the proceeds from that piece alone." She gave a high, meaningless laugh.

Max sneaked a glance at his watch, wondering how long he had to stay before leaving would be rude. His sixth sense, the perfect courtesy that governed his movements, had deserted him, leaving him subject to the gaucheries of ordinary mortals. He never peeked at his watch at functions, and at any prior funeral he would have deftly pried Martha Gildersleeve from her victim. Instead he stood helplessly by while she tortured Mrs. Caudwell and other bystanders alike.

He glanced at his watch again. Only two minutes had passed since his last look. No wonder people kept their eyes on their watches at dull meetings; they couldn't believe the clock could move so slowly.

He inched stealthily toward the door, exchanging empty remarks with the staff members and trustees he passed. Nothing negative was said about Lotty to his face, but the comments cut off at his approach added to his misery.

He was almost at the exit when two newcomers appeared. Most of the group looked at them with indifferent curiosity, but Max suddenly felt an absurd stir of elation. Victoria, looking sane and modern in a navy suit, stood in the doorway, eyebrows raised, scanning the room. At her elbow was a police sergeant Max had met with her a few times. The man was in charge of Caudwell's death, too: it was that unpleasant association that kept the name momentarily from his mind.

V. I. finally spotted Max near the door and gave him a discreet sign. He went to her at once.

"I think we may have the goods," she murmured. "Can you get everyone to go? We just want the family, Mrs. Gildersleeve, and Gioia."

"*You* may have the goods," the police sergeant growled. "I'm here unofficially and reluctantly."

"But you're here," Warshawski grinned, and Max wondered how he ever could have found the look predatory. His own spirits rose enormously at her smile. "You know in your heart of hearts that arresting Lotty was just plain dumb. And now I'm going to make you look real smart. In public, too."

Max felt his suave sophistication return with the rush of elation that an ailing diva must have when she finds her voice again. A touch here, a word there, and the guests disappeared like the hosts of Sennacherib. Meanwhile he solicitously escorted first Martha Gildersleeve, then Mrs. Caudwell to adjacent armchairs, got the brother to fetch coffee for Mrs. Gildersleeve, the daughter and son to look after the widow.

With Gioia he could be a bit more ruthless, telling him to wait because the police had something important to ask him. When the last guest had melted away, the immunologist stood nervously at the window rattling his change over and over in his pockets. The jingling suddenly was the only sound in the room. Gioia reddened and clasped his hands behind his back.

Victoria came into the room beaming like a governess with a delightful treat in store for her charges. She introduced herself to the Caudwells.

"You know Sergeant McGonnigal, I'm sure, after this last week. I'm a private investigator. Since I don't have any legal standing, you're not required to answer any questions I have. So I'm not going to ask you any questions. I'm just going to treat you to a travelogue. I wish I had slides, but you'll have to imagine the visuals while the audio track moves along."

"A private investigator!" Steve's mouth formed an exaggerated "O"; his eyes widened in amazement. "Just like Bogie."

He was speaking, as usual, to his sister. She gave her high-pitched laugh and said, "We'll win first prize in the 'How I Spent My Winter Vacation' contests. Our daddy was murdered. Zowie. Then his most valuable possession was snatched. Powie. But he'd already stolen it from the Jewish doctor who killed him. Yowie! And then a P. I. to wrap it all up. Yowie! Zowie! Powie!"

"Deborah, please," Mrs. Caudwell sighed. "I know you're excited, sweetie, but not right now, okay?"

"Your children keep you young, don't they, ma'am?" Victoria said. "How can you ever feel old when your kids stay seven all their lives?"

"Oo, ow, she bites, Debbie, watch out, she bites!" Steve cried.

McGonnigal made an involuntary movement, as though re-
straining himself from smacking the younger man. "Ms. Warshawski is right—you are under no obligation to answer any of
her questions. But you're bright people, all of you. You know I
wouldn't be here if the police didn't take her ideas seriously. So
let's have a little quiet and listen to what she's got on her mind."

Victoria seated herself in an armchair near Mrs. Caudwell's.
McGonnigal moved to the door and leaned against the jamb.
Deborah and Steve whispered and poked each other until one
or both of them shrieked. They then made their faces prim and
sat with their hands folded on their laps, looking like bright-
eyed choirboys.

Griffen hovered near Mrs. Caudwell. "You know you don't
have to say anything, Vivian. In fact, I think you should return
to your hotel and lie down. The stress of the funeral—then
these strangers—"

Mrs. Caudwell's lips curled bravely below the bottom of her
veil. "It's all right, Grif. If I managed to survive everything else,
one more thing isn't going to do me in."

"Great." Victoria accepted a cup of coffee from Max. "Let me
just sketch events for you as I saw them last week. Like everyone
else in Chicago, I read about Dr. Caudwell's murder and saw it
on television. Since I know a number of people attached to
Beth Israel, I may have paid more attention to it than the
average viewer, but I didn't get personally involved until Dr.
Herschel's arrest on Tuesday."

She swallowed some coffee and set the cup on the table next
to her with a small snap. "I have known Dr. Herschel for close
to twenty years. It is inconceivable that she would commit such
a murder, as those who know her well should have realized at
once. I don't fault the police, but others should have known
better. She is hot-tempered. I'm not saying killing is beyond
her—I don't think it's beyond any of us. She might have taken
the statue and smashed Dr. Caudwell's head in, in the heat of
rage. But it beggars belief to think she went home, brooded
over her injustices, packed a dose of prescription tranquilizer,
and headed back to the Gold Coast with murder in mind."

Max felt his cheeks turn hot at her words. He started to
interject a protest but bit it back.

"Dr. Herschel refused to make a statement all week, but this afternoon, when I got back from my travels, she finally agreed to talk to me. Sergeant McGonnigal was with me. She doesn't deny that she returned to Dr. Caudwell's apartment at ten that night—she went back to apologize for her outburst and to try to plead with him to return the statue. He didn't answer when the doorman called up, and on impulse she went around to the back of the building, got in through the service entrance, and waited for some time outside the apartment door. When he neither answered the doorbell nor returned home himself, she finally went away around eleven o'clock. The children, of course, were having a night on the town."

"*She* says," Gioia interjected.

"Agreed." V. I. smiled. "I make no bones about being a partisan. I accept her version. The more so because the only reason she didn't give it a week ago was that she herself was protecting an old friend. She thought perhaps this friend had bestirred himself on her behalf and killed Caudwell to avenge deadly insults against her. It was only when I persuaded her that these suspicions were as unmerited as—well, as accusations against herself—that she agreed to talk."

Max bit his lip and busied himself with getting more coffee for the three women. Victoria waited for him to finish before continuing.

"When I finally got a detailed account of what took place at Caudwell's party, I heard about three people with an ax to grind. One always has to ask, what ax and how big a grindstone? That's what I've spent the weekend finding out. You might as well know that I've been to Little Rock and to Havelock, North Carolina."

Gioia began jingling the coins in his pockets again. Mrs. Caudwell said softly, "Grif, I am feeling a little faint. Perhaps—"

"Home you go, Mom," Steve cried out with alacrity.

"In a few minutes, Mrs. Caudwell," the sergeant said from the doorway. "Get her feet up, Warshawski."

For a moment Max was afraid that Steve or Deborah was going to attack Victoria, but McGonnigal moved over to the widow's chair and the children sat down again. Little drops of sweat dotted Griffen's balding head; Gioia's face had a greenish sheen, foliage on top of his redwood neck.

"The thing that leapt out at me," Victoria continued calmly, as though there had been no interruption, "was Caudwell's remark to Dr. Gioia. The doctor was clearly upset, but people were so focused on Lotty and the statue that they didn't pay any attention to that.

"So I went to Little Rock, Arkansas, on Saturday and found the Paul Nierman whose name Caudwell had mentioned to Gioia. Nierman lived in the same fraternity with Gioia when they were undergraduates together twenty-five years ago. And he took Dr. Gioia's anatomy and physiology exams his junior year when Gioia was in danger of academic probation, so he could stay on the football team.

"Well, that seemed unpleasant, perhaps disgraceful. But there's no question that Gioia did all his own work in medical school, passed his boards, and so on. So I didn't think the board would demand a resignation for this youthful indiscretion. The question was whether Gioia thought they would, and if he would have killed to prevent Caudwell making it public."

She paused, and the immunologist blurted out, "No. No. But Caudwell—Caudwell knew I'd opposed his appointment. He and I—our approaches to medicine were very opposite. And as soon as he said Nierman's name to me, I knew he'd found out and that he'd torment me with it forever. I—I went back to his place Sunday night to have it out with him. I was more determined than Dr. Herschel and got into his unit through the kitchen entrance—he hadn't locked that.

"I went to his study, but he was already dead. I couldn't believe it. It absolutely terrified me. I could see he'd been strangled and—well, it's no secret that I'm strong enough to have done it. I wasn't thinking straight. I just got clean away from there—I think I've been running ever since."

"You!" McGonnigal shouted. "How come we haven't heard about this before?"

"Because you insisted on focusing on Dr. Herschel," V. I. said nastily. "I knew he'd been there because the doorman told me. He would have told you if you'd asked."

"This is terrible," Mrs. Gildersleeve interjected. "I am going to talk to the board tomorrow and demand the resignations of Dr. Gioia and Dr. Herschel."

"Do," Victoria agreed cordially. "Tell them the reason you got to stay for this was because Murray Ryerson at the *Herald-Star* was doing a little checking for me here in Chicago. He found out that part of the reason you were so jealous of Caudwell's collection is that you're living terribly in debt. I won't humiliate you in public by telling people what your money has gone to, but you've had to sell your husband's art collection and you have a third mortgage on your house. A valuable statue with no documented history would have taken care of everything."

Martha Gildersleeve shrank inside her sable. "You don't know anything about this."

"Well, Murray talked to Pablo and Eduardo. . . . Yes, I won't say anything else. So anyway, Murray checked whether Gioia or Mrs. Gildersleeve had the statue. They didn't, so—"

"You've been in my house?" Mrs. Gildersleeve shrieked.

V. I. shook her head. "Not me. Murray Ryerson." She looked apologetically at the sergeant. "I knew you'd never get a warrant for me, since you'd made an arrest. And you'd never have got it in time, anyway."

She looked at her coffee cup, saw it was empty and put it down again. Max took it from the table and filled it for her a third time. His fingertips were itching with nervous irritation; some of the coffee landed on his trouser leg.

"I talked to Murray Saturday night from Little Rock. When he came up empty here, I headed for North Carolina. To Havelock, where Griffen and Lewis Caudwell grew up and where Mrs. Caudwell still lives. And I saw the house where Griffen lives, and talked to the doctor who treats Mrs. Caudwell, and—"

"You really are a pooper snooper, aren't you," Steve said.

"Pooper snooper, pooper snooper," Deborah chanted. "Don't get enough thrills of your own so you have to live on other people's shit."

"Yeah, the neighbors talked to me about you two." Victoria looked at them with contemptuous indulgence. "You've been a two-person wolfpack terrifying most of the people around you since you were three. But the folks in Havelock admired how you always stuck up for your mother. You thought your father got her addicted to tranquilizers and then left her high and dry. So you brought her newest version with you and were all set— you just needed to decide when to give it to him. Dr. Herschel's outburst over the statue played right into your hands. You figured your father had stolen it from your uncle to begin with—why not send it back to him and let Dr. Herschel take the rap?"

"It wasn't like that," Steve said, red spots burning in his cheeks.

"What was it like, son?" McGonnigal had moved next to him.

"Don't talk to them—they're tricking you," Deborah shrieked. "The pooper snooper and her gopher gooper."

"She—Mommy used to love us before Daddy made her take all this shit. Then she went away. We just wanted him to see what it was like. We started putting Xanax in his coffee and stuff—we wanted to see if he'd fuck up during surgery, let his life get ruined. But then he was sleeping there in the study after his stupid-ass party, and we thought we'd just let him sleep through his morning surgery. Sleep forever, you know, it was so easy, we used his own Harvard necktie. I was so fucking sick of hearing 'Early to bed, early to rise' from him. And we sent the statue to Uncle Grif. I suppose the pooper snooper found it there. He can sell it and Mother can be all right again."

"Grandpa stole it from Jews and Daddy stole it from Grif, so we thought it worked out perfectly if we stole it from Daddy," Deborah cried. She leaned her blond head next to her brother's and shrieked with laughter.

V

Max watched the line of Lotty's legs change as she stood on tiptoe to reach a brandy snifter. Short, muscular from years of racing at top speed from one point to the next, maybe they weren't as svelte as the long legs of modern American girls, but he preferred them. He waited until her feet were securely planted before making his announcement.

"The board is bringing in Justin Hardwick for a final interview for chief of staff."

"Max!" She whirled, the Bengal fire sparkling in her eyes. "I know this Hardwick and he is another like Caudwell, looking for cost-cutting and no poverty patients. I won't have it."

"We've got you and Gioia and a dozen others bringing in so many nonpaying patients that we're not going to survive another five years at the present rate. I figure it's a balancing act. We need someone who can see that the hospital survives so that you and Art can practice medicine the way you want to. And when he knows what happened to his predecessor, he'll be very careful not to stir up our resident tigress."

"Max!" She was hurt and astonished at the same time. "Oh. You're joking. I see. It's not very funny to me, you know."

"My dear, we've got to learn to laugh about it—it's the only way we'll ever be able to forgive ourselves for our terrible misjudgments." He stepped over to put an arm around her. "Now where is this remarkable surprise you promised to show me?"

She shot him a look of pure mischief, Lotty on a dare as he first remembered meeting her at eighteen. His hold on her tightened and he followed her to her bedroom. In a glass case in the corner, complete with a humidity-controlled system, stood the Pietro Andromache.

Max looked at the beautiful, anguished face. I understand your sorrows, she seemed to say to him. I understand your grief for your mother, your family, your history, but it's all right to let go of them, to live in the present and hope for the future. It's not a betrayal.

Tears pricked his eyelids, but he demanded, "How did you get this? I was told the police had it under lock and key until lawyers decided on the disposition of Caudwell's estate."

"Victoria," Lotty said shortly. "I told her the problem and she got it for me. On the condition that I not ask how she did it. And Max, you know—*damned* well that it was not Caudwell's to dispose of."

It was Lotty's. Of course it was. Max wondered briefly how Joseph the Second had come by it to begin with. For that matter, what had Lotty's great-great-grandfather done to earn it from the emperor? Max looked into Lotty's tiger eyes and kept such reflections to himself. Instead, he inspected Hector's foot where the filler had been carefully scraped away to reveal the old chip.

BILL PRONZINI

INCIDENT IN A NEIGHBORHOOD TAVERN

Although the private eye has flourished in the novels and short stories of the 1980s, few of today's private eye writers appreciate the need for a good puzzle as much as Bill Pronzini. His Nameless Detective novels and tales are among the best real detective stories being written today. This one brought Pronzini his fifth Edgar nomination from MWA, the first for a Nameless story. It appeared in the third anthology of the Private Eye Writers of America and in Pronzini's own collection of fifty of his short-shorts, Small Felonies (St. Martin's Press).

When the holdup went down I was sitting at the near end of the Foghorn Tavern's scarred mahogany bar talking to the owner, Matt Candiotti.

It was a little before seven of a midweek evening, lull time in working-class neighborhood saloons like this one. Blue-collar locals would jam the place from four until about six-thirty, when the last of them headed home for dinner; the hard-core drinkers wouldn't begin filtering back in until about seven-thirty or eight. Right now there were only two customers, and the jukebox and computer hockey games were quiet. The TV over the back bar was on but with the sound turned down to a tolerable level. One of the customers, a porky guy in his fifties, drinking Anchor Steam out of the bottle, was watching the last of the NBC national news. The other customer, an equally porky and middle-aged female barfly, half in the bag on red wine, was trying to convince him to pay attention to her instead of Tom Brokaw.

I had a draft beer in front of me, but that wasn't the reason I was there. I'd come to ask Candiotti, as I had asked two dozen other merchants here in the Outer Mission, if he could offer any leads on the rash of burglaries that were plaguing small businesses in the neighborhood. The police hadn't come up with anything positive after six weeks, so a couple of the victims had gotten up a fund and hired me to see what I could find out. They'd picked me because I had been born and raised in the Outer Mission, I still had friends and shirttail relatives living here, and I understood the neighborhood a good deal better than any other private detective in San Francisco.

But so far I wasn't having any more luck than the SFPD. None of the merchants I'd spoken with today had given me any new ideas, and Candiotti was proving to be no exception. He stood slicing limes into wedges as we talked. They might have been onions the way his long, mournful face was screwed up, like a man trying to hold back tears. His gray-stubbled jowls wobbled every time he shook his head. He reminded me of a tired old hound, friendly and sad, as if life had dealt him a few kicks but not quite enough to rob him of his good nature.

"Wish I could help," he said. "But, hell, I don't hear nothing. Must be pros from Hunters Point or the Fillmore, hah?"

Hunters Point and the Fillmore were black sections of the city, which was a pretty good indicator of where his head was at. I said, "Some of the others figure it for a local talent."

"Out of this neighborhood, you mean?"

I nodded, drank some of my draft.

"Nah, I doubt it," he said. "Guys that organized, they don't shit where they eat. Too smart, you know?"

"Maybe. Any break-ins or attempted break-ins here?"

"Not so far. I got bars on all the windows, double dead-bolt locks on the storeroom door off the alley. Besides, what's for them to steal besides a few cases of whiskey?"

"You don't keep cash on the premises overnight?"

"Fifty bucks in the till," Candiotto said, "that's all, that's my limit. Everything else goes out of here when I close up, down to the night deposit at the B of A on Mission. My mama didn't raise no airheads." He scraped the lime wedges off his board, into a plastic container, and racked the serrated knife he'd been using. "One thing I did hear," he said. "I heard some of the loot turned up down in San Jose. You know about that?"

"Not much of a lead there. Secondhand dealer named Pitman had a few pieces of stereo equipment stolen from the factory outlet store on Geneva. Said he bought it from a guy at the San Jose flea market, somebody he didn't know, never saw before."

"Yeah, sure," Candiotto said wryly. "What do the cops think?"

"That Pitman bought it off a fence."

"Makes sense. So maybe the boosters are from San Jose, hah?"

"Could be," I said, and that was when the kid walked in.

He brought bad air in with him; I sensed it right away and so did Candiotti. We both glanced at the door when it opened, the way you do, but we didn't look away again once we saw him. He was in his early twenties, dark skinned, dressed in chinos, a cotton windbreaker, sharp-toed shoes polished to a high gloss. But it was his eyes that put the chill on my neck, the sudden clutch of tension down low in my belly. They were bright, jumpy, on the wild side, and in the dim light of the Foghorn's interior, the pupils were so small they seemed nonexistent. He had one hand in his jacket pocket, and I knew it was clamped around a gun even before he took it out and showed it to us.

He came up to the bar a few feet on my left, the gun jabbing the air in front of him. He couldn't hold it steady; it kept jerking up and down, from side to side, as if it had a kind of spasmodic life of its own. Behind me, at the other end of the bar, I heard Anchor Steam suck in his breath, the barfly make a sound like a stifled moan. I eased back a little on the stool, watching the gun and the kid's eyes flick back from Candiotti to me to the two customers and back around again. Candiotti didn't move at all, just stood there staring with his hound's face screwed up in that holding-back-tears way.

"All right all right," the kid said. His voice was high pitched, excited, and there was drool at one corner of his mouth. You couldn't get much more stoned than he was and still function. Coke, crack, speed—maybe a combination. The gun that kept flicking this way and that was a goddamn Saturday night special. "Listen good, man, everybody listen good and I don't want to kill none of you, man, but I will if I got to, you believe it?"

None of us said anything. None of us moved.

The kid had a folded-up paper sack in one pocket; he dragged it out with his free hand, dropped it, broke quickly at the middle to pick it up without lowering his gaze. When he straightened again there was sweat on his forehead, more drool coming out of his mouth. He threw the sack on the bar.

"Put the money in there, Mr. Cyclone Man," he said to Candiotti. "All the money in the register but not the coins; I don't want the fuckin' coins, you hear me?"

Candiotti nodded; reached out slowly, caught up the sack, turned toward the back bar with his shoulders hunched up against his neck. When he punched No Sale on the register, the ringing thump of the cash drawer sliding open seemed overloud in the electric hush. For a few seconds the kid watched him scoop bills into the paper sack; then his eyes and the gun skittered my way again. I had looked into the muzzle of a handgun before and it was the same feeling each time; dull fear, helplessness, a kind of naked vulnerability.

"Your wallet on the bar, man, all your cash." The gun barrel and the wild eyes flicked away again, down the length of the plank, before I could move to comply. "You down there, dude, you and fat mama put your money on the bar. All of it, hurry up."

Each of us did as we were told. While I was getting my wallet out I managed to slide my right foot off the stool, onto the brass rail, and to get my right hand pressed tight against the beveled edge of the bar. If I had to make any sudden moves, I would need the leverage.

Candiotti finished loading the sack, turned from the register. There was a grayish cast to his face now—the wet gray color of fear. The kid said to him, "Pick up their money, put it in the sack with the rest. Come on come on come on!"

Candiotti went to the far end of the plank, scooped up the wallets belonging to Anchor Steam and the woman; then he came back my way, added my wallet to the contents of the paper sack, put the sack down carefully in front of the kid.

"Okay," the kid said, "okay all right." He glanced over his shoulder at the street door, as if he'd heard something there; but it stayed closed. He jerked his head around again. In his sweaty agitation the Saturday night special almost slipped free of his fingers; he fumbled a tighter grip on it, and when it didn't go off I let the breath I had been holding come out thin and slow between my teeth. The muscles in my shoulders and back were drawn so tight I was afraid they might cramp.

The kid reached out for the sack, dragged it in against his body. But he made no move to leave with it. Instead he said, "Now we go get the big pile, man."

Candiotti opened his mouth, closed it again. His eyes were almost as big and starey as the kid's.

"Come on, Mr. Cyclone Man, the safe, the safe in your office. We goin' back there *now.*"

"No money in that safe," Candiotti said in a thin, scratchy voice. "Nothing valuable."

"Oh man I'll kill you man I'll blow your fuckin' head off! I ain't playin' no games I want that money!"

He took two steps forward, jabbing with the gun up close to Candiotti's gray face. Candiotti backed off a step, brought his hands up, took a tremulous breath.

"All right," he said, "but I got to get the key to the office. It's in the register."

"Hurry up hurry up!"

Candiotti turned back to the register, rang it open, rummaged inside with his left hand. But with his right hand, shielded from the kid by his body, he eased up the top on a large wooden cigar box adjacent. The hand disappeared inside; came out again with metal in it, glinting in the back bar lights. I saw it and I wanted to yell at him, but it wouldn't have done any good, would only have warned the kid . . . and he was already turning with it, bringing it up with both hands now—the damn gun of his own he'd had hidden inside the cigar box. There was no time for me to do anything but shove away from the bar and sideways off the stool just as Candiotti opened fire.

The state he was in, the kid didn't realize what was happening until it was too late for him to react; he never even got a shot off. Candiotti's first slug knocked him halfway around, and one of the three others that followed it opened up his face like a piece of ripe fruit smacked by a hammer. He was dead before his body, driven backward, slammed into the cigarette machine near the door, slid down it to the floor.

The half-drunk woman was yelling in broken shrieks, as if she couldn't get enough air for a sustained scream. When I came up out of my crouch I saw that Anchor Steam had hold of her, clinging to her as much for support as in an effort to calm her down. Candiotti stood flat-footed, his arms down at his sides, the gun out of sight below the bar, staring at the bloody remains of the kid as if he couldn't believe what he was seeing, couldn't believe what he'd done.

Some of the tension in me eased as I went to the door, found the lock on its security gate, fastened it before anybody could come in off the street. The Saturday night special was still clutched in the kid's hand; I bent, pulled it free with my thumb, and forefinger, broke the cylinder. It was loaded, all right—five cartridges. I dropped it into my jacket pocket, thought about checking the kid's clothing for identification, didn't do it. It wasn't any of my business, now, who he'd been. And I did not want to touch him or any part of him. There was a queasiness in my stomach, a fluttery weakness behind my knees—the same delayed reaction I always had to violence and death—and touching him would only make it worse.

To keep from looking at the red ruin of the kid's face, I pivoted back to the bar. Candiotti hadn't moved. Anchor Steam had gotten the woman to stop screeching and had coaxed her over to one of the handful of tables near the jukebox; now she was sobbing, "I've got to go home, I'm gonna be sick if I don't go home." But she didn't make any move to get up and neither did Anchor Steam.

I walked over near Candiotti, pushed hard words at him in an undertone. "That was a damn fool thing to do. You could have got us all killed."

"I know," he said. "I know."

"Why'd you do it?"

"I thought . . . hell, you saw the way he was waving that piece of his. . . ."

"Yeah," I said. "Call the police. Nine-eleven."

"Nine-eleven. Okay."

"Put that gun of yours down first. On the bar."

He did that. There was a phone on the back bar; he went away to it in shaky strides. While he was talking to the Emergency operator I picked up his weapon, saw that it was a .32 Charter Arms revolver. I held it in my hand until Candiotti finished with the call, set it down again as he came back to where I stood.

"They'll have somebody here in five minutes," he said.

I said, "You know that kid?"

"Christ, no."

"Ever see him before? Here or anywhere else?"

"No."

"So how did he know about your safe?"

Candiotti blinked at me. "What?"

"The safe in your office. Street kid like that . . . how'd he know about it?"

"How should I know? What difference does it make?"

"He seemed to think you keep big money in that safe."

"Well, I don't. There's nothing in it."

"That's right, you told me you don't keep more than fifty bucks on the premises overnight. In the till."

"Yeah."

"Then why have you got a safe, if it's empty?"

Candiotti's eyes narrowed. "I used to keep my receipts in it, all right? Before all these burglaries started. Then I figured I'd be smarter to take the money to the bank every night."

"Sure, that explains it," I said. "Still, a kid like that, looking for a big score to feed his habit, he wasn't just after what was in the till and our wallets. No, it was as if he'd gotten wind of a heavy stash—a grand or more."

Nothing from Candiotti.

I watched him for a time. Then I said, "Big risk you took, using that .32 of yours. How come you didn't make your play the first time you went to the register? How come you waited until the kid mentioned your office safe?"

"I didn't like the way he was acting, like he might start shooting any second. I figured it was our only chance. Listen, what're you getting at, hah?"

"Another funny thing," I said, "is the way he called you 'Mr. Cyclone Man.' Now why would a hopped-up kid use a term like that to a bar owner he didn't know?"

"How the hell should I know?"

"Cyclone," I said. "What's a cyclone but a big destructive wind? Only one other thing I can think of."

"Yeah? What's that?"

"A fence. A cyclone fence."

Candiotti made a fidgety movement. Some of the wet gray pallor was beginning to spread across his cheeks again, like a fungus.

I said, "And a fence is somebody who receives and distributes stolen goods. A Mr. Fence Man. But then you know that, don't you, Candiotti? We were talking about that kind of fence before the kid came in . . . how Pitman, down in San Jose, bought some hot stereo equipment off of one. That fence could just as easily be operating here in San Francisco, though. Right here in this neighborhood, in fact. Hell, suppose the stuff taken in all those burglaries never left the neighborhood. Suppose it was brought to a place nearby and stored until it could be trucked out to other cities—a tavern storeroom, for instance. Might even be some of it is *still* in that storeroom. And the money he got for the rest he'd keep locked up in his safe, right? Who'd figure it? Except maybe a poor junkie who picked up a whisper on the street somewhere—"

Candiotti made a sudden grab for the .32, caught it up, backed up a step with it leveled at my chest. "You smart son of a bitch," he said. "I ought to kill you, too."

"In front of witnesses? With the police due any minute?"

He glanced over at the two customers. The woman was still sobbing, lost in a bleak outpouring of self-pity; but Anchor Steam was staring our way, and from the expression on his face he'd heard every word of my exchange with Candiotti

"There's still enough time for me to get clear," Candiotti said grimly. He was talking to himself, not to me. Sweat had plastered his lank hair to his forehead; the revolver was not quite steady in his hand. "Lock you up in my office, you and those two back there . . ."

"I don't think so," I said.

"Goddamn you, you think I won't use this gun again?"

"I *know* you won't use it. I emptied out the last two cartridges while you were on the phone."

I took the two shells out of my left-hand jacket pocket and held them up where he could see them. At the same time I got the kid's Saturday night special out of the other pocket, held it loosely pointed in his direction. "You want to put your piece down now, Candiotti? You're not going anywhere, not for a long time."

He put it down—dropped it clattering onto the bartop. And as he did his sad hound's face screwed up again, only this time he didn't even try to keep the wetness from leaking out of his eyes. He was leaning against the bar, crying like the woman, submerged in his own outpouring of self-pity, when the cops showed up a little while later.

THE YEARBOOK OF THE MYSTERY & SUSPENSE STORY

THE YEARS BEST
MYSTERY & SUSPENSE NOVELS

Robert Barnard, *At Death's Door* (Scribners)
Michael Collins, *Red Rosa* (Donald I. Fine)
Len Deighton, *Spy Hook* (Knopf)
Don DeLillo, *Libra* (Viking)
Pete Dexter, *Paris Trout* (Random House)
Antonia Fraser, *Your Royal Hostage* (Antheneum)
Elizabeth George, *A Great Deliverance* (Bantam)
Ellen Godfrey, *Murder Behind Locked Doors* (St. Martin's)
Sue Grafton, *"E" Is for Evidence* (Holt)
Graham Greene, *The Captain and the Enemy* (Viking)
Thomas Harris, *The Silence of the Lambs* (St. Martin's)
Jeremiah Healy, *Swan Dive* (Harper & Row)
Tony Hillerman, *A Thief of Time* (Harper & Row)
Elmore Leonard, *Freaky Deaky* (Arbor House/Morrow)
John Lutz, *Kiss* (Holt)
Ed McBain, *The House That Jack Built* (Holt)
Douglas McBriarty, *Snowshot* (Walker)
John Mortimer, *Summer's Lease* (Viking)
Marcia Muller, *Eye of the Storm* (Mysterious Press)
Sara Paretsky, *Blood Shot* (Delacorte)
Bill Pronzini, *Shackles* (St. Martin's)
Edward Stewart, *Privileged Lives* (Delacorte)
Peter Straub, *Koko* (Dutton)
Andrew Vachss, *Blue Belle* (Knopf)
Judith Van Gieson, *North of the Border* (Walker)
Anne Wingate, *Death by Deception* (Walker)

BIBLIOGRAPHY

I. Collections

Abbreviations:
AHMM—*Alfred Hitchcock's Mystery Magazine*
EQMM—*Ellery Queen's Mystery Magazine*

(Correction: On last year's list I identified "Justin Case" as a pseudonym of Robert Leslie Bellem, as stated in a standard mystery reference book. Douglas G. Greene and Bill Pronzini have informed me that "Justin Case" was most often a pseudonym of Hugh B. Cave.)

1. Alcott, Louisa May. *A Double Life: Newly Discovered Thrillers of Louisa May Alcott.* Boston: Little Brown. Five novelettes, mainly criminous, in a third collection of unknown Alcott thrillers. Edited by Madeleine B. Stern, Joel Myerson, and Daniel Shealy.
2. Archer, Jeffrey. *A Twist in the Tail.* New York: Simon & Schuster. Twelve stories, some criminous.
3. Braun, Lilian Jackson. *The Cat Who Had 14 Tales.* New York: Jove Books. Fourteen stories about cats, some fantasy but including five stories from *EQMM.*
4. Brown, Frederic. *Nightmare in Darkness.* Miami Beach: Dennis McMillan Publications. Nine stories from the pulps, plus the original ending of Brown's novel *The Screaming Mimi.*
5. _____. *Selling Death Short.* Missoula, Montana: Dennis McMillan Publications. Ten stories from the pulps, 1940–55, introduced by Francis M. Nevins, Jr.
6. _____. *Three-Corpse Parlay.* Missoula, Montana: Dennis McMillan Publications. Thirteen stories from the pulps, introduced by Max Allan Collins.
7. _____. *Who Was That Blonde I Saw You Kill Last Night?* Miami Beach: Dennis McMillan Publications. Ten stories from the pulps.

8. Corris, Peter. *Heroin Annie and Other Cliff Hardy Stories.* New York: Fawcett. First published in Australia in 1984.

9. ———. *The Big Drop.* New York: Fawcett. More Cliff Hardy stories.

10. Crowley, Aleister. *The Scrutinies of Simon Iff.* Chicago: Teitan Press. Six stories about a mystic detective, first published as by "Edward Kelly" in *The International,* 1917–18.

11. Daly, Carroll John. *The Adventures of Race Williams.* New York: Mysterious Press. Five novelettes from *Dime Detective,* 1935–36. Introduction by Robert Weinberg.

12. ———. *The Adventures of Satan Hall.* New York: Mysterious Press. Four novelettes from *Detective Fiction Weekly,* 1932–34. Introduction by Robert Weinberg.

13. Estleman, Loren D. *General Murders.* Boston: Houghton Mifflin. Ten stories from various sources about Detroit private eye Amos Walker.

14. Gardner, Martin. *The No-Sided Professor.* Buffalo: Prometheus Books. Twenty-eight stories, some fantasy. Includes six detective stories, 1987.

15. Gilbert, Michael. *Young Petrella.* New York: Harper & Row. Sixteen stories about the early cases of Detective Inspector Petrella, some from prior Gilbert collections.

16. Hanson, Joseph. *Bohannon's Book.* Woodstock, VT: Foul Play/Countryman Press. Five novelettes about a former California sheriff, from *EQMM* and *AHMM.*

17. Highsmith, Patricia. *Mermaids on the Golf Course.* New York: Penzler Books. Eleven stories, some criminous. First published in England in 1985.

18. ———. *The Black House.* New York: Penzler Books. Eleven stories, some fantasy. First published in England in 1981.

19. Lovisi, Gary. *The Nemesis.* Brooklyn, NY (P.O. Box 28-0209): Gryphon Publications. Three new short stories in the pulp tradition, about a modern masked avenger.

20. Lutz, John. *Better Mousetraps: The Best Mystery Stories of John Lutz.* New York: St. Martin's Press. Thirty-five stories from *EQMM, AHMM,* and other sources. Introduction and checklist by Francis M. Nevins, Jr.

21. Martin, Janet Letnes. *Shirley Holmquist & Aunt Wilma:*

Whodunit? Hastings, MN: Martin House Publications. Fourteen short-short Sherlockian parodies, set against a background of Scandinavian life in Minnesota.

22. Nebel, Frederick. *The Adventures of Cardigan.* New York: Mysterious Press. Six novelettes from *Dime Detective,* 1933–35. Introduction by Robert Weinberg.

23. Peters, Ellis. *A Rare Benedictine.* London: Headline. Three novelettes about Brother Cadfael, from *Winter's Crimes.*

24. Pronzini, Bill. *Small Felonies.* New York: St. Martin's Press. Fifty short-short stories, eight of them new.

25. Rendell, Ruth. *Collected Stories.* New York: Pantheon. Thirty-eight stories comprising all of her short fiction through 1986, previously collected in four separate volumes.

26. Sanders, Lawrence. *Timothy's Game.* New York: Putnam. Three novelettes about Wall Street investigator Timothy Cone.

27. Searls, Hank. *The Adventures of Mike Blair.* New York: Mysterious Press. Seven stories and novelettes from *Dime Detective* and other pulps, 1949–50. Introduction by the author, afterword by Robert Weinberg.

28. Thompson, Jim. *Fireworks: The Lost Writings of Jim Thompson.* New York: Donald I. Fine. Thirty-four short essays and tales, including seven stories from mystery magazines. Edited by Robert Polito and Michael McCauley.

29. Treat, Lawrence. *Crime and Puzzlement 3.* Boston: David R. Godine. Twenty-four brief picture mysteries.

30. Woolrich, Cornell. *Rear Window and Other Stories.* London: Simon & Schuster. Thirteen stories and novelettes. Introduction by Richard Rayner.

II. Anthologies

1. Adrian, Jack, ed. *Crime at Christmas.* Wellingborough, England: Equation/Thorsons. Eighteen stories, two new.

2. Asimov, Isaac, Martin H. Greenberg, and Charles G. Waugh, eds. *The Best Crime Stories of the 19th Century.* New York: Dembner Books. Fifteen stories, 1834–99.

3. Bruccoli, Matthew J., and Richard Layman, eds. *A Matter of Crime, Vol. 3.* San Diego: Harcourt Brace Jovanovich. Fourteen new stories plus an interview with George V. Higgins.

4. ———. *A Matter of Crime, Vol. 4.* San Diego: Harcourt Brace Jovanovich. Ten new stories plus an interview with Andrew Vachss and an excerpt from his unpublished first novel. The final volume of an anthology series.

5. Godfrey, Thomas, ed. *English Country House Murders.* New York: Mysterious Press. Twenty-two stories, mainly British.

6. ———. *Murder at the Opera.* London: Michael O'Mara Books. Eleven stories from various sources.

7. Gorman, Ed, ed. *The Second Black Lizard Anthology of Crime Fiction.* Berkeley, CA: Black Lizard/Creative Arts. Thirty-eight stories, three new, plus a novel by Peter Rabe.

8. *Great Murder Mysteries.* London: Octopus. Sixty-six stories, mainly British, some fantasy. No editor credited. (U.S. edition distributed by Chartwell Books, Secaucus, NJ.)

9. Greenberg, Martin H., ed. *Masterpieces of Mystery and Suspense.* New York: St. Martin's Press. Forty stories by well-known writers, from a variety of sources. (Earlier edition distributed by Doubleday Book Clubs, 1988.)

10. ———, and Francis M. Nevins, Jr., eds. *Mr. President, Private Eye.* Twelve new stories in which former American presidents become involved in crimes.

11. ———, Charles G. Waugh, and Frank D. McSherry, Jr., eds. *Red Jack.* New York: DAW Books. Eight stories, some fantasy, about Jack the Ripper, plus a novel by Ellery Queen, *A Study in Terror.*

12. Greenberg, Rosalind M., Martin Harry Greenberg, and Charles G. Waugh, eds. *14 Vicious Valentines.* New York: Avon Books. Fourteen Valentine's Day stories, twelve new, including a few fantasies.

13. Hale, Hilary, ed. *Winter's Crimes 20.* London: Macmillan. Nine new stories in an annual anthology series, one previously published in America in *EQMM.*

14. Harris, Herbert, ed. *John Creasey's Crime Collection 1988.* London: Gollancz. Fifteen stories, four new, in the annual anthology from the Crime Writers' Association.

15. Hoch, Edward D., ed. *The Year's Best Mystery and Suspense Stories 1988.* New York: Walker. Fourteen of the best stories published during 1987.

16. Jaffery, Sheldon, ed. *Selected Tales of Grim and Grue from the Horror Pulps.* Bowling Green, OH: Bowling Green State University Popular Press. Eight stories and novelettes from the "weird menace" pulps of the 1930s, with an introduction and index of ten such magazines by Robert Kenneth Jones.

17. Jones, Richard Glyn, ed. *Solved!* New York: Peter Bedrick. A dozen well-known mystery writers offer their solutions to classic true crimes.

18. Jordan, Cathleen, ed. *Alfred Hitchcock's Most Wanted: The First Lineup.* New York: Davis Publications. Twenty-one of the best stories from *AHMM,* 1980–85.

19. _____. *Alfred Hitchcock's Shrouds and Pockets.* New York: Davis Publications. Twenty-nine stories from *AHMM.*

20. _____, and Cynthia Manson, eds. *Tales from Alfred Hitchcock's Mystery Magazine.* New York: Morrow. Twenty stories from *AHMM,* 1982–88, packaged for young adult readers.

21. Muller, Marcia, Bill Pronzini, and Martin H. Greenberg, eds. *Lady on the Case.* New York: Bonanza Books. Twenty-one stories, one new, plus a novel by Stuart Palmer, all featuring women detectives.

22. Preiss, Byron, ed. *Raymond Chandler's Philip Marlowe.* New York: Knopf. Twenty-three new stories by leading mystery writers, using Chandler's famed private eye as the protagonist, plus a story by Chandler himself. Introduction by Frank MacShane.

23. Pronzini, Bill, and Martin H. Greenberg, eds. *Baker's Dozen: 13 Short Detective Novels.* New York: Bonanza Books. Thirteen novelettes and short novels, 1936–83.

24. _____. *Cloak and Dagger.* New York: Avenel Books. Thirty-five espionage stories from the past hundred years.

25. _____. *Criminal Elements.* New York: Ivy Books/Ballantine. Thirteen stories, one new, in the third volume of an anthology series.

26. _____. *Homicidal Acts.* New York: Ivy Books/ Ballantine.

Fourteen stories in the fourth volume of an anthology series.

27. _____. *The Mammoth Book of Private Eye Stories.* New York: Carroll & Graf. Twenty-six stories and novelettes from various sources.

28. Randisi, Robert J., ed. *An Eye for Justice.* New York: Mysterious Press. Thirteen new stories in the third anthology from the Private Eye Writers of America.

29. Sullivan, Eleanor, ed. *Ellery Queen's Media Favorites.* New York: Davis Publications. Nineteen stories, mainly from *EQMM*, which have been adapted for films, television, or radio.

30. _____. *Ellery Queen's More Media Favorites.* New York: Davis Publications. Fifteen stories and two brief plays, mainly from *EQMM*, which have been adapted to other media.

31. van de Wetering, Janwillem, ed. *Distant Danger.* New York: Wynwood Press. Sixteen stories, two new, in the annual anthology from the Mystery Writers of America.

32. Waugh, Carol-Lynn Rossel, Martin Harry Greenberg, and Isaac Asimov, eds. *The Sport of Crime.* New York: Lynx Books. Nineteen stories about crime and sports.

33. Waugh, Carol-Lynn Rossel, Martin H. Greenberg, and Frank D. McSherry, eds. *Murder and Mystery in Chicago.* New York: Dembner Books. Eleven stories, 1938–86, from various sources.

34. Zahava, Irene, ed. *The Womansleuth Anthology: Contemporary Mystery Stories by Women.* Freedom, CA: The Crossing Press. Twelve new stories with women sleuths.

III. Nonfiction

1. Bargainner, Earl F., ed. *Comic Crime.* Bowling Green, OH: Bowling Green State University Popular Press. Eleven new essays on humor in the mystery.

2. Benson, Raymond. *The James Bond Bedside Companion.* New York: Dodd Mead. An updated edition of a comprehensive guide first published in 1984.

3. Browne, Ray B. *The Spirit of Australia: The Crime Fiction of Arthur W. Upfield.* Bowling Green, OH: Bowling Green State University Popular Press. A detailed study of Upfield's Inspector Napoleon Bonaparte novels and his other fiction.
4. Cawelti, John G., and Bruce A. Rosenberg. *The Spy Story.* Chicago: University of Chicago Press. A study of leading spy novelists.
5. Collins, Max Allen, and John Javna. *The Best of Crime and Detective TV.* New York: Harmony. A guide to the best mystery TV shows, as chosen by top mystery writers.
6. Cook, Michael L., and Stephen T. Miller. *Mystery, Detective and Espionage Fiction: A Checklist of Fiction in U.S. Pulp Magazines, 1915–1974.* New York: Garland. A two-volume listing of the contents of 360 pulp titles, covering nearly 9,000 issues and over 58,000 stories. The second volume is an author index.
7. Dale, Alzina Stone, and Barbara Sloan Hendershott. *Mystery Reader's Walking Guide: England.* Lincolnwood, IL: Passport Books. Fourteen walking tours of southern England, outside London, with mention of several hundred mystery novels and short stories set in the region.
8. Goulart, Ron. *The Dime Detective.* New York: Mysterious Press. A history of the detective pulp magazines.
9. Horning, Jane. *The Mystery Lover's Book of Quotations.* New York: Mysterious Press. More than 1,600 quotations from the world's great crime writers, indexed by title, author, and subject.
10. Hubin, Allen J. *1981–1985 Supplement to Crime Fiction, 1789–1980.* New York: Garland. A comprehensive bibliography continuing Hubin's landmark work, with additional listings covering film adaptations.
11. Klein, Kathleen Gregory. *The Woman Detective: Gender & Genre.* Urbana, IL: University of Illinois Press. A study of female detectives in fiction, from 1864 to the present.
12. McArdle, Phil and Karen. *Fatal Fascination.* Boston: Houghton Mifflin. A study of police work in real life and as portrayed in fiction.
13. Nevins, Francis M., Jr. *Cornell Woolrich: First You Dream, Then You Die.* New York: Mysterious Press. A massive

biography and critical study of all Woolrich's novels and stories, with complete checklists. Includes checklists of all movie, TV, and radio adaptations.

14. Nichols, Victoria, and Susan Thompson. *Silk Stalkings: When Women Write of Murder.* Berkeley, CA: Black Lizard/ Creative Arts. A survey of series characters created by women authors, with checklists.

15. Oleksiw, Susan. *A Reader's Guide to the Classic British Mystery.* Boston: G.K. Hall. An annotated checklist of more than 1,440 novels by 121 authors, with additional lists of series characters, occupations, settings, etc.

16. O'Prey, Paul. *A Reader's Guide to Graham Greene.* New York: Thames & Hudson. A study of Greene's novels and major short stories.

17. Rader, Barbara A., and Howard G. Zettler, eds. *The Sleuth and the Scholar: Origins, Evolution, and Current Trends in Detective Fiction.* Westport, CT: Greenwood Press. Ten new essays on detective fiction. Foreword by Robin W. Winks.

18. Reddy, Maureen T. *Sisters in Crime.* New York: Ungar/ Continuum. A study of feminism and the detective novel.

19. Sampson, Robert. *Spider.* Bowling Green, OH: Bowling Green State University Popular Press. Detailed study of a pulp magazine character popular 1933–43, with a checklist of all fiction in *The Spider* magazine.

20. ———. *Yesterday's Faces, Volume 4: The Solvers.* Bowling Green, OH: Bowling Green State University Popular Press. A study of series detectives in the pulp magazines.

21. Shine, Walter and Jean. *A MacDonald Potpourri.* Gainesville, FL: University of Florida Libraries. Checklists and assorted bibliographic facts about all of John D. MacDonald's books.

22. Tuska, Jon. *In Manors and Alleys: A Casebook on the American Detective Film.* Westport, CT: Greenwood Press. A study of the transformation of popular fictional detectives to the screen.

23. Winks, Robin W., ed. *Detective Fiction: A Collection of Critical Essays.* Woodstock, VT: Foul Play/Countryman. Re-

vised and expanded edition of a book first published in 1980.

24. Woeller, Waltraud, and Bruce Cassiday. *The Literature of Crime and Detection.* New York: Ungar. An illustrated history from antiquity to the present, enlarged and adapted from an earlier edition published in Germany in 1984.

AWARDS

Mystery Writers of America

Best novel: Stuart M. Kaminsky, *A Cold Red Sunrise* (Scribners)

Best first novel: David Stout, *Carolina Skeleton* (Mysterious Press)

Best original paperback: Timothy Findley, *The Telling of Lies* (Dell)

Best fact crime: Harry N. MacLean, *In Broad Daylight* (Harper & Row)

Best critical/biographical work: Francis M. Nevins, Jr.: *Cornell Woolrich: First You Dream, Then You Die* (Mysterious Press)

Best young adult novel: Sonia Levitin, *Incident at Loring Groves* (Dial)

Best juvenile: Willo Davis Roberts, *Megan's Island* (Atheneum)

Best short story: Bill Crenshaw, "Flicks" (*Alfred Hitchcock's Mystery Magazine*)

Best episode in a TV series: Gary Hopkins, "The Devil's Foot" (*Mystery! The Return of Sherlock Holmes*)

Best television feature: David J. Kinghorn, "Man Against the Mob" (NBC)

Best motion picture: *The Thin Blue Line* (Miramax)

Grandmaster: Hillary Waugh

Ellery Queen Award: Richard Levinson and William Link

Special Edgar: Joan Kahn

Special Raven: *Sheer Madness* (drama)

Special Raven: Bouchercon Mystery Conventions

Robert L. Fish Memorial Award: Linda O. Johnston, "Different Drummers" (*Ellery Queen's Mystery Magazine*)

Crime Writers Association (London)

Gold Dagger: Michael Dibdin, *Ratking* (Faber; U.S. edition: Bantam)

Silver Dagger: Sara Paretsky, *Toxic Shock* (Gollancz; U.S. edition: *Blood Shot,* Delacorte)

John Creasey Memorial Award: Janet Neel, *Death's Bright Angel* (Constable)

Gold Dagger for Nonfiction: Bernard Wasserstein, *The Secret Lives of Trebitch Lincoln* (Yale University Press)

Punch Prize for Funniest Crime Novel: Nancy Livingston, *Death in a Distant Land* (Gollancz)

Ellery Queen's Mystery Magazine Readers Award

Clark Howard, "The Dakar Run" (*EQMM*, August)

Private Eye Writers of America (for 1987)

Best novel: Ben Schutz, *A Tax in Blood* (Tor)

Best first novel: Michael Allegretto, *Death on the Rocks* (Scribners)

Best paperback novel: L. J. Washburn, *Wild Night* (Tor)

Best short story: Ed Gorman, "Turn Away" (*Black Lizard Anthology of Crime Fiction*)

Life achievement award: Robert Wade

Life achievement award: Dennis Lynds

Anthony Awards (for 1987)

Best novel: Tony Hillerman, *Skinwalkers* (Harper & Row)

Best first novel: Gillian Roberts, *Caught Dead in Philadelphia* (Scribners)

Best paperback original: Robert Crais, *The Monkey's Raincoat* (Bantam)

Best short story: Robert Barnard, "Breakfast Television" (*Ellery Queen's Mystery Magazine*)

Best movie: *The Big Easy*

Best television series: *Mystery!* (PBS)

NECROLOGY

1. Norma Ainsworth (?–1987). Author and editor of juvenile mysteries.
2. John Ball (1911–1988). Well-known author of the Virgil Tibbs books and other mysteries, beginning with his Edgar-winning first novel *In the Heat of the Night* (1965).
3. John Bingham (1908–1988). Pseudonym of Michael Ward, British author of seventeen suspense novels, notably *My Name Is Michael Sibley* (1952) and *The Tender Poisoner* [British title: *Five Roundabouts to Heaven* (1953)].
4. Frank Bonham (1914–1988). Western writer who authored three paperback mysteries in the early 1960s.
5. Christianna Brand (1907–1988). Well-known British author of some twenty novels and short story collections. Best remembered for her seven novels about Inspector Cockrill, including the classic *Green for Danger* (1944).
6. Michael L. Cook (?–1988). Mystery fan and author/compiler of *Mystery, Detective and Espionage Magazines* (1983), *Monthly Murders* (1982), a checklist of fiction in digest-size magazines, and *Mystery, Detective and Espionage Fiction* (1988), a checklist of fiction in pulp magazines.
7. William R. Cox (1901–1988). Western and mystery writer, author of nine paperback mysteries, 1954–73, notably *Death on Location* (1962).
8. Dr. Theodore S. Drachman (1904–1988). Author of four medical mysteries beginning with *Cry Plague!* (1953).
9. Randall Garrett (1927–1987). Well-known science fiction writer, author of the "Lord Darcy" mysteries set in an alternate universe.
10. Noel B. Gerson (1913–1988). Author of nine crime-suspense novels, some published as by "Samuel Edwards" and "Leon Phillips," as well as numerous western and historical novels.
11. Geoffrey Household (1900–1988). Well-known British author of more than twenty suspense and intrigue novels,

notably *Rogue Male* (1939), *A Rough Shoot* (1951), and *Watcher in the Shadows* (1960).

12. Veronica Parker Johns (1907–1988). Author of five mystery novels, notably *Murder by the Day* (1953), and eleven short stories.

13. Lane Kauffmann (1921–1988). Author of two suspense novels, *The Perfectionist* (1954) and *Waldo* (1960).

14. Louis L'Amour (1908–1988). Famed western writer. Some of his early pulp detective stories (1947–1952) were collected in *The Hills of Homicide* (1983).

15. Elizabeth Linington (1921–1988). Popular author under her own name, and as "Dell Shannon," "Leslie Egan," and "Anne Blaisdell," of some one hundred crime novels, mainly police procedurals. Her most famous series, under the Shannon name, featured Lt. Luis Mendoza of the Los Angeles Police Department.

16. Margerie Bonner Lowry (1905?–1988). Widow of writer Malcolm Lowry, she published two mystery novels—*The Shapes That Creep* and *The Last Twist of the Knife*—under her maiden name of Bonner in 1946.

17. Edward Mathis (1927–1988). Author of five novels, mainly about detective Dan Roman, starting with *From a High Place* (1985).

18. James McConnell (1915–1988). British author of some twenty-five suspense novels as "Douglas Rutherford," notably *Flight into Peril* (1952), plus two novels coauthored with Francis Durbridge as "Paul Temple."

19. Catherine Lucile Moore (1911–1987). As C. L. Moore this well-known science fiction writer authored a future mystery novel, *Doomsday Morning* (1957) and two short stories in *AHMM* and *The Man from U.N.C.L.E. Magazine.*

20. David Atlee Phillips (1922–1988). Retired CIA agent who authored a single espionage novel, *The Carlos Contract* (1978).

21. E. Hoffmann Price (1898–1988). Fantasy and adventure writer who authored a single hardboiled detective novel, *The Case of the Cancelled Redhead* (ca. 1952) under the pseudonym "Hamlin Daly."

22. Jerome Prince (1907–1988). Former Dean of Brooklyn

Law School; coauthor with his brother, Dr. Harold Prince, of several short stories, mainly in *EQMM*, 1944–1950.

23. Joel Townsley Rogers (1896–1987?). Pulp writer and novelist best known for the classic *The Red Right Hand* (1945).

24. Flora Rheta Schreiber (1918–1988). Author of the fact crime book, *The Shoemaker*.

25. Terrence L. Smith (1942–1988). Author of eight mystery novels starting with *The Thief Who Came to Dinner* (1971), some under the pseudonym of "Philips Lore." Son of the late mystery writer Charles Merrill Smith.

26. Bryce Walton (1918–1988). Author of more than a hundred short stories and novelettes, which appeared in *Black Mask*, *EQMM*, *AHMM*, *Manhunt*, *Mike Shayne*, and other publications.

27. Charles Willeford (1919–1988). Author of four novels about Miami detective sergeant Hoke Moseley, starting with *Miami Blues* (1984). Also published an earlier crime novel as "Will Charles."

HONOR ROLL

Allyn, Doug, "Bloodlines," *AHMM,* February

———, "Déjà Vu," *AHMM,* June

———, "Lancaster's Ghost," *AHMM,* mid-December

Banse, Timothy, "The Dreadful Lemon Pie," *The Second Black Lizard Anthology of Crime Fiction*

Bendel, Stephanie Kay, "The Woman in the Shadows," *Distant Danger*

Beres, Michael, "The Plant Lady," *EQMM,* January

Brett, Simon, "Stardust Kill," *Raymond Chandler's Philip Marlowe.*

Byrd, Elizabeth, "Prodigal Grandson," *EQMM,* August

Chan, C.M., "The Dressing Table Murder," *AHMM,* October

Church, James Cabell, "Road Kill," *A Matter of Crime #3*

Clayton, Deborah Hillyard, "The Move," *EQMM,* mid-December

Collins, Lorraine, "The Nature of the Beast," *EQMM,* October

*Collins, Michael, "Crime and Punishment," *A Matter of Crime #3*

Crais, Robert, "The Man Who Knew Dick Bong," *Raymond Chandler's Philip Marlowe*

Crawford, Dan, "A Double Run in Clubs," *EQMM,* March

*Crenshaw, Bill, "Flicks," *AHMM,* August

Dearmore, Ellen, "The Adventure of the Perpetual Husbands," *The Womansleuth Anthology*

Doorley, Lawrence, "Mrs. Ralston's Old Flame, a Yale Man," *AHMM,* June

*Estleman, Loren D., "The Crooked Way," *A Matter of Crime #3*

*Gorman, Edward, "The Reason Why," *Criminal Elements*

Grafton, Sue, "Non Sung Smoke," *An Eye For Justice*

Hoch, Edward D., "The Theft of the Faded Flag," *EQMM,* September

———, "The Problem of the Black Roadster," *EQMM,* November

Starred stories are included in this volume. All dates are 1988.

*_____, "The Spy and the Guy Fawkes Bombing," *EQMM*, December

Holding, James G., "Exit the Dragon," *AHMM*, May

Howard, Clark, "The Color of Death," *EQMM*, June

*_____, "The Dakar Run," *EQMM*, August

_____, "Lie Down with the Lamb," *A Matter of Crime #4*

*Johnston, Linda O., "Different Drummers," *EQMM*, July

Kaminsky, Stuart M., "Bitter Lemons," *Raymond Chandler's Philip Marlowe*

Livingston, B., "Thou Shalt Not," *A Matter of Crime #3*

Lovesey, Peter, "The Pomeranian Poisoning," *EQMM*, August

*_____, "The Wasp," *EQMM*, November

*Martin, Carl, "Fatherly Love," *EQMM*, July

_____, "Found Money," *EQMM*, December

Montserrat, Maria de, "The Sunday Bird," *EQMM*, August

Nolan, William F., "The Cure," *The Horror Show*, Spring

Obermayr, Erich, "A Matter of Blood and Wax," *AHMM*, February

O'Neil, Dennis, "Margaret You Mourn For," *EQMM*, November

*O'Neill, Judith, "Bridey's Caller," *AHMM*, May

*Paretsky, Sara, "The Case of the Peitro Andromache," *AHMM*, December

Powell, James, "The Cerebus Emerald," *EQMM*, October

*Pronzini, Bill, "Incident in a Neighborhood Tavern," *An Eye for Justice*

_____, "Something Wrong," *Small Felonies*

Reasoner, James M., "In the Blood," *A Matter of Crime #3*

Russell, Lee, "The Man at the Back of the Bus," *AHMM*, December

Russell, Martin, "The Lesson," *EQMM*, May

Sheffield, Charles, "The Heart of Ahura Mazda," *AHMM*, November

Sorrels, Roy, "Message for Dr. Mattie," *Woman's World*, April 26

Stevens, B.K., "True Detective," *AHMM*, June

Stodghill, Dick, "The Old Squad," *AHMM*, December

Stuart, Ian, "Françoise," *EQMM*, January

Todd, Karen L., "Finders, Weepers," *A Matter of Crime #3*

Turnbull, Peter, "Not at All Like the Scorpion," *EQMM*, April

Wasylyk, Stephen, "The Thawing of Gerald McGreedy," *AHMM,*
    July
————, "The Alley," *AHMM,* November
West, William Kyer, "Hector's Passing," *AHMM,* September
Wyckoff, Will, "A Christmas Story," *The Second Black Lizard
    Anthology of Crime Fiction*
Zimler, Robert L., "Takeout Order," *AHMM,* March